WHERE THERE'S SMOKE 2:

When the Smoke Clears

WHERE THERE'S SMOKE 2:

When the Smoke Clears

TERRA LITTLE

www.urbanbooks.net

Urban Books, LLC
1199 Straight Path
West Babylon, NY 11704

ISBN-13: 978-1-60162-262-4
ISBN-10: 1-60162-262-7

First Printing February 2010
Printed in the United States of America

10 9 8 7 6 5 4 3 2 1

Distributed by Kensington Publishing Corp.
Submit Wholesale Orders to:
Kensington Publishing Corp.
C/O Penguin Group (USA) Inc.
Attention: Order Processing
405 Murray Hill Parkway
East Rutherford, NJ 07073-2316
Phone: 1-800-526-0275
Fax: 1-800-227-9604

Dedication

This book is dedicated to my family, especially my mother, Lavelma Little. Mommy, for everything you've ever done for me and everything you continue to do, this one's for you.

Acknowledgments

A big thank you goes out to all the readers who asked for this sequel and to all the readers who have reached out to me in support of its predecessor, *Where There's Smoke.* In one way or another, you helped me breathe life into the characters and I'm grateful that you love them as much as I do.

Another big thank you goes out to all the hardworking online venues that help spread the word about African-American authors and books: RAWSISTAZ Literary Group, APOOO Books, and Urban Reviews, just to name a few. Also, to all the book clubs that support, encourage, uplift, and promote. I look forward to many more years of mixing business with pleasure.

And last, but certainly not least, an incredibly big thank you goes out to my agent, Pam Strickler of Pam Strickler Author Management. A good agent is like an aspirin—having one decreases the risk of a heart attack.

I leave you with a reflective thought: God is an awesome god.

CHAPTER ONE

ALEC

I had a flashback. Thought I was back in time, in a place where nothing and no one was safe; not me, not my stash, not my cash, nothing. Back then, I had the Robin-wood Housing Projects on lock, pushing weight from one corner to the next and looking over my shoulder every step of the way. I managed to get away with the diabolical lifestyle I was living for three or four years. I was forced to get my head on straight. I was Smoke and you couldn't find me in the club with 50 Cent, but you could find me on any given day, cruising around my domicile in a freshly waxed SUV, laying low and checking my rearview mirror for static.

For a brief moment, I imagined that the black Nissan with even blacker windows that was riding my bumper right about now was bringing static along with it and then I remembered that I was living a static-free life and had been for something like twenty years. So I did a roll call. License and insurance? Check. Registration and certificate of sale? Check. Was my house in order? Check. Was my house *really* in order? Check.

Yeah, right.

I made a quick, unexpected right turn and shook my head. The black Nissan was right behind me and pissing me off a little more every time it inched up on the bumper of my new truck. For the past twenty minutes it had been doing that, barely stopping in time enough to avoid rear-ending me and following me so closely that it could've been riding in the bed of my truck. I took it on a circular tour through a neighborhood I did not live in, led it across a busy discount store parking lot and made it wait for me while I filled my gas tank and went inside the station to get a soda. Then I came back outside, hopped up in my truck and started the parade all over again.

When I passed the grocery store I was supposed to be going to for the third time, I grabbed my cell phone from the passenger seat and dialed like a maniac. The phone rang three times on the other end before someone finally picked up.

"What are you doing?" I said straight out of the gate. I did not have time for this today.

Truth be told, I wasn't a stranger to the black Nissan. This was about the fiftieth time I had caught it following me, but never for this long and never like this. If I didn't know better, I would swear it was planning on going home with me and really starting some confusion, the likes of which I didn't need nor could I ill afford. I could've kicked my own ass for allowing the situation to go on for as long as it had been going on.

I thought about a saying that my father used to say before he got a wild hair up his butt and decided to croak when I was thirteen. He used to say: "Son, never shit where you lay your head." Young buck that I was, the lesson in what he said didn't quite sink in until I started looking twice at women and contemplating the possibilities.

Even then, it had taken me a minute or two to fully understand the value of keeping my homefront peaceful.

Here I was, forty years old and telling my own son the same thing, thinking I was passing down pearls of wisdom, father to son and all that, and shit personified was following me around the city in a black Nissan every other day. And shit in a skirt, on top of that. Apparently, I hadn't learned the lesson that I thought I'd learned.

"I don't know what you mean," Diana Daniels purred in my ear. "How are you, baby?"

"Dee . . ." I took a breath for patience and had to chuckle at myself. "This crap you're doing; you know it has to stop, right?"

"You make me do this, Alec. This is the only way I get to see you anymore. You stopped coming to me, so I have to come to you."

"I stopped coming to you for a reason." I tucked the phone between my head and shoulder and busted a wide, spur of the moment U-turn. Damned if she didn't bust one too, and speed up. A police cruiser passed me on my left and I debated catching the chump's attention, so he could pull my Glenn Close wannabe over and give me time to get the hell out of dodge. It figured that Mr. Officer was too busy yakking on his cell phone to notice a tax-paying citizen needing some assistance.

"Because you have Anne now?"

"Something like that, yeah." I stopped for a red light and felt a bump from behind. Wrong answer. "You've got problems, you know that?"

"No, baby, I think you're the one with problems." Diana tapped her horn and then waved to me through her open sunroof—with her middle finger. "I wonder what Anne would say if she knew where you were two weeks ago, Alec? Wonder what she'd say if she knew . . ."

"You know what?"

"That you had your pants down around your ankles and your . . ."

"You need to chill out, Dee."

". . . in my mouth," she finished, laughing. "Don't tell me you're scared of that bitch?"

"I'm starting to think I need to be scared of you."

"Oh, so I'm crazy now?"

"It's been four years," I reminded her in case she had forgotten. "I'm where I want to be. I think I told you that. And stop bumping my fucking truck."

"It's been two months since your dick was where it wanted to be, Alec. You know you need to quit deluding yourself and admit you made a mistake when you dumped me for that whore you call a housewife."

"I've made some mistakes, but getting with Anne wasn't one of them, Dee. Stop following me."

"Stop fucking me, Alec, and I might think about it."

I turned into the grocery store parking lot and slowed my roll, with her right on my bumper. She was really taking it to the extreme today. Usually, she trailed me just long enough for me to notice her and then she turned off somewhere and disappeared. Today, she was trying the hell out of my patience and making me wonder just how twisted in the head she really was. Obviously, more twisted than I had given her credit for.

She was right though, I had fucked her. A grand total of two times since me and Anne had hooked up and both times were stick and runs. She caught me tripping one night when I ran out to rent a couple of movies and talked me into following her behind the video store to talk. At least that's what she said. But she wasn't wearing panties and I ended up having a conversation with the wrong lips, and using the wrong head. The second time, she showed up at the junior high school where I taught Honors Algebra classes and bent over my desk. Her panties were missing in action then, too. I hadn't touched her since then, not that it made what I had done any less wrong, but there it was.

Two weeks ago, she showed up at my school again, wanting a repeat and I showed her the door. Then, I came out of the school a little while later and found my rear license plate missing and a note from her in its place. I had to go to her place to get my plate and she gave me a blowjob for my trouble.

She wasn't in too big of a hurry to let me forget what we'd done, either. Like I really needed help remembering. Every time I looked at myself in the mirror, I remembered what I'd done and asked myself what I could've been thinking. I knew what I had been thinking *with*, but what I'd been thinking *about* was anybody's guess. I couldn't even claim to be a greedy man, because greed hadn't factored into any of what happened. It wasn't like Anne was selfish with her loving, so what the hell?

That's what I asked Diana. "What the hell?"

"That's what I want to know," she said. "What the hell are you with her for if you can't keep it zipped up?"

As much as I wanted to have an answer to that question, I didn't and she knew it, so I didn't even try to come up with one. I pulled into a parking space, threw my truck into park and tried to think about the situation objectively.

Four years ago, I was dating Diana when I ran up on Anne, hiding out in Illinois with my sixteen-year-old son. Wait, scratch that. Anne ran up on me with my son in tow and seriously rocked my world. She hadn't wanted anything from me except help straightening out my son. Once I got over the shock of having a son in the first place, I

signed on to help her as much as I could. I wasn't expecting Anne and me to start rolling around in bed together
and falling in love, but we did.

For a minute, I was dealing with both Anne and Diana
and then Anne put the smack down on a brotha and I
made a decision. What else could I do? It was either Anne
or Diana and damned if I could see myself being without
Anne. The problem was, Diana couldn't seem to see herself being without me. So, for the past four years, I'd had a
stalker that I couldn't shake for nothing.

"Damn," I said out loud without meaning to. Anne was
not the type of woman to put up with even a tad bit of
shit. I knew that going in and in case I didn't, she hurried
up and told me what the deal was. If she found out about
Diana, my house would be so out of order that Hurricane
Katrina would look like a spread worthy of *Good House-
keeping* in comparison. Anne was nobody's joke and how
I managed to forget that, I didn't have the foggiest.

Dirty Diana was breathing in my ear like the character
in *Girl 6*. I turned my head and looked at her car, shook
my head again. "You don't love her," she whispered in my
ear.

"I don't love you," I told her and meant it. "And you
know it."

"Well, you had better start figuring out where to find
some love for me, Alec, because I've got something over
here that belongs to you. Something you can't deny even
if you wanted to."

"Go home, Dee, okay? Stop following me and go home."
As far as I was concerned the conversation was over. I
snapped my cell shut and dropped it in my pocket.

I got out of my truck and circled around to the passenger side back door. Diana's Nissan hadn't moved, so I decided to pretend it wasn't there. I opened the door,
reached in and picked up my daughter like she was pre-

cious cargo. Even in sleep she knew her daddy's touch, knew she could wipe her nose on my cheek and finish drooling down the side of my neck and nobody would say a damn thing to her, least of all me. This was the stuff I lived for.

I was smelling the curve of my baby's neck when I heard Diana's car easing up behind me. Something told me to look over my shoulder. I did, and then I jumped ten feet to the left to avoid being run over by the crazy bitch. She burned rubber flying past me and turned a corner on two wheels. An oncoming car almost rammed her from the side as she merged into traffic illegally and flew out of sight.

A few seconds later, my cell phone rang and I didn't have to look at the caller ID to know who it was. I snatched it out of my pocket and put it to my ear. I was so motherfucking mad, I couldn't see straight.

I didn't give her a chance to say anything. "If you had hurt my daughter, I would've blown your fucking brains out and gladly gone back to jail." She was quiet and I was too angry to take a second and think about what the silence might mean. "You hear me, Dee?"

More silence. Then, "Smoke?"

My head snapped back on my neck so hard I heard bones popping. I stopped right where I was standing in the middle of the grocery store parking lot and counted to ten. "Anne?"

"Dee, as in Diana?"

"Yeah, baby, she . . ."

"Where are you and where is my daughter?"

"Iris is right here and I'm at the store, where I'm supposed to be."

"Okaaaay. . . ." I could hear the wheels in Anne's head spinning. "And how does Diana factor into that?"

"Ran into her," I lied. A smiling door greeter had a cart

waiting for me just inside the automatic doors and I took it with a forced smile in return. It wasn't his fault I was on the hot seat. I pushed it off to the side and took the phone away from my ear to check the call waiting caller ID. I had an incoming call. "Hold on a second, baby, okay?"

"Smoke . . ."

"Hold on," I said and pushed a button to take me to the incoming call. "What the fuck is your problem? You could've . . ."

She cut me off at the throat and at the knees. "I think I'm pregnant, Alec."

I'm glad somebody had the foresight to snatch my daughter from my arms before I started sinking to the floor. I caught myself before I landed on my ass and fell against the wall behind me. Then I reached out and stopped the complete stranger who was holding my baby from moving out of my sight, working my cell with my free hand.

I switched back over to Anne. "Anne?" Nothing but dead air. "Anne?"

She had hung up.

CHAPTER TWO

ISAIAH

Somebody passed me another drink and I took it straight to the head. I figured if there was one of those little dissolving date rape pills in the bottom of the cup, I was out of luck. I was feeling a little too mellow to remember exactly how many I'd had and I didn't have the foggiest idea what I was drinking. I just knew that whatever it was, was about to sit a brotha right on his butt in a very few minutes.

I found a wall to lean up against so I didn't have to remember how to stand up and checked out the scene. Honeys on top of honeys, with a brotha or two thrown into the mix here and there to bring some balance to a situation that was perfect just the way it was. Even the ugliest dude in the place was bound to get laid tonight. I was nowhere near ugly, so what did that say about me?

Kentucky State University had more than its share of fine female undergrads and probably three-fourths of the ones to watch were in the house tonight. Friday night Kappa House parties were legendary on campus and some of the same sistas who sat in class and put the *N* in nerd were the very ones who showed up after dark and put the *L* in legendary. Quiet as it was kept, I didn't think I had ever seen so many fine black women together in one place in my whole life. I thought I had peeped my share, but . . . damn.

I was a senior in high school the first time I toured the campus. KSU's basketball scout was riding me about accepting a scholarship, so me and my old dude drove down here from Indiana to take a look around and see what we thought about KSU. They were one of three schools throwing full rides at me. Even though I was moaning and groaning about wanting to go somewhere more metropolitan, my old dude dragged me down here anyway. Old dude was asking all the important need-to-know questions and peeking around corners and what not, and I was taking in the scenery. Trying to keep my tongue from dragging the ground, for real. I came home and decided to go along with my mama—New York was too far away and so was Utah. A historically black university was where it was at and suddenly, I was down for KSU.

Did the man upstairs break the mold after he made the black woman or what?

"What's up, Zay?"

And here was one such example of exactly what I was talking about. Five-foot-six, body tighter than a drum and titties like Jell-O. A chemistry major, planning on being some kind of doctor and smart enough to pull it off too. Her parents were big-time church folks, her pops was the preacher at one of them fire and brimstone churches down in Mississippi somewhere, and she could quote the Bible backward and forward. Only problem was, she was prone to using the Lord's name in vain when it was convenient for her. *Holy shit*, this and *goddamn*, that. And, oh yeah, my personal favorite: *God, you fuck me good.* I just knew her pops wouldn't approve of his baby girl's nice-nasty mouth. But me? I didn't have the slightest problem with it.

When her parents got a hair up their butts and decided to visit, she jumped into loose fitting khakis and oxford cloth shirts, remembered that she wore wire-rimmed glasses and put those mugs on. She pulled her hair up in a tight ponytail and called me Isaiah when she saw me on campus. But no sooner than their Jaguar was out of sight, I was back to being Zay, she was back in a demin miniskirt that was frayed around the hem and closer to her ass than ninety-nine was to a hundred and she was hunting me down at the Friday night Kappa frat parties.

"You," I said as I covered a quiet belch with my fist. "You looking for me?"

"You know I was." She took my drink and helped herself to a sip. Then, she leaned over and set the cup on the steps. Since my hands were empty, I filled them with her ass and tasted the strawberry flavored lip gloss on her lips. "What were you and Missy Davis over here talking about a little while ago?"

"Same thing you and Bruce were over there talking about a little while ago," I said. "You didn't think I was peeping you, did you? Over there getting your mack on."

"If you were peeping me like you say you were, you would've seen me check him. I didn't see you over here setting Missy straight, though."

"I handled my business."

"Yeah, right."

I didn't have anything to prove, but I still pulled out the folded piece of paper Missy had scribbled her number on and slipped in my pocket, and pushed it in the vee of her shirt, right between her tits. "Now what?" We stared at each other.

The music changed up and a slow groove replaced Ludacris' hollering about coming for the number one spot.

She rolled her head around on her shoulders, ran her fingers through her waist-length wavy hair and started swaying from side to side. I watched her lips pucker like she was kissing the air and I wanted to lick those bad boys.

She saw me looking and grinned. "Ooooh, that's my jam, boo. Dance with me?"

Everywhere I looked, couples were bumping and grinding, damn near having intercourse on the dance floor and not caring who was watching. I spotted Bruce's punk ass pushing up on somebody else's woman and shook my head. And some chick I had seen before but didn't know was so high she was slowly coming out of her clothes, tripping on E and straight out of her mind. She pulled her bra off, shook her tits for everybody and then took off running, with her big, ugly boyfriend right behind her. I could've told him she was off the chain, E or no E, but he didn't ask me, so I kept my mouth shut and my eyes open.

Any other time I would've tuned in to the hilarious reality show unfolding all around me, but I had other, infinitely more important business to attend to. I eased up on my dance partner from behind and spread my fingers out on her thighs. She reached up and wrapped her arms around my neck and we grooved like that through three slow jams.

The last thing I intended on doing when I came to college was hooking myself up with one girl and being monogamous, but that's exactly what I was doing. Don't get me wrong, a brotha was tempted all the time and there were plenty of opportunities to get my creep on, but right about now I was about as full as a tick. No sense in being greedy.

I was sucking on her neck when Ice Cube blasted through the speakers and everybody went back to humping and pumping. We kept on slow grooving and that's how I knew it was time to go.

My boy Tommy's room was on the top floor of the frat house and he was down in Florida. I stuck my head in his room and made sure the coast was clear and then it was on. As soon as I locked the door behind us, she was on me and I was on her, both of us reaching for my zipper and laughing when our fingers got tangled up together.

I fell back against the wall, my mouth dropped open and my eyes slammed shut. Good thing the music was pounding full blast, because I was doing some serious hissing and grunting. Toes curling and all that. Baby girl's mouth was a lethal weapon and I think she knew it. But just in case she didn't, I told her.

When I could talk.

"Baby boy like dat, eh?"

"Baby boy 'bout to tear your ass up." I gripped her waist and spun her around, walked her over to the bed and bent her over. I tongued her ass cheeks until she started chanting in her native Jamaican tongue. She knew it drove me crazy.

"Oooh, dat's it baby. Do dat shit, eh? Yeah baby, jus' like dat."

I wrapped my hands up in her hair and pulled her head back, hit a secret spot on her neck with my teeth and tongue and made her cum. My fingers got lost in her heat and I damn near came myself. I wanted to taste her, but I couldn't make myself wait that long.

I was sexing a sista from the islands and I had been since a month after the fall semester started. Freshman year she was dating a dude named Jared. Sophomore year she was engaged to the chump and planning on getting married. Then he tripped and got caught slipping with one of her so-called friends, a high-yellow chick named Stefani from around the way. I had been lusting after her since day one and I didn't sleep when her sorry-ass man lost his place. Ten minutes after she took the ring off, I swooped in and started whispering in her ear. It had been on ever since. Nobody was saying we were going together or anything like that, but nobody was saying we weren't, either. Things were just kind of understood between us.

Erica was her name and for the most part brothas didn't test the waters. They knew she was mine. Every now and again, Missy Davis or some other chick tried to step to me, but I was cool rolling like I was. Then there was punk niggas like Bruce, who didn't believe fat meat was greasy, always trying to push up on her when he thought I wasn't looking. But I was never not looking though, because I guess you could say I was . . . seriously infatuated.

"Hold up," I hissed through clenched teeth. She was straddling me, rolling her hips round and round in the air over my dick and feeding me mouthfuls of her tits. I was so caught up that I had almost sent the chief in without backup, which was something I never did. She had me twisted in the head. I hurried up and rolled on a condom.

After that, it was all over for me. I didn't hear anymore music, anymore more bass, anymore anything, except for moans and groans, and gasps and hisses. Tongues were everywhere, hands all over the place and I just knew we was gon' break Tommy's headboard clean in half.

"Shhh." I flipped her over on her back and put my hand over her mouth. "Make somebody think I'm killing you in here."

She threw her head back and cracked up, which was just as bad as all the screaming and clowning she was doing a few minutes ago. But she was cute with it though—hair spread out across the mattress, teeth white as hell, light brown slanted eyes shining out of her face and skin the color of midnight.

Yeah, Erica was dark skinned. One of them Jamaican sistas that brothas lost their minds over. That is, if they had even a little bit of sense. The blacker the berry, the sweeter the juice? Shit, my boo was so sweet that I had to swallow her in sips. Stupid Jared didn't know what he had and that's the truth. Or maybe he did know and that's why he was always giving a brotha the evil eye, thinking I was going to stand down or something. What the hell ever. He messed around and fell for the okey-doke, slipped and tripped with a sista who had been around the block more times than a used Buick. Come to think of it, I think I had even tapped Stefani once or twice during freshman year. He had to feel stupid, but that wasn't my problem. But now, if he tried to come crying back to Erica, that *was* going to be my problem.

"Zay!"

I snatched my foot out of somebody's clutches and picked up where I left off snoring. Sometime during the night, me and Erica had slipped underneath the covers and made ourselves at home in Tommy's bed. I had planned on taking a short nap to knock the edge off, then sneaking her back to her dorm and heading to mine, but as soon as my head hit the pillow, I was down for the count.

"Zay!" I felt my foot being yanked again. And then, "Nigga, wake yo' ass up! Laying up like you Alice in Wonderland or some shit. Doolittle 'bout to do a house check and he know damn well you ain't Tommy."

I took a pillow from over my face and cracked one eye open, looked around the room until I spotted my boy Cyril standing at the foot of the bed. "Doolittle?"

Doolittle was the pet name we had given one of the deans, because he wore thick glasses and carried a Persian cat named Sylvia around with him all the time. He was the least coolest of all the school's staff and I couldn't figure out how he had ended up being appointed frat delegate, of all things. No doubt one person's idea of a cruel joke that had turned out to be everybody else's worst nightmare. Doolittle was one of the few and the proud. He wasn't a Marine, but he took his job seriously. His real name was Percival Began, but everyone called him Doolittle, even my parents.

"Damn right, Doolittle, nigga. Get 'cho good sleeping ass up."

Erica decided that she wanted to wake up just then and Cyril's eyes got big when she went to squirming around underneath the covers. She raised her head from my stomach and crawled up my body like a snake. Her head was the first thing to pop out and then her shoulders and then . . .

"Oh, snap, I didn't know you had a shorty in here with you!"

I caught her just before her tits would've greeted Cyril and held the covers in place. "Hold up, baby, we got company." She glanced over her shoulder at Cyril, groaned and pressed her face into my neck. I ran my hands up her back and had a thought. "Wait a minute. I locked the door, so how did you get up in here?"

He held up a key ring and jingled it. "You know I had to do a sweep before Doolittle brought his nosy ass up in here. We had about half the campus up in this piece. Oh, and remind me later on to tell you what I walked in on down the hall, too."

Erica stretched and started chewing on my neck. Cyril looked away and scratched his head, grinning. "You got about fifteen minutes to get some ghost."

"That's plenty of time," she crooned after Cyril was gone.

"Have you met Doolittle?" I sat up and looked around for our clothes, spotted her thong and handed it to her. Doolittle was likely to pop up at any minute and the last thing I needed was to be caught with my dick hanging out, literally. I could see the next issue of the school's newspaper slash gossip rag now: CO-CAPTAIN OF THE BASKETBALL TEAM SUSPENDED FOR INDECENT EXPOSURE. Plus, let me tell it, Doolittle had some sugar in his tank and I wasn't trying to be running around in his dreams anytime soon if I could help it. I got up, found my jeans and shook them out.

"Remember when we were actually small enough to think this was fun?"

I turned around just in time to catch Erica jumping up and down on Tommy's bed like a five-year-old. Hair flying all over the place, titties bouncing and a big smile on her face. I couldn't help laughing, even if Tommy's bed was taking some serious abuse. "Girl, quit playing and put some clothes on."

Another thing I didn't need was for Doolittle to catch me tripping and go running to my parents. My old dude was cool about things like this, but my mama? I wouldn't put it past my mama to drive down here and show her ass in the middle of the student center. She was out of control like that and it wouldn't be a damn thing my old dude could do to stop her. I guess she thought I spent all my time studying and playing ball, because she hadn't once asked me if I had a girlfriend or if I was even dating. I wondered what she'd think of Erica. Then, I wondered why I was wondering something like that and reached for my shirt.

Erica dropped down to her knees, bounced twice and then popped back up to her feet.

The bed was squeaking like crazy, but she was having a ball. Me, I was having a ball watching her clown. She was probably going to graduate Summa Cum Laude and she was mad smart, but she was nowhere near stuck up, which was another reason I liked me some Erica. Maybe the main one. She was a straight fool when she wanted to be.

"Tommy is going to tap that ass when he finds out what

you did to his bed," I said as I pulled my shirt over my head. I picked up her skirt and tossed it to her. Then I sent her bra flying through the air in her direction.

"No mon tap de ass but you, baby," she joked, still bouncing.

I guess I was used to tossing basketballs across the court, because my attempt at tossing a frilly bra was less than impressive. My mouth dropped open as I watched Erica reach out for it, lose her balance and go spinning off the bed. She landed flat on her butt in the middle of the floor, looking around like she had fallen down a rabbit hole.

I wanted to laugh so loud and so badly I had to cover my mouth for a good ten seconds. Then I ran over to her and played like I didn't want to crack up. I squatted down in front of her and looked into her eyes. "Um . . . you . . . um . . . you all right?"

We stared at each other and I waited for her to tear up and start whining about her butt hurting or her wrist being sprained or something. She sucked in a breath and then I sucked in a breath. She looked away and sucked her teeth, and I put a finger to my lips to keep them closed.

We stayed like that for a minute.

"That was embarrassing," Erica said in her best chemistry lab voice.

"I told you to quit playing and put your clothes on but *noooo* . . ."

She saw the grin lurking on my face and frowned. "You think this is funny?"

"Not really, no. I don't think it's funny. Not real funny, anyway." I held up two fingers with less than an inch of space between them. "Maybe a little bit funny, but *funny* funny? Nah."

"You know what, Isaiah?"

"What, Erica?"

"I think its real funny."

"Oh . . . okay."

Next thing I knew, she was on her back, laughing like a fool. Making more noise than a little bit and making my dick hard without even trying to.

"Hello?" A voice called out and shut Erica right up. "Hello? Is someone up here?"

I got to my feet and did a Carl Lewis over to the door. Doolittle was in the house and on his way up the stairs. "Damn!" I glared at Erica over my shoulder. Suddenly, she was in a hurry to get dressed. "Messing with you. Oh, now you want to get dressed?"

She was moving so fast that she couldn't catch up with herself. She kept fumbling with the button fly on her skirt, couldn't figure out what manual dexterity was for nothing. Finally, she gave up, pushed her hands through her hair and blew out a frustrated breath. Then, she flopped down on the bed and finished cracking up.

Doolittle walked in the room and caught us both laughing so hard that we were crying.

CHAPTER THREE

ANNE

Smoke was pretending like he didn't see me standing right in front of him, motioning for him to give me the phone. I'd heard the first part of the conversation and from the comments he was making and the questions he was asking, I put two and two together and figured out that someone from Isaiah's school was on the phone. What I couldn't figure out was why he wouldn't let me talk.

"What was that about?" I asked as soon as he hung up. "Is Isaiah okay? Is he hurt?"

"Isaiah is fine. Please calm down before you give yourself a stroke." He went over to the stove and peeked inside a covered skillet. "You need to check on this chicken, too. I like it well done, but burnt is another thing. I don't know why you just didn't go ahead and fry it. I mean, I'm all for gourmet meals, but I *would* like to eat before it's time to go to bed."

I rolled my eyes at his back and shooed him out of my way. "I am frying it, just not with breading." I flipped leg quarters over and tossed in sliced bell peppers and onions. Then I turned down the fire and propped a hand on my hip. "Who was that calling and what did they want, Smoke?"

"Isaiah is fine, Anne," he said as he kept reading the paper. Like I was working his nerves. I thought about slinging the spatula I was holding across the room and braining his behind.

This was typical Smoke. Always in "I'm the man of the house" mode, which was really starting to piss me off. At first, I thought it was sexy, the way he stepped in and handled everything, so I didn't have to do much but stand back and watch him work. But now, four years into being with him, I was beginning to feel like my presence in his life was strictly for ornamental purposes; like I didn't have a voice when it came to important household decisions. Smoke said it and it shall be done.

He was about to make me tell him a thing or two, I knew that much. I wasn't used to being out of the loop in my own home and I was starting to realize just how out of the loop I really was. Take this situation, for instance. Here I was, questioning him about what was going on with our son and getting clipped—abbreviated responses to my questions. The kind of responses people gave other people when they didn't want them to know something, or anything at all. And that just wasn't right. If something important was going on with Isaiah, I had every right to be as informed about it as he did. Probably even more so, since I had raised Isaiah by myself for the first sixteen years of his life.

I wondered if he actually thought I couldn't look in his hazel-gray eyes and tell when he was being less than truthful with me, if he thought I couldn't see the shift in them just before he opened his mouth and uttered a falsehood. Among other things, Isaiah had inherited his father's eyes and I'd had sixteen years worth of deception detection training before Smoke came into the picture. At this point, I could do more than see a lie coming, I could smell it a mile away.

These days, I was smelling more lies than I cared to admit, which was another thing that was really pissing me off. Somewhere along the way I had turned into one of those women who pretended not to see what was right in front of their faces just to keep the peace. I could've pulled Smoke's behind to the carpet about plenty of other mess and plenty of other times, Isaiah be damned, but I hadn't. Not yet, anyway.

Another instance: Diana Daniels. She was the woman Smoke was involved with when I bum-rushed him four years ago and offered to let him be a father to my son. Isaiah was running around with the wrong crowd and experimenting with drugs, sliding down a slippery slope in school and in general, scaring the mess out of me every other day. So I remembered what I knew about his father and tracked Smoke down. I needed help straightening out my son and Smoke was my last hope.

He came through for Isaiah like gangbusters, I had to give him his due. But what he had done to me was another story. Now I wasn't the type of woman to be running around with another woman's man, but that's exactly what I had done with Smoke. He and Diana were doing whatever they were doing and on the flipside of that, he and I were, well . . . spelling it out isn't all that necessary. Suffice it to say, we were busy deciding that we wanted to be together.

I thought he'd made a decision he could live with by choosing to pursue our relationship, but lately, I wasn't so sure. Diana's name was popping up in the course of conversation more and more, and I was beginning to suspect that there was more going on than met the eye. My eye, anyway, because the Lord knew Smoke was as tight-lipped as ever. I questioned him about what was going on with Diana and got the same clipped and abbreviated answers that I got for damn near everything else.

I flipped the chicken again and dropped the skillet lid in place with a nice little clang. Just thinking about it made me want to splash some hot oil on Smoke's butt. I had warned him a long time ago not to mess with me, but apparently he hadn't listened. He had talked a lot of that "I love you baby" mess, but he hadn't really been listening to me. I saw that now. I was doing just fine on my own. I hadn't needed a man in my bed or in my life, but for him, I had opened myself up and now I was starting to regret it a little more each day.

True enough, Diana was already in the picture when I came along. But that bastard was a big boy and I hadn't made him do anything he didn't want to do. If anything, the reverse was true. He was the one who decided to break things off with Diana to be with me. He was the one who had the bright idea for me to leave Chicago and move back to Indiana, so we could be together 24-7. And he was the one who decided that we wanted more children. Just like he decided everything else.

What I had decided to do was go along with everything because I loved him. And when I decided that I loved him, Diana Daniels had to go. Off she went and good riddance. But was she really gone? That was the million-dollar question. If the answer to that question wasn't one I could live with, I was out of here.

I told myself I was over reacting, riding on a newfound jealous streak, but I wasn't crazy for real. I knew what I was doing. I was biding my time and getting my life back in order. I had a job lined up, which would allow me to live the way I was living before Smoke, and I had a slowly expanding savings account to fall back on. I was no stranger to taking care of business and that was something Smoke must have forgotten. If he kept trying to play me, I was taking my daughter and leaving his ass in the dust.

My thoughts returned to the kitchen a little at a time and I realized that Smoke was in the midst of saying something to me. I tuned back in and tried to keep up. "What is this you're saying about money?"

"I was asking you if you sent Zay the money to fly home, instead of riding the bus."

"No." I transferred chicken from the skillet to a platter, turned the fire down and caught Smoke's eyes. "I thought you sent him some extra cash and just didn't tell me about it." *The same way you neglect to tell me about everything else.*

"We agreed on a monthly amount."

"We did," I said slowly. "You've been known to change your mind from time to time, though."

"As have you."

"Touché. But I've stuck to our original agreement." I walked into the pantry and walked back out with a bag of potatoes. I took four from the bag, dropped them in the sink and retraced my steps, staring at Smoke as I went. "Stuck to it to the letter, too. Have you?"

"Are we having the same conversation?"

"I don't know, are we?"

"You tell me. I'm trying to find out where Zay is suddenly getting all this extra money from."

"Not from me." I froze in the middle of scraping potato skins and listened extra hard for a few seconds. Iris was awake and from the sound of it, having a bowel movement, the little rat. "I send him what we agreed on and not a penny more. If you ask me, he needs to get a part-time job."

"I don't want him working right now," Smoke decided for the both of us. "He's on the last leg of his engineering degree and this isn't the time for him to start slipping. He'll be starting his internship in a hot little minute, anyway. He can wait."

"As you wish," I mumbled under my breath and reached for a strainer to rinse the potatoes. I saw Smoke watching me from the corner of my eye and did a double take. "What?"

"Are you pissed with me about something, Anne?"

"I don't know, Smoke. You tell me. Am I?" I wiped my hands on a dishtowel and walked out of the kitchen.

My daughter was crying, which was exactly what I felt like doing. As I went to go and see about her, I wished my crap was as easy to wipe up and toss away as hers was. Children didn't know how easy they had it.

Most couples had rituals they performed with each other, regardless of what was going on around them and Smoke and I were no different. A volcano could erupt at four o'clock in the morning, the rest of the city could be busy evacuating and he would swear up and down there was time enough for us to make love before we started packing. We could live in a bubble in the middle of the Atlantic Ocean, with water all around us as far as the eye could see, and he would still come into the shower with me every night and every morning, ostensibly to conserve water. We could argue, fight and fuss all day long, but when the house was locked up for the night and the baby was asleep, we put the fighting aside, lowered our voices and did us.

Nighttime was my personal favorite, because it was peaceful. Iris usually dropped off to sleep around eight and she rarely woke up before six the next morning. The phone rarely rang and when it did, we let it go to voicemail. After a warm shower, I was loose and my mind was idling in neutral, ready for whatever, but sluggish with it.

And Smoke was right there with me, being the Smoke I had fallen in love with—street smooth, laid back and tuned in to me like a transistor radio. When he was like that, it was easy for me to forget that I was pissed with him for one reason or another. It was all too easy for him to sweet talk me into doing just about anything.

Like sitting up in a tank top and a thong, playing Xbox video games and eating greasy pizza at ten o'clock at night.

"Stay in your own lane, Smoke!"

I shifted around on the mattress until I was lying on my stomach at the foot of the bed, closer to the television and able to look over his shoulder to see what he was doing with his control that I wasn't doing with mine. I watched him push buttons and twirl the stick around for a few seconds and decided that he was somehow cheating.

"Show me how to make my car go up on two wheels like yours is doing."

He glanced back at me over his shoulder. "Can't do it. Next thing you'll be wanting to know is how I always kick your ass at drag racing and if I told you that, I'd have to kill you."

I reached for the glass of iced tea sweating on the floor by his hip and took a sip. I pushed at his shoulder. "Please, Smoke . . ."

Smoke put the game on pause and swallowed a mouthful of beer, stared at me for long seconds and then shook his head, laughing. "Come here."

He didn't have to tell me twice. I hurried up and hopped off the bed and into his lap. I made myself extra comfortable and took a bite out of the slice of pizza he was bringing to his mouth.

"What is this you're wearing on your skin? Smelling like I need to be eating you instead of this pizza."

"Shea butter," I said and picked up his beer by accident.

It was halfway to my mouth before I realized what I was doing. I froze and stared at it and Smoke froze and stared at me.

"That's the same scent that got me into trouble in the first place. Damn shea butter," he said a few seconds later. He reached up and touched the bottle. "Take a sip if you want to, Anne."

"I don't want to."

"Then put it down."

"I meant to pick up the iced tea, Smoke. You know I don't drink."

"I know."

I was never much of a drinker, so it wasn't like I was worried about falling off the wagon and having to repeat the twelve steps. But I was afraid the chances of me developing a taste for alcohol and becoming addicted to it were higher than most other people's chances, simply by virtue of who and what I was. To avoid that, I had sworn off controlled substances in any form when I swore off crack cocaine over twenty years ago. I hadn't wanted to go from being a crackhead to being a drunk, hadn't wanted to trade one drug for another and lose myself so soon after I had finally found myself. That was my greatest fear.

I spent the tail end of my teenage years smoking crack cocaine like a speed demon, daring myself to die and waiting for death to set me free. The Grim Reaper never came for me though, but my Aunt Bobbi did. She came all the way from Mississippi with her Bible in hand, and snatched me up by my collar. When I knew enough to take a look around me, I was back in Mississippi with her, roaming around her house like a thief, looking for anything I could sell for some crack.

If I let myself think about that time in my life long enough, I remember that she was a husky woman compared to my own skin and bones. I was no match for her strength when she was forced to use it against me. That woman tossed me around her house like a rubber ball and didn't miss a beat quoting scripture and praying for my sorry butt while she was doing it. I would make a run for the door and find myself flying through time and space in the opposite direction. Two o'clock in the morning and she'd just magically be there, standing over me, waiting for me to finish the thought I was entertaining about crawling out of the window.

I liked to romanticize my time with Aunt Bobbi, make it seem like we were just two biddies piddling around her house and enjoying each other's company. But the truth of the matter was that we were at war, I was her POW and she was nothing but heaven in human form.

On her deathbed, I promised her that I would never be an addict again. To keep that promise, I hadn't even accepted the drugs they offered me when I was in labor this last time with Iris.

"Anne." I transferred my attention from the beer in my hand to Smoke's face. "You ever had a beer before?"

We stared at each other. "Once or twice."

"Did you like it?"

I shook my head. "Doesn't matter if I liked it or not."

"What do you think is going to happen if you take a sip?"

"Smoke . . ."

"You think one sip will make you an alcoholic?"

"I don't know and I'm not going to find out."

"You trust me, baby?"

"What does that have to do with anything?" I was confused.

"Do you?"

"Smoke . . ."

"You think I would give you something that would hurt you? You think I would stand back and watch you do something to yourself that would hurt you?"

The look in my eyes said everything. Smoke searched them leisurely, read my thoughts and nodded slowly. When I was strung out, I bought my drugs from him exclusively and I had given him my virginity when I ran out of money. Those drugs had hurt me and he had given them to me. "We're not those people anymore, Anne."

"I know that."

"Smoke, the dope man is dead and so is sad little Breanne Phillips."

"I know that, too."

"Do you?" he snapped. "But you still think I would hurt you intentionally? You don't think I have your back?"

"You're confusing me," I said.

And he was, poking at me and hitting me with questions that he wanted answers to before I had a chance to think about what I wanted to say. Thinking quickly on my feet wasn't one of my strong points when it came to looking inside of myself and figuring things out. A year of intensive inpatient drug treatment had not only flushed drugs out of my system, but it had also forced me to really look at myself for the first time in my life. I figured out way back then that I needed to stay focused on things that I could reach out and touch, things outside of myself, in order to leave the past where it belonged.

"I know all that." I pushed my hands through my locks and reigned in my temper. "How did we go from playing a damn video game to you trying to convince me to take a drink?"

"I'm not trying to convince you to do anything. I just want you to be convinced about what's going on between you and me."

"Would I be here if I wasn't?"

He tipped his head to one side and considered me. "Would you?"

I pretended to think about it for a second. "I'm not even going to dignify that with a response. Oh wait, yes, I will. What the hell kind of crazy question is that?"

"I love you, Anne," he said and laughed. One of his hands reached for the beer and the other closed around a fistful of my locks. He stuck the tip of his tongue inside the bottle, turned it up to get a taste and then transferred his tongue from the bottle to my mouth. I went on autopilot and opened my mouth as wide as I could.

"See what you do to me?" I swiped his spit from under my bottom lip and scratched my head like I was just coming out of a daze. "That damn tongue of yours is dangerous. I forgot all about the beer you just force-fed me. Barely tasted it. What are you doing?"

He tipped the bottle up again. Pressed his lips against mine and waited. We locked eyes and I shook my head, no. He winked and nodded his head, yes. A drop of liquid rolled down my chin and made its way down my neck. The next drop rolled sideways and pooled in the corner of my mouth. I caught it with the tip of my tongue and swallowed in my own time.

"Stop being silly, Smoke." Another drop landed and I licked it away. "Stop it. It's not even cold anymore. Nobody in their right mind wants to drink warm beer from somebody else's mo . . . aahh!" As Isaiah would say, I got caught tripping and got a mouthful of warm beer along with Smoke's tongue. It was all I could do to keep from choking and still keep up with him when he took the kiss deep.

He pulled back and sucked my bottom lip inside his mouth. "What did you think?"

I made a face. "Too warm to tell. Wait . . . I wasn't trying to say I wanted more, Smoke. Look . . ." I sighed and opened my mouth again.

"What did it taste like?"

"Like you."

"Really?"

"Yeah."

"You drunk yet?"

"No."

"You want some more?"

"No." I reached for the game control and handed it to him. "I want you to show me how to make my car go up on two wheels. You thought I forgot, didn't you?" I switched the game from PAUSE to PLAY and sat back in his lap.

I raced my red Lamborghini against Smoke's blue Mazarati for thirty minutes straight and finally managed to win. I suspected he let me win, though. He tossed his control down and told me I'd won, but the point tracker in the corner of the television screen said something completely different.

I cocked a brow and looked back at him. "Don't let me win out of pity."

"I'm letting you win because I love you."

"Still . . ."

"Say it back to me, Anne."

"I do say it back to you."

"Say it now then."

"Say what?"

"Tell me you love me."

"I do and you know it."

"Then say it."

"I just did." I had to pee, so I got up and went to the bathroom. Smoke had shut the game down, turned off the television and the lamps, and climbed in bed by the time I walked back into the bedroom, ready to bob and weave again. I looked at his reflection in the mirror as I gathered my locks into a ponytail and snapped a rubberband around them.

"You love me, Smoke?" I said as I made my way across the room toward the bed.

"All day long."

I stepped out of my thong first and then I pulled my tank top over my head. I slipped between the sheets buck naked and draped a leg over his. He was hard as a rock and needing some attention.

"Show me," I said and I let him.

CHAPTER FOUR

ALEC

Six months Diana and I had dated and we'd had sex so many times and so many ways that I lost count after the first couple of months. But I didn't think we had ever really made love to each other. We had smacked and grabbed, and grunted and groaned, but the concept of love was conspicuously missing. Furthermore, neither of us had thought to stop knocking boots long enough to notice that it was missing. I could only speak for myself, but I knew I hadn't given a flying shit one way or the other. She got hers, I got mine and in and around that we got along.

Truthfully, my relationship with Diana was superficial as hell and just something to do, since I wasn't doing anything or anyone else at the time. I cared about her, but I cared about her the same way I cared about watching my saturated fat intake. When I had an appointment with my doctor, I worried about what the blood test results would reveal. Then, after I got a clean bill of health, I came home, ordered a Meat Lover's pizza and washed it down with a cold beer. Conscious and then unconscious—like that and in that order.

So why had I allowed myself to slip and trip with her the way I had? Again. I hadn't come up with an answer to that question yet. But I did know that I regretted it with everything in me. Besides the fact that she was psycho, which was something I should've seen a long time ago, she refused to go away and I needed her to do that so my guilt could go with her.

I thought about her, bent over my desk with no panties on and her skirt up around her waist, and shook my head to clear the image from my mind. Thought about me running up in her, hitting it so hard that it sounded like somebody was in the room with us, clapping, and felt needles of shame pricking my face. I hadn't fucked her because I couldn't walk away from what she was offering me. I had fucked her because she begged me to, because said she *needed* to be fucked and by *me*. Until I got with Anne, I didn't know much about needing someone. Wanting? Hell yeah, but needing? What was that?

I knew like a motherfucker now, though. Rolling over at four in the morning and sighing as I pushed inside of Anne was about me needing to connect with her. Busting in on her showers and watching her watch me soap her body was about me needing to know what every part of her body looked and felt like. Listening to her talk for hours about things she needed to find other women to talk to about, was about me needing to walk around inside her head. Me wanting to hear her say she loved me as much as I loved her was about me needing to know that she was here with me and not locked down inside of herself, where I suspected she was most of the time.

Four years ago, you couldn't have told me I would be worried about what a woman I was dealing with was thinking and feeling about me and our relationship. You couldn't have told me I would be wondering if what I was doing was enough and feeling like, somehow, it wasn't.

Anne was still a mystery to me, so introverted and diffi-
cult to reach sometimes that I felt like I had to work
harder to make her see me. To see us. We were good together. Damn good, if you asked me and when I got her
underneath me in bed. I tried to break my back showing
her that.

I gave her everything I had and watched the fruits of my
labor unfold before me. She squeezed me from the inside
out and her mouth dropped open in surprise. I saw the
trembling start in her neck and make its way down her
body to her legs. I heard her recite my favorite letter of
the alphabet in a high-pitched voice that told me she was
going to sleep like a baby tonight. Then, I let myself go
and filled her up.

I left her lying there searching for her lost breath and
went to stand over the toilet. I looked at myself in the mirror for a second and then I reached up and hit the switch
for darkness. Cancel that image. Sometimes Anne made
me so angry that I couldn't stand to see the depth of it on
my face.

I walked out of the bedroom and into the kitchen before I flipped open my cellphone and put it to my ear. "I
thought I told you I'd be in touch?"

Diana sighed into the phone and blew her nose noisily.
"I was waiting for you to call me, but then it occurred to
me that you weren't planning on doing that anytime soon.
Have you thought about what I told you?"

"Can't think about much of anything else. When do you
see a doctor?" I spotted yesterday's mail on the counter
and snatched it up. My hands needed to be doing something other than shaking right about now. If Anne walked
in the kitchen . . .

"I'll get around to it . . . eventually." She sounded like
she couldn't care less.

"What?"

"I said I'll get around to making an appointment in the next day or two. I'll let you know when and what time, so we can go together."

"I don't think so." I shot a look over my shoulder at the doorway and kept flipping through envelopes. A bill, another bill, a lingerie catalog, cigarette coupons and yet another bill. The last envelope was from our bank. "I'm not getting ready to start this shit with you, Dee. Find out what you need to find out and we'll go from there." I tossed the coupons in the trash and set the catalog to the side for Anne, sat down with the bank statement and started reading.

"I know you don't think I'm about to go through this pregnancy alone, Alec?"

"I didn't say that, but I know you don't think I'm about to drop my responsibilities over here and come running over there whenever you call. That's not how this is going to go."

She was quiet for a few seconds. "Have you told Anne?"

"No, and I don't plan to until I know there's something to tell, so don't get any bright ideas about the flow of things over here."

"I just want you to step up to the plate and accept your responsibility to me and our baby. You don't think she'd want to know you have another baby on the way?"

"The only thing I'm thinking right now is that you need to hop, skip and jump to the doctor. Everything after that will take care of itself."

"I bet she won't be too happy with you, boo. But you know what? That's okay with me, because you need to be over here with me, anyway. This baby was meant to bring us back together."

I scanned the last line at the bottom of the page and

sucked in a sharp breath. I stood up so fast the chair fell over behind me. I was tripping so hard that I almost took my cell phone back into the bedroom with me. I caught myself in the hallway and came up short. "Another thing you need to do is accept the fact that I'm with Anne now, Dee," I whispered into the phone.

"Tell that to your dick . . ."

I cut her off, sick of hearing talk of my dick coming from her mouth. "Save it. I'll be in touch. Meantime, go to the doctor."

"Alec . . ."

"I'll be in touch," I said and snapped the phone closed.

"Anne!" She jumped and then pulled the covers up around her neck, thinking that she was about to snuggle in. I didn't think so. I walked around the bed and snatched the covers back. She curled into a ball and I started pinching her butt cheeks. "Anne, wake your ass up, okay? Ain't that much sleep in the world and I know you hear me calling you."

"Stop, Smoke. Don't you have to be at work in a few minutes?" Anne mumbled into my pillow. "Ouch, Smoke! Did you hear me tell you to stop? Ouch!"

"It's the last day of school before Thanksgiving break," I told her. "I don't have to go in at all if I don't want to." I kept pinching until she slapped my hands away and opened one eye to stare at me. "Sit up and look at this. Tell me if I'm losing my mind or not." I paced back and forth while she read.

"Who's making all these deposits?" She was just as shocked as I had been a few minutes ago. She sat all the way up and folded her legs Indian style, spreading the pages out on the mattress in front of her.

"You?" I suggested. She twisted her lips to one side and looked at me like I was crazy. "Well, it's not me."

"So if it's not you and it's not me, then that leaves . . ."

"Isaiah," I finished for her. "Where the hell did he get eight thousand dollars?" I tried not to sound like I was accusing Anne, but it wasn't working.

"I don't know, Smoke. Hell, if he got it from me why would he turn around and deposit it right back into an account I have full access to? If I'm sneaking it to him, I mean? And," she held up a finger, "if I had eight thousand dollars to give away, why would I give it to him instead of buying that Ralph Lauren luggage set I've had my eye on since last year?"

She had a point. But still . . . "Ain't nothing wrong with the Louis Vuitton luggage you already have," I felt it important to point out. She made a jacked up face. "Anne, I swear to God . . ."

"Anne, I swear to God," she mimicked me as she rolled to her feet. "Forget the luggage, Smoke. Tell me why my son is suddenly tossing money around like a . . ." She froze halfway to the bathroom and turned toward me slowly, eyes big. "What if he's selling drugs?"

"Do you listen to yourself when you talk? That's the last thing I'm worried about."

One of the last things, anyway. I hadn't planned on mentioning it to Anne, but the possibility that Isaiah was selling had briefly entered my mind. I tried to picture him selling a little weed here and there to some students and probably a few teachers, but the picture wouldn't gel. If anybody knew about the foolishness of getting caught up with drugs, Isaiah did. Anne and I had made sure of that.

When I rolled up into his life, he was dabbling with weed, swigging from forty ounce bottles of cheap malt liquor and, according to Anne, experimenting with Ecstasy. I hurried up and straightened him out. I told him I'd fuck his world up if I ever caught him drunk or high again and then I dared him to try me.

Not that I needed to drive the point home too hard, because finding out that Anne was once addicted to crack cocaine was what had twisted up his head in the first place. All the smoking and drinking he was doing was his way of letting her know that he was angry and hurt. Once we had dealt with those issues and I had helped him see that becoming an addict himself wasn't the way to express his feelings, the smoking and drinking stopped.

Plus, he knew that I used to sell drugs and he knew I had almost gone to prison for a long time because of it. He couldn't be that stupid.

I said that to Anne. "He couldn't be that stupid."

"What about the cell phone he bought you for your birthday? You should've known something was up when he gave it to you, Smoke. I told you that damn thing cost at least three hundred dollars, but *noooo*, you were too busy salivating all over your new Blackberry."

"And where is your iPod, Anne?" She went to stuttering and stammering. "That's what I thought. That little piece of junk was somewhere in the vicinity of two hundred bucks, too. I don't see you refusing to take it jogging with you."

"I'm not giving it back," she said and made me crack up.

"Then keep your lips off my Blackberry." I glanced at my watch and followed her into the bathroom. I needed to be in my truck and halfway to work right now, but I never left home without handling my business first and foremost. I backed Anne up against the vanity and slipped my tongue in her mouth. Pulled back slowly and caught her eyes. "When Zay gets home, let me handle him."

"This could be serious, Smoke."

"Look at my face." She did. "Don't I look like I'm serious? Zay's ass is mine. I'm finding out where the money came from if I have to beat him down to get it out of him. What time does his flight get in this afternoon?"

"Two, I think."

"I'll be home by three," I said and stole one last kiss. My Blackberry vibrated in my pocket and I glanced at the caller ID on my way out the door. Diana again. I sent the call straight to voicemail and wished I could send her to hell on the same bus.

ISAIAH

Dude pulled in a mouthful of thick smoke and tried to pass me the blunt he was killing. I shook my head and sent him a lopsided smile when his eyebrows rose. He tried to act like he was confused by me, but he knew the deal. I didn't indulge and I told him that every time he offered me a hit. I figured the weed must've been affecting his memory, because this made the third time I had declined and then grinned at him.

"You worried about your coach dropping you?" dude asked and took another hit.

I sipped my soda and glanced at the clock. I had to be at the airport in a hot little minute and I still needed to run back to my dorm to shower and change clothes. There was no way in the world I was stepping inside the airport smelling like chronic. And don't even talk about me rolling up on my mama reeking.

"I'm cool."

Plus, I wasn't jeopardizing my scholarship for man, woman or child. I came to KSU on a full ride. Books, room and board, meals, everything, and as long as I kept my game tight on the court, it was all good. I had taken the Breds to the state championships for the past two years and if I had my way, we were going one more time before I pulled my degree. Taking a hit off of a blunt when I knew

I could be dropped at any time of the day or night didn't even interest me a little bit.

Dude walked in slow motion across his hotel room and stuck his head inside a mini refrigerator. He came back to the couch where I was sitting with two beers and offered me one. I took it and set it on the floor by my feet.

"Damn, you ain't drinking, either?" He knocked back half of his beer in one long gulp and belched. He was straight fucked up and funny to watch—smiling like Sylvester the Cat. "What you want to do then? You want me to tell you some shit about the draft that's coming up? You already know we want your ass, so don't even trip about that."

Dig this, dude's name was Marion, of all things. Marion Witherspoon. My coach had introduced me to several NBA scouts from different teams this past season and they had all expressed interest in recruiting me, but Marion was a strange breed. He had gone above and beyond the call of duty and started lacing a brotha with all kinds of perks—a new BlackBerry that I gave to my old dude, a top of the line iPod that I passed along to my mama, weekend rental cars, and loot. I tried to turn down the money he tossed my way, but he wouldn't hear of it. So I banked it and waited for the day he started talking noise about me owing him something. He was convinced that I was going to be a Mountaineer, but I hadn't even thought that far ahead. A couple of other teams had piqued my interest too, so I was keeping my options wide open. He was sticking like glue to a couple of other dudes on my team too, and they were spending the money he gave them, but I was waiting to see what was really up with him.

Marion was cool and all that, but he was the only scout that I knew of who hung out with students on his own time, smoking himself silly and drinking so much that he got straight tore down. He had been around for most of the academic year, chilling in an extended-stay hotel room and getting comfortable as hell. I thought that was curious.

"A scout from Tennessee came down to watch my tapes," I said.

"From Tennessee?" He looked shocked. "Those mother-fuckers? They ain't gon' treat your ass half as good as we will, I'm telling you. How much was their signing bonus?"

"Five hundred." I was still having trouble wrapping my lips around half a million dollars.

I mean, I knew pro ballers made five, hell, ten times more than that every year, but it was still more money than I'd ever had in my life. And the topic of what my yearly salary would be hadn't even come up yet. Five hundred grand was just a for starters, a thanks for shopping here type thing.

"So what you want to do? You want to go with them chumps, Zay?"

"I'm not going with anybody until I get my hands on my degree," I said and laughed. He had reached for his beer three times and missed it by a mile each time. "I'm keeping my options open right now."

"Yeah, well, just don't forget the Mountaineers been hooking your ass up while them other motherfuckers ain't been doing shit." Marion tapped me on my leg and tipped his head. "I been keeping you straight, haven't I? Shit, you count up all the money you got, you probably owe me about twenty grand or some shit."

Here we go, I thought. I sat up and braced my elbows on my thighs, looking at him like, *don't even try it.* "More like ten," I said. "You want it back?"

We stared at each other and he was the first to look away, laughing like I had cracked the joke of the century.

"Oh, I see you one of those mathematical motherfuckers. That's right, you getting a degree in architecture or some shit, ain't you?"

"Engineering."

"All that shit is Swahili to me. I'm so damn hungry, I could eat me three pussies right about now." He sat up and patted his shirt pockets and then he leaned back and patted his front pant pockets. "Where the fuck is my wallet?" I picked it up from the coffee table in front of us and handed it to him. "Oh shit, I'm tripping. Come on, nigga, let's go get us some juicy ass steaks and some fat-ass baked potatoes."

He was so high he had forgotten that we'd just eaten steaks and baked potatoes a bit over an hour ago, for lunch. Dude smoked entirely too much weed. I checked my watch and stood up. "Can't do it. I need to be at the airport in a minute or two, so I better roll."

"Oh, okay, that's cool. Hold up though, I need you to drop something off for me real quick."

I looked at the backpack he passed me curiously. "What's up with this?"

"It's a backpack, nigga. Drop it off at Chandler Hall for me, Zay. You know that little cat named Cullen?" I nodded slowly. "Him. Give it to him for me."

"What's in it?"

"Man, don't worry about all that, okay? You done made drops for your boy before, so don't even trip. You going home for Thanksgiving break?"

"Yeah." I thought about the padded envelope I had dropped off to a cat named Darius a few weeks back and then I thought about the messenger bag I had dropped off to a dude we called Hicks earlier this week. I hoped Marion didn't think I was all the way stupid.

"Gon' hang out with your pops and shit?"

"A little bit, yeah."

"Cool." He opened the door and stood back. "I put you a couple of bills in the front pocket, so you'll have a little spending change. Cullen should be looking out for you."

I gave him daps and slung the backpack over my shoulder. I didn't know what he had me toting off to Cullen, but whatever it was, wasn't heavy enough to be books, I knew that much.

In the car with Erica on my way to the airport, I had a flashback to high school and the situation I had gotten myself into with a crazy nigga named Hood. I wasn't trying to go there again, so I pulled out my cell phone and dialed Marion's cell. He picked up on the fourth ring.

"Check it," I said and laid a hand on Erica's thigh. "That was the last package I'm dropping off somewhere for you."

"Did you look and see what it was?"

"Nah, but I'm not stupid though."

"Nah, you ain't no stupid motherfucker, that's for damn sure. It's cool, Zay. We cool?"

I folded my cell phone closed and dropped it back in my pocket. Rolled my head around on my neck and looked at my baby. "Are you going to miss your man?"

She cracked a smile and slid me a glance. "You could always take me home with you, so I can meet your superhero parents."

"I could," I said. "And I will. One of these days I'm going to surprise you and toss you to the wolf, better known as my mama. Now, my old dude, he's cool. But my mama, she'll eat you for breakfast, lunch and dinner." I laid my other hand on my chest and chuckled like the spoiled brat that I was. "She don't play about her special baby boy. Can't just no anybody step to her talking about they're my woman. Especially since she thinks I'm still a virgin."

"Then I know she'll hate my guts," Erica said and we cracked up. Then she got quiet for a minute. "Did I ever tell you that Jared's mother told him not to marry me because I was too dark? She was worried about what her grandbabies would look like."

I sat up in the passenger seat, eyes got big. "He told you she said that?" That dude was even more stupid than I thought.

"When I dumped him." She sent me a sideways look.

"That dude ain't even worth talking about," I said and meant it.

"Your mama might feel the same way."

I thought about it and then I thought about it some more. I couldn't help laying my head back on my neck and hollering with laughter.

"What's so funny?"

"Nothing." I leaned sideways and sucked on her bicep softly. "Inside joke. I might tell it to you one day if you keep treating me right."

My mama was waiting for me at the gate, looking like a fifteen-year-old in hip hugging jeans and a green and gold KSU Thorobreds T-shirt. She saw me and came running, pushing a stroller in front of her.

"The green and gold," I joked just before she jumped up in my arms and hugged my neck so hard that I almost choked. I planted a smacking kiss on her puckered lips, squeezed her until she laughed and set her on her feet. "Hey, boo-boo. Why is it that I'm getting older and every time I see you, you look younger than the time before?"

I couldn't find a wrinkle anywhere on my mama's face. Her locks were pulled back into a ponytail, giving me a clear view of smooth skin and big, liquid brown eyes. She was a tiny little thing too, short and thin like Will Smith's wife, with eyes like Betty Boop's. Back in high school, all my friends had called my mama a dime piece, which meant that she was fine and they hadn't never lied. A couple of them had gone so far as to flirt with her when I wasn't looking. My high school basketball coach had even taken her out to dinner once or twice.

I think she knew she had it going on, too. It was in every move she made, the way she walked and talked. The way she looked up at a brotha with those eyes of hers and crinkled her nose when she laughed. I had seen her let loose on my old dude and watched him damn near break his neck trying to get her whatever she asked for. Cracked me up every time. She was such a big flirt that she didn't know how to turn it off.

I thought about what Erica had said and chuckled to myself. My mama was just as dark as Erica was and every bit as pretty. They looked more like mother and daughter than me and my mama looked like mother and son. Wait, scratch that. They looked more like sisters, if anything.

"Boy, please." She was blushing up to the roots of her hair and grinning from ear to ear.

"You still the prettiest woman I ever seen." I laid it on thick because I liked to see her eyes shine the way they were shining now. I loved me some my mama. I'd kill a nigga for her little ass and wouldn't think twice about it.

I dropped down to my haunches and stared at my second favorite lady. Her eyes lit up when she saw me and she almost fell on her face trying to get out of her stroller and into my arms. I unsnapped her and snatched her little butt up with one hand. "Don't start drooling and shit," I told her before I laid her little wet lips right on top of mine, drool and all.

"Watch your mouth, Isaiah."

"Excuse me, mama."

Home sweet home.

CHAPTER FIVE

ANNE

Isaiah hadn't been home a good twenty-four hours before my sister Laverne started calling, wanting to have a family dinner. The second time Smoke brought me the phone, telling me that she was on the line yakking about dinner plans, I had barely restrained myself from reminding her that a family was actually needed in order to have a family dinner. And I do mean barely.

Since I'd moved back to Indiana, Laverne and my mother had been on me like stink on shit, wanting to hang around, offering to babysit, Iris, whenever I needed them to and calling me for no reason at all. I still thought one of them was secretly terminally ill and needing me to give them a vital organ, but Smoke believed their motives were pure. He said that they just wanted to be in my life and I couldn't figure out for the life of me, why. And why now?

Growing up in the same house with my mother and sister was like being an ice cube in hell. To say I hated Laverne was putting it mildly. And my mother? I wasn't going there right now. No love lost though, you can believe that.

Of the three of us, I was the odd ball. The black sheep,

figuratively and literally. Both Laverne and my mother were light-skinned, like matching sticks of butter, with wavy, fine hair. Then, there was little old me, looking like a Hershey's chocolate bar, with a mop of thick, coarse hair sticking out from my head. That's why my locks were so gorgeous today, because I had the right type of hair for them. No lie, my locks were the bomb, but I am digressing.

I shook myself and focused on Iris' messy face. She had turkey and rice dinner smeared across her mouth and up the side of her face and I thought I saw Tutti-Frutti dessert along her hairline. "You eat just like your daddy, you know that?" I received a smile in response to my question. "Act like food is the beginning, the middle and the end of the world. You have to see it, taste it and wear it."

She slung her pacifier at me and reached for the spoon I was holding, growling like she really thought she could take me down for not moving fast enough. "Alright, piggy, give me a minute, okay?" I scooped up more turkey and rice and narrowed my eyes at her. "I'll bet you aren't even listening to me, are you? Here I am spilling my guts and you can't even spare me a few minutes of your time. You don't love me, do you, special baby?"

I was convinced that she understood every word I said to her. She heard me say the *L* word and stretched her arms out to me, reaching for my face with her little sticky, gooey fingers. I dodged them and leaned in to kiss her lips. She took two more spoonfuls of food, then she pushed the spoon away and started talking Russian.

"Oh, you want me to keep going?" She got excited. "Okay then," I said. "Where was I?"

Black Breanne, black Breanne, hair so thick, hair so wild, looks like a Zulu child. That's what the other kids used to call me. Called me that until I was in the eleventh grade. Laverne too. She made it so that I could never escape the cruel things other kids said to me. She made it so that I was not only miserable all day at school, but I was miserable all night at home, too.

She wasn't by herself though. My mother was right there with her, telling me how black and ashy I was, how funny looking I was, because my butt tooted out behind me and my chest was flat. She wasn't big on putting her hands on us, but my mother's tongue had cut me up from the top of my head to the soles of my feet, every damn day of my miserable life.

I came to always expect the middle finger from my mother, but Laverne was inconsistent with her torture, which was confusing. Sometimes, she was actually nice to me and we got along just fine, but other times, she was a hot little mess. She opened her mouth and sounded just like my mother, calling me black and ugly, telling me that no boy would ever want me, because I was too ugly to get one to look at me. I couldn't keep up with her mood swings.

I never told her that two of her boyfriends had flirted with me when she was out of the room and I never told her that one of them had actually gone so far as to try to kiss me. She would've really lost her mind then and I would've had to hurt her.

I never had to fight so much in my life, as much as I had to fight Laverne. When we went at each other, we'd spin from one room to the next, until our entire apartment bore witness to the fact that a knock-down drag-out had taken place. We fought like we were strangers just meeting for the first time—like we didn't give a damn if the other person lived or died. She talked about my skin so much that whenever I got my hands on hers I tried to rake it off of her with my bare hands. I was convinced that underneath all that high-yellow skin was a demon and I always tried to expose her for what she was.

I suffered for those fights, too. Because the sad fact of the matter was that Laverne was always one of those people who let their mouths write a check that their asses couldn't cash. She couldn't fight worth a damn and before it was all over and done with, I'd have her behind under my foot, begging me not to kick her anymore. Then, when my mother came home and saw what I had done to Laverne's pretty face, I'd find myself outside, rain, snow, sleet or shine, sitting on the front stoop waiting for her to decide when I could come back inside. Once or twice, it was after midnight when I finally heard the lock sliding free. Toward the end, my mother would put me out of our apartment and instead of sitting there, I'd go walking around the housing project where we lived. That's how I happened upon my first hit off of a crack pipe.

I saw his face in my mind, the guy who stopped the girl who was crying so hard that snot was running down her chin and asked her why she was crying. That girl, the one he stopped, had seen him around the neighborhood a few times and she knew he lived a couple of buildings over. She didn't know his name, but she didn't really need to know it to know that she liked what he said to her. Wanted it to be true so badly that she believed him and went with him when he promised her that he had something to make her feel better.

That something was crack cocaine and it made me feel like Superwoman, Xena Warrior Princess and one of the X-Men all rolled into one. For about twenty minutes, that is, while the high was good and strong, and then I felt like crap again. So this is what I did. I stayed high most of the time. I stole, begged, lied and stole some more to get high and when the money ran out, I gave Smoke my virginity for yet another rock.

Bastard that he was back then, he took it. I couldn't even begin to estimate the number of times that I went to him looking for a high. But I do know that I never bought my drugs from anyone else, so when I ended up pregnant, there was no question about whose child I was carrying.

Then came Aunt Bobbi and the rest, as they say, is history. I was somewhere around three months pregnant when I went away with her and I never looked back. I never planned on coming back to Indiana before there was a death in the family and I had to pick out somebody's casket, but here I was—in love and shacking with a man who had me doing all kinds of things that I said I would never do.

"Ain't that some mess?" I set the bowl I had been feeding Iris from in the sink and filled it with tap water. I looked across the room at her and smiled. I had always sworn up and down that I didn't know if I could love another child as much as I loved my son. I'd doubted I had that kind of love left in me after Isaiah. But my Iris, she proved to me that mothers had about fifty hearts beating in their chests and that each child claimed a whole one for themselves. I wondered what other line my mother had been standing in when the man upstairs was giving out hearts. Probably the line for good hair or some other such silliness.

"You think we have time for a quick nap?" She looked at me like I was crazy. "No? Well, what about a bath?" She showed me her gums. "Oh, you like the sound of that, huh? We can't splash and play around today though." I glanced at the kitchen clock and sighed long and hard. "We need to hurry up and get ready for dinner. They're coming soon for us and it just wouldn't do for us to look anything less than our absolute best, now would it?"

* * *

There were three things that you could always count on happening when black families congregated: an impromptu card or domino game, somebody getting drunk and showing his or her ass, and at least one argument between grown folks who were supposed to know better. Not necessarily in that order, but guaranteed entertainment nonetheless. Sometimes, these events happened in rapid succession and sometimes they evolved slowly, one after another throughout the course of said congregating. There was no way to predict these things.

Since we'd told everyone three o'clock and by four over half of those invited were in attendance, with no signs of a disturbance evident, I came to the conclusion that we were on a gradual throughout the evening schedule. But we were coming along nicely.

I took a pan of corn bread from the oven and looked to my left. Smoke's brother, Jake was rooting around in the all-purpose drawer, looking for the deck of cards that Smoke had sent him in search of. He finally found them and gave me a triumphant grin on his way out of the kitchen. One down, I thought as I wiped my hands on a dishtowel and went back into the den, where everyone else was.

By six o'clock, we had a house full. There was Smoke's brother, Don, and his wife, Liz, their two kids and two other ones that had arrived with Smoke's other brother, Jake, and his girlfriend. The kids were hers and her name was Kee-Kee. One look at Jake's face and I knew he was in lust, full throttle. Kee-Kee's butt was huge and his eyes followed it everywhere it went. That was probably why he couldn't see the woman's bad-ass kids running through my house like vigilantes. And forget about him saying something to Kee-Kee, so she could say something to

them, so I didn't have to. He was transfixed by her der-
riere, practically blinded by it.

Jake was clearly one of those people who didn't like to
correct other people's children, but Smoke had no such
qualms. Kee-Kee's kids took one turn too many around his
expensive stereo equipment and it was on. By the time he
got done with them, they were sitting in front of the big
screen being nice and quiet and watching *Big Mama's
House II* like it was the first movie they had ever seen.

Isaiah sat in a recliner with his Big Mama on his lap.
They were looking through a photo album that he had
brought home with him and he was pointing out the high-
lights to her. Jeff, Don's oldest and Isaiah's partner in
crime, was secluded in a corner whispering into the cordless phone. He looked up as I passed and winked. He even
had the nerve to blow me a kiss, with his mannish self. I
laughed even though I didn't need to and made my way
over to where Smoke was sprawled out on one end of the
couch.

My mother was sitting in the other recliner and Laverne
was holding court at the other end of the couch. Neither
of them had said very much since they had arrived and
greeted everyone. They were content to watch everyone
else and to smile when someone cracked a stale joke,
which was often because Jake didn't know when to quit.
Laverne's daughters had attached themselves to Don's
daughter in what appeared to be a slight case of hero wor-
ship and Iris was still in the throes of a nap that she
needed to be awakened from if I hoped to get any sleep
tonight.

I glanced at my watch and asked Smoke to make the
announcement that dinner was ready. He nodded and
leaned forward to set his empty beer bottle on the coffee
table at the same time that Laverne leaned forward with

the same intention. I did a quick mental count and then asked myself if she'd had three or four beers already. Eventually, I came to the conclusion that she had just finished beer number three.

Laverne drunk? Was she spectacle number two in progress? Interesting. Maybe the inevitable argument would unfold between her and Kee-Kee. There had been a brief exchange of words earlier between the two women after Kee-Kee's daughter had pushed Laverne's daughter. I wondered if Laverne had brushed up on her fighting technique over the years and hoped I wouldn't have to find out.

"We need to say grace," Big Mama announced. She uncurled herself from Isaiah's lap and got to her feet. She sent Jeff a meaningful glance and pointed to the big screen. "Turn that thing off, somebody, please."

We all linked hands and formed a large circle, heads bowed.

"Father . . ." Big Mama began.

Iris's pitiful sounding cry came through the baby monitor loud and clear. Everyone's head turned in the direction of the end table where it sat.

"Can I get her?"

I looked at my mother like I didn't know who she was. "No, I'll get her," I said and stepped back from the circle. Two steps from being out of the room, Laverne's voice hit me between my shoulder blades.

"Why can't mama get her, Bree? She just wants to spend some time with at least one of your children before she dies."

"What?" I turned around in slow motion and stared at Laverne. I shook my head, confused. "What are you talking about, Laverne?"

"I'm just saying, mama's been trying to hold that baby since we got here and you've come up with one excuse after another for why she can't. Did it ever occur to you that you're hurting her feelings?"

Anger jumped on my back so quickly that I didn't know it was there until I opened my mouth and sliced the air with it. "You don't know anything about hurt feelings, Laverne. You never did, so that makes you just about the last person qualified to speak on the subject."

"Here we go," Isaiah mumbled under his breath and laid his head back to stare at the ceiling. You could've heard a pin drop, the room was so quiet.

"Bree . . ."

"And stop calling me Bree."

Laverne's eyes got big, her weight shifted to one side and a hand went to her hip. "Why should I? That's your damn name, isn't it? Breanne Melanie Phillips."

"Oh? I thought it was Zulu Girl?"

She looked tired. "Bree . . ." She shook her head.

I looked at my mother and pointed to her sidekick. "What about you? Why are you letting her do all the talking for you? That's new, isn't it?"

"Anne."

I looked at Big Mama and the look on her face was enough to make me feel like I was twelve years old again.

"Why don't you go and get everything ready in the kitchen?" she suggested. "Alec?"

"Yes, ma'am?"

"Go and see about your daughter, okay? Isaiah?"

"Ma'am?"

"Lead us in prayer, please?" We didn't move fast enough and she sent a look around the room that had me skipping toward the kitchen, Smoke excusing himself from the room to go and see about Iris, and Isaiah clearing his throat, head bowed. They didn't call her five-foot-two inch, red-haired self, Big Mama, for nothing.

Five minutes later, I walked into the den and caught

Smoke passing my daughter to my mother and damn near dropped the glass of soda I was sipping from. He swooped in just in time to take the glass from me and slip an arm around my waist.

"Let me talk to you for a minute," he said and led me out of the room.

As soon as he had closed the bedroom door behind us I started spitting and hissing. "What are you doing, Smoke? You know how I feel about this!"

"Anne, the woman just wants to hold her granddaughter. Baby, you're tripping, okay?"

"Tripping?" I fell back and waved my arms in the air. "I'm tripping? You know good and well what she's capable of and I'll be damned if I stand back and let her mistreat Iris. She's evil, Smoke. I told you that. Now move so I can go out there and get my baby." I tried to step around him, but he wasn't having it. We did a two-step and then I stood back and folded my arms across my chest, glaring at him.

"Don't you think it's time you let the past go?"

"And how," I paused to swallow the lump in my throat, "do you propose I do that?" I was so angry that I was shaking with it, had tears in my eyes. "Am I supposed to forget what they did to me? Act like it didn't happen?"

"It's eating you up, Anne," Smoke said. "You need to . . ."

I cut him off with the asthma attack that I thought I was having.

ALEC

I caught Anne before she hit the floor and dragged her over to the bed. She was shaking like a leaf and gasping for air. Scaring the shit out of me and making me want to crack up at the same time. I knew there was nothing really wrong with her, except for the fact that she needed to calm down. But seeing her put on a show was always extra special, because she didn't do it very often. One of these days though, she was going to give herself a real heart attack, trying to win an Emmy.

"Sit down, Anne, damn." I stooped down in front of her and made her look at me. "You know you need to quit, don't you?"

"She could be out there whispering something foul in Iris's ear right now. And you saw how many beers Laverne drank. While you're in here harassing me, they could . . ."

"Zay is out there," I told her. "So is Big Mama and everybody else. Iris is fine." I searched her face for long seconds. "You might not be, though. I thought you said you were going to try with them."

"I am trying. They're here, aren't they?"

"They've been here over two hours and you haven't said a total of that many words to them, Anne. I saw you run your mother out of the kitchen, too. You got them following you around with their eyes, begging you to pay some attention to them."

I had been peeping Anne's mother and sister out all evening and they were so desperate for Anne's attention that I was starting to feel sorry for them. Especially her mother, since she was the one Anne shot down the quickest and the hardest whenever she reached out. I saw the look on her face when Anne told her that there was nothing she could do to help in the kitchen but then turned around and asked Big Mama to slice tomatoes for the salad. I read the despair in Laverne's eyes when she and Anne were having their little scrimmage a minute ago. They wanted in and Anne was doing a stellar job of keeping them as far out as possible.

What Anne failed to realize and what I couldn't seem to make her see was that she was hurting herself the most. She had so much anger and hurt bottled up inside of her that it was taking everything in her to feed it and keep it alive and thriving. She would deny it until her dying day, but I saw the way she looked at her people when she didn't think anybody was looking at her. She wanted to do something too, she just didn't quite know what that something was.

Meanwhile, I was doing what I could to help Anne's mother and sister out. They had their own ways of chipping away at Anne's armor and I had mine. Whereas, theirs didn't seem to be gaining them too much ground, my methods of persuasion had the benefit of a more personal and up-close advantage. I figured the least I could do was provide some necessary distraction when it was needed.

I sent Anne back out to the den without a trace of lip gloss on her lips, but with a noticeably calmer vibe. She slid a look over to where Iris was crawling all over Laverne on the couch, sucked in a sharp breath and switched into the kitchen. I heard some pots and pans taking a beating and found Zay's eyes across the room.

"She thinks I'm gon' hurt my own grandbaby?" Anne's mother tipped up on me and asked quietly. Even though she was light, bright and damn near white, I could still see Anne in her face, especially around the mouth and chin.

"She'll be all right." I hoped I was telling the truth. I hated to admit it, but every now and again, I caught myself wondering how she could've treated Anne the way she had and expected anything less than the treatment she was receiving in return. "Me and Isaiah are working on her."

"I know you are and we appreciate it, me and Laverne. Breanne always was a hardheaded little thang. Thinking I'm gon' do something wrong to my own grandbaby," she huffed. "She knows better than that."

"She . . ."

Jake's raised voice floated out of the kitchen. "Negro, how you gon' grab up all the drumsticks?"

"Because I'm grown, that's how," Don replied in a voice that was just as loud. "Any other time your ass wants a breast. Now, all of a sudden you want the drumsticks?"

"You need to leave some for somebody else. What if one of these kids wants a drumstick?"

Anne butted in, talking softly. "There's more drumsticks."

"Naw, what you need to do is stop trying to show off for Kee-Kee and these bad-ass kids of hers. You should'a been doing all this hollering when they were running around here like hyenas."

I dropped my head in my hand and very quietly cracked up. Beside me, Anne's mother was smiling and shaking her head. "Those kids do need some home training," she said and chuckled behind her hand.

"Excuse me?" Kee-Kee.

"Excuse me?" Don mimicked her squeaky, high-pitched voice perfectly and had me and Anne's mother falling against each other, laughing. "Did I stutter? Your kids need their little butts whipped. I can't put it any plainer than that."

"I can put my foot up your ass though." I figured she was ghetto, but damn. "Don't nobody talk about my damn kids."

"Baby, calm down," Jake said, sounding silly.

I took two steps in the direction of the kitchen and froze. The next voice I heard threw me for a loop.

Don's wife was one of those every Sunday going to church, usher board president kind of women. But I could've sworn I heard her earrings hitting the floor just before she said, "You want to put your foot up somebody's ass, why don't you try mine? Jake, you better get this strumpet."

"Ha!" Laverne blurted out.

"What the hell you laughing at?" Kee-Kee was on Laverne's case now.

"You, strumpet. And another thing, if your kid puts her hands on my kid again, I'm putting my hands on her, so you better watch her."

"Oh, now hold up," Jake was saying, but I thought it was a little too late to be trying to make peace. Sounded like Kee-Kee was on everybody's shit list right about now.

I headed to the kitchen to find Iris and make sure she was out of the line of fire. Kee-Kee's kids be damned. If mine got hurt, even if it was by accident, I was going to have to unlock my pistol and put some fire in somebody's ass. A foot wouldn't be good enough.

As soon as I stepped in the kitchen, Anne held up three fingers and looked around the room with her eyebrows raised. She had warned me, but I wouldn't listen. And we still had Thanksgiving to get through.

We waited until the day before Zay was flying back to Kentucky to come hard at him. I liked to be prepared for whatever, liked to have all the facts and all the necessary evidence to support my position before I went running up in somebody's space, so I laid low while he was home for spring break and bided my time.

The good news was that I hadn't found anything to make me think that Zay was using drugs. I'd searched his room from top to bottom this morning while he was out running with Anne and I hadn't found so much as a roach clip. This wasn't necessarily conclusive evidence, but it was enough to regulate my breathing. Just like some folks never left home without their Mastercards, a user never strayed too far from the nest without some sort of supply and Zay's room was clean.

The bad news was that the bank account he had full access to was out of order. Again. He had deposited another thousand dollars the same day he came home last week. I hadn't mentioned it to Anne yet, because I wanted to get Zay alone in a corner somewhere and find out what the deal was before I brought her into the mix. I couldn't begin to imagine where he was getting the money, but I refused to consider the possibility that he was pushing weight. He had to know that I would fuck his world up if that was the case, so trying me on the issue was definitely not in his best interests.

I had to come at him for this four years ago and I doubted that he would forget the circumstances under which we first met anytime soon. He was sixteen before I knew he even existed, but when I found out, I didn't hesitate to bust up in his space and toss him on his head. Anne was damn near going crazy, wondering what to do about all the smoking and drinking he was doing, his bad grades and the hoodlums he was running around with. But me? I had the perfect solution.

I picked Isaiah up by the back of his neck and I never let him go. True enough, me and Anne were tangled up in a knot at the time, but I never let Isaiah stray too far from my range of vision no matter how hard me and Anne were going at each other. He was up close and personal with a little dope-slinging thug named Hood, but I hurried up and announced myself as his new best friend. Broke that so-called friendship up quick, fast and in a hurry.

Back then Zay was a forty-ounce drinking, blunt smoking fool. Getting so high that he couldn't remember what he was doing from one day to the next, which almost got him killed. He made the mistake of thinking that Hood was cool people, when that little thug really had designs on taking my son down the drain along with him. He hadn't counted on me though. Hood didn't know what hit him when he ran up on me, talking shit. I tried to put that fool's head to bed. Then, I got with Isaiah.

Hell no, he couldn't be selling drugs, I thought as I

pulled my cell phone from my pocket and dialed methodically. I took it into my bedroom with me and closed the door for privacy. Anne had supersonic hearing.

"What the hell you want with me, Smoke?"

"What's up, Dino? Long time no hear." I couldn't stop a smile from spreading across my face. Me and Dino went way back to the days when I was selling and selling hard. He had started me in the game and taught me the all-important ropes. Brought me up from running weight from corner to corner to running things, period. Though I was all the way out of the game and had been for years, we still kept in touch.

"Whatever, nigga. You the one over there playing happy family and shit. What's up with my baby girl, she cool?"

Not too many people knew that Dino's birth name was Ira, not even Anne. She thought that I'd suggested the name to her because it began with an *I* like Isaiah's name and I let her keep thinking that. The truth was that Iris was named for the brotha who had paved the way for me to step down from the dope game free and clear and without a bullet in my skull. He had taken me on as a liability and staked his name on the fact that I could be trusted to keep who and what I knew to myself.

Naming one of my children after him was the least I could do. "Yeah," I said. "Getting fat and spoiled as hell. She was seven months last week."

"What did Anne think about them diamond earrings I sent my baby for Christmas?"

"Haven't gotten around to showing them to her yet. You know better than to buy a baby two-carat diamond earrings. You thought she was going to wear them now?"

"Hell, they insured. I bet you didn't even tell Anne I bought them, did you?"

"I'm working my way around to it," I said and laughed.

"You done turned into a old punk ass nigga, Smoke. Anne got your ass so whipped it ain't even funny. She must be putting it down on you."

"All damn day long." He took the phone from his ear and barked at somebody, told them to step back and wait until he was done on the phone. I recognized the tone. "You need to go?"

"Motherfuckers trying my patience over here. What's up with you, son? Tell a nigga what you want with me already."

"Oh, I can't call just to check on you?"

"Time is money, Smoke. You know that shit. Plus, a brotha stays on the phone too long and motherfuckers think I ain't paying attention to they asses. Speak up, bruh."

"I need you to do some checking for me," I told him. "Isaiah is . . ."

"Zay?" he cut me off. "What the fuck is he into now? I'ma tell you what, I'm 'bout ready to beat his ass like he stole something myself. I thought he was off in school some motherfucking where."

"Kentucky State University," I enunciated clearly and perfectly. "You got people there?"

"I got people everywhere, son. You think Zay is off into some shit he don't need to be off into?"

"That's what I need you to tell me, Dino. Put a clock on him for a minute and see what time it is."

"I'ma do better than that," Dino said. "I'ma make a run down to Kentucky my motherfucking self. I need to get down that way anyway. Give me a day or two and I'll get back with you. Cool?"

"Cool."

"A'ight then, Smoke. Peace."

My plan was to wait until I heard back from Dino to approach Isaiah about the money. Meanwhile, I needed to pull his coat about something else. I came out of my bedroom, found my brothers in the kitchen raiding the refrigerator and harassing Anne, and told them it was time to roll.

CHAPTER SIX

ISAIAH

I looked to my left and saw my Uncle Jake coming out the front door. Looked over my shoulder and saw my old dude coming through the garage toward me. Then, my Uncle Don came from around the side of the house, moving in on my right. Something was up.

Jeff and me slid each other knowing looks.

"What's up, da?" I said as soon as my old dude was up on me and breathing down the back of my neck. Next thing I knew, he was sniffing me with a big smile on his face. I had to laugh. "You're tripping."

"Nah, youngblood, I assert that it is you who is tripping, slipping and every damn thing else. Why you got Dolittle calling the house, talking about he caught you and some hoochie laying up in the frat house? You're lucky I got to the phone before your mother did, because you know she thinks you don't know what pussy is, right? Plus, I had to argue with her about why I wouldn't say what the call was about, so you owe me big." My old dude poked me in my back and sucked his teeth. "You owe me so big, it ain't even cute."

"Dolittle is full of shit." I dribbled the basketball Jeff and me had been tossing around over to the hoop and went in for a layup. "Everybody was dressed when he walked in the room. Nobody was laying up."

"Oh, so we do smell pussy?"

I froze with the ball and stared at my Uncle Don. My old dude was liable to say anything at any time, but my Uncle Don was usually a little more conservative, what with his bible thumping wife and everything. Had he just said pussy? "You been drinking?"

He held up the bottle of beer he was carrying around with him and shook it. "Don't try to get off the subject, boy. Who is the hoochie?"

That was the second time that word had been said and just like the first time that I heard it, it hit me the wrong way. Erica was a lot of things, but a hoochie wasn't one of them. I shot the ball to Jeff and stood back while he sank a jump shot. Then I reached up and scratched my head slowly. "She's not a hoochie, so chill with that."

Jake narrowed his eyes at me as he took a gigantic bite of his ham and cheese sandwich.

"You in love, Zay?"

"I ain't saying all that."

"Then, what the hell are you saying? Who is this hoochie?"

I caught the ball with one hand and used the other one to lean up against Jake's Range Rover, looking at my Uncle Don like he was crazy. "Erica." I could've sworn I felt my dick stirring just from the sound of her name. She was the main reason that I was ready to get back to school. It had been a week and a brotha was overdue.

"Naw, Smoke, that ain't a stripper's name." Jake shoved half of his sandwich in his mouth and almost choked on it trying not to laugh. Then Jeff threw his head back and cracked up, which really pissed me off. That fool knew about Erica two days after I knew about her and he had even met her once before, so he knew what the deal was. The hoochie shit was nowhere near funny.

"Erica, who?" my old dude wanted to know. He folded his arms across his chest and leaned a hip against the house. "Who are her people? Where is she from? What's her story and are you wrapping your shit up like you need to be wrapping it up?"

"Da. Duh."

"Da, my ass. I'm not trying to be anybody's grandfather no time soon Zay, and you know it doesn't take much for your mother to run for the knives."

"You ain't never lied," I cosigned and dribbled the ball back over to the hoop. I sank four out of five shots before I said, "Her father is some kind of big time evangelist in Mississippi. Got one of them churches with a thousand members or something like that. Her mom is into social work, I think."

"You done pulled you a southern gal?" Jake hollered, laying on a heavy accent that sounded more Irish than southern.

"Well now, you know what they say about them southern women." Don took a seat on the bumper of the Rover and started grinning like Grady from *Sanford and Son*. "Those are some hospitable sistas—really hospitable."

I rolled my eyes and kept hooping. "They moved to Mississippi when she was little. She's from the islands."

"Is she a sista?"

"What else?" I would've heard my old dude's sigh of relief even if I had been born without ears.

"Because you know your mother's motto. If she can't use the comb, don't . . ."

"Bring her home," I finished and we cracked up. "Ain't no problem there, trust."

"Sistas from the islands ain't no joke."

"Da, please." Jeff finally found his voice. "Ya'll need to stop with this good cop, bad cop stuff. Me and Zay grown ass men."

"Talk that grown ass men shit to me when I'm done paying your college tuition and you put a degree in my hand, boy," Uncle Don told him. "And shut up too, because I'm not two seconds off your ass, as it is."

"What did I do?"

"The question is, who did you do? And where?"

Now it was my turn to crack up. I dropped the ball, took two steps to the side and tried to fall out, I was laughing so hard. I had told that fool not to trip, but no, you couldn't tell him nothing. He looked like a deer caught in headlights.

"Lisa told?"

"You know damn well five dollars wasn't going to keep Lisa's money-hungry mouth closed. Hell, I had to give her a twenty just to keep her from telling your mother I was the one who ate some of the wedding cake she made for one of her coworkers. Why would you even *think* about bringing Sister Hempstead up in my house to screw? A hotel down the street and around the corner and you took her to your bedroom? What if that had been your mother who walked in and caught you with your ass in the air?"

That was exactly what I had asked him. Sister Hempstead was hot to trot, damn near forty years old and engaged to Brother Carlton all day long. Now, I didn't see nothing wrong with Jeff tightening her up every now and again, but he should've done it as far away from home as possible. I had told that fool not to shit where he laid his head, especially since he had been tagging Sister Hempstead on the regular ever since he turned eighteen and she stopped worrying about catching a case.

"See, this is why it don't pay to have kids." We all turned to look at Jake. "Every other minute, they got something going on. Zay is running around here laying up with hoochies from the islands and Jeff's got a ho from the church with her legs wrapped around his neck." He shook his head like he was confused. "But what I can't figure out is how my nephews are managing to get more pussy than I am?"

"I keep telling ya'll, Erica is not a hoochie."

"Whatever, Zay. Just make sure Doolittle doesn't ring my phone again."

"And Sister Hempstead is not a . . ."

"Boy, if you stand there and tell that lie you're crazier than I thought." Jeff tried to walk past Uncle Don, but he stopped him with a hand on his shoulder. "And you need to stop grinning up in Brother Carlton's face every time you see him, too. You might think fucking another man's woman is cool right now, but some day you might think it's a reason to take somebody's head off. You dig?"

"I know you ain't done, Don," Smoke butted in. "Because I think we need to go a little deeper with this shit."

"I think so, too," Uncle Jake said, still chewing on his sandwich and looking silly.

"You're right, you're right. Sit 'cho ass down, boy, and let me holla at you for a minute," Uncle Don told Jeff.

"Look, da," Jeff started in. "I'm cool . . ."

"You need me to help you sit down?"

Behind him, Smoke motioned for me to sit down, too. Jeff and I looked at each other and didn't say nothing. I mean, what could we say to that? He sat down first and then I followed suit. It was going to be a long afternoon.

ANNE

Hands Are Not For Hitting wanted me and they wanted me badly. I still hadn't quite figured out how they had known where to find me but over the last year they had been courting me so intensely that I was beginning to be uncomfortable with their level of interest. If I hadn't already done extensive research on the organization, I would've sworn they were some kind of cult out to brainwash me and make me drink purple Kool-Aid. They were that persistent.

While I was living in Chicago, I had founded the *Olive Branch*, a full service wellness center for women from all walks of life. Because I was a former addict, the center specialized in providing substance abuse counseling, AA meetings and life skills counseling to women who were new to living sober. I felt it was my duty to give back some of what I had received while I was in the year-long inpatient drug program that saved my life. Isaiah had never known or seen me as an addict, but I remembered vividly who and what I was before getting clean, and I desperately wanted to share what I'd learned with those who were still in that time and place.

Making the decision to sell the center and move to Indiana was one of the hardest things I'd ever had to do, but I had to look at the situation objectively. I weighed the pros and cons and finally admitted to myself that I was an all or nothing kind of person. Smoke was of the mind that I could run the center from a distance, but I knew better. If I couldn't be totally involved with the center, less than that simply wouldn't do. So I sold it to the state of Illinois for a lovely profit and cried nonstop for two weeks afterward.

Finding out about and preparing for Iris had kept me from going stir-crazy for a while, but lately, I was becoming more and more restless. Just like when Isaiah was a baby, I needed to be doing something to stimulate myself intellectually at the same time that I was caring for my child. Back then that something was finishing my high school education and going on to college. In the here and

now, it looked like that something would be my acceptance of the administrative position *Hands* was literally
begging me to take.

Of the sixty battered women's shelters and thirty transitional housing complexes they operated all over the country, five safe house shelters and three transitional housing
apartment complexes were located in Indiana. My job, if I
chose to accept the position, would be to oversee those
entities and the staff that worked in them. The salary wasn't
the greatest for the level of responsibility I'd have, but I
didn't really care about that so much as I cared about the
opportunity to make a difference. Two hundred grand a
year would allow me to do that and at least live comfort-
ably in the process.

Another plus, and probably the deciding factor for me,
was that I could make my own schedule and work from
home when I felt like I needed or wanted to. They called
me and told me that little piece of information. Suddenly,
I was a lot more interested than I had been all the other
times they had contacted me. I talked it over with Smoke
and we decided that I needed to start taking what *Hands*
was offering me more seriously.

I stopped with all the vague responses and shucking
and jiving, and finally let them pin me down on an exact
date and time to come in for an interview. More like an in-
terrogation, I thought as I tossed my briefcase into the
passenger seat and followed it inside my car. I had been
hemmed up all morning, facing off with a three-person fir-
ing squad, fielding questions on everything from my edu-
cational history to my choice of breakfast cereals. One of
the last things I had done for the *Olive Branch* was orga-
nize a multi-million dollar fund raiser, which had attracted media attention from all over the country. They
wanted a play-by-play on how I'd managed to pull it off
and that in itself, had taken me an hour to discuss as

vaguely as I could. I didn't believe in revealing valuable secrets of the trade.

When it was all said and done though, I walked out of the meeting with a firm job offer on the table and my tentative slash firm acceptance right beside it. I started my car, shifted into DRIVE and cut the wheel. Then my cell phone rang. I shifted back into PARK and wrestled with my briefcase, trying to pin down its whereabouts. I finally wrapped my hand around it and checked the caller ID. I didn't recognize the number.

"This is Anne Phillips."

"I know who this is," the caller said. "This is Diana Daniels."

I lost my stride for a second, but I got it back before I had a chance to really miss it. "What can I do for you, Diana?"

Flossie. I hadn't had the occasion to cross her path since the time me and Smoke had run into her at a dinner-dance thing we had gone to a year or so back. Good music, mediocre food and when I looked around, Diana Daniels was up in my face. Falling out of her dress and slightly tipsy, making like we had something other than how she could go somewhere and die a slow death to talk about. If I hadn't been five months along with Iris, I would've snapped the hand she kept touching my stomach with clean in half. Bitch.

"You can give Alec a message for me."

"And that would be?"

"Tell him I have a doctor's appointment scheduled for Thursday of next week and I think we'll be able to listen to the baby's heartbeat then."

"Excuse me?"

"He didn't tell you?"

"You tell me," I said.

"Alec and I are having a baby, Anne. I thought he

would've told you by now, since I told him I was pregnant a week ago. No, that's not right. It was probably closer to two weeks ago."

"Ah." Some things were starting to make sense now. "Oh that? Yeah, I do remember him saying something about you lying about being pregnant, but I must have forgotten about it, since I've been so busy planning the wedding and everything." I listened to Diana suck in a sharp breath and let myself smile, though I had murder on my mind.

"What wedding?"

"Mine and Alec's, bitch. You didn't think he was coming back to you, did you? Just because he slipped up and messed around with you once doesn't mean . . ."

"Twice," she hissed. "I had your man twice, so what now?"

I'd found out exactly what I wanted to know, that was what. No wonder the whore was a gym teacher, she was so simple it was almost funny. Nothing but perky tits, a wide, fiendish smile and empty space between her ears. "Nothing now." I chuckled like I wasn't understanding the question. "We'll pay child support and expect regular visitation, that's what. After the paternity test . . ."

"BITCH!" Diana screamed at the top of her lungs in my ear. I took my cell from my ear and stared at it. "BITCH, BITCH, BITCH . . ."

I had been a bitch four consecutive times when I disconnected from the psycho and bypassed stopping to have a manicure and pedicure in favor of going straight home, where Smoke was waiting for me. We were planning on taking in a movie and having a romantic dinner afterward, but that was out the window now, wasn't it?

As far as Diana Daniels was concerned, one thing she needed to hurry up and learn about me was that I hadn't let a woman get the best of me in over twenty years and I wasn't about to start now. Smoke was a different story though. He had obviously been getting the best of me for a hot little minute now and I was too blind to see it.

I dropped my briefcase on the bed, checked to make sure Iris was sleeping soundly and then I followed the sound of the shower into the bathroom adjoining our bedroom. I stood there for a few minutes, watching him move around behind the frosted glass and taking deep breaths, so I wouldn't lose it and plug in a hair dryer. Then I made a "Bill Bixby-Incredible Hulk, turning green because I'm furious" move.

I scared the shit out of Smoke, opening the shower door the way I did. He spun around with his mouth hanging open and his dick swinging. "Woman, you were about to get a beatdown, running up on a brotha like that."

I didn't smile when he smiled, nor did I take a deep relieved breath when he took a deep relieved breath. Instead, I stepped halfway inside the shower in my six hundred dollar Michael Kors pantsuit, my two hundred dollar DKNY silk shell and my three hundred dollar Farragamo pumps, and slapped the shit out of Smoke. Then I said, "Diana said for me to tell you it's a boy. Congratu-fucking-lations."

He came tripping out of the bathroom with a towel pressed up against the family jewels and dripping all over the carpet. "Run that by me again?"

I ignored him and kept on doing what I was doing, which was easing Iris off of our bed and into my arms. I stood still and waited for her to settle back into sleep and then I tiptoed her down the hallway to her own room. When I came back to our bedroom, Smoke was stepping into boxers and eyeing the doorway warily. I closed the door behind me, stepped out of my heels and shrugged off my jacket. I took my earrings off and laid them on the armoire. Then I rushed Smoke like a stealth bomber.

"What the hell . . . ?"

I succeeded in driving him back into the dresser before he caught my hands and tried to pull me into him. I wasn't aware that I had started crying until I pushed him away from me and had to wipe my face with my hands, so I could see him clearly. "I love you, Anne. I want to be with you, Anne. I don't want anyone but you, Anne. Marry me, Anne. Isn't that the shit you said to me, Smoke?"

"I know what I said. Baby, listen to me, this is not what it looks like, okay?"

He came toward me with his hands out and I stopped him with a look. "If dying right here and now is what you want to do, then you go right ahead and put your hands on me."

"I haven't been creeping around with Diana the whole time we've been together. If she said that, she was lying."

"Oh, I got that part, Smoke. The silly whore was only too happy to tell me that she had my man twice and apparently, this last time she got . . ." I paused to punch him in his chest, . . . "pregnant. So not only were you screwing her, but you were screwing her without protection. Bringing that whore home to share with me!"

"That's not how it was."

"So you didn't screw her twice?"

"Yes, but . . ."

"And you used condoms both times?"

His mouth opened, snapped shut and then opened again. "No, but . . ."

"So you willingly put my life in danger, is that right?"

"If you would just listen to me for a minute, I can explain. I wasn't running around with Diana behind your back. What happened between her and I was nothing. Didn't mean shit to me."

"But you did it anyway." I pushed a hand through my locks and closed my eyes against new tears. I couldn't believe I was standing here, letting him see how devastated I was. Couldn't believe something like this was what it took for me to realize how completely I had given myself to him. Couldn't believe . . . "Two times, Smoke? You can call one time a mistake, but two? You knew what you were doing. You went to her looking for sex."

"I didn't go to Diana looking for anything. She kept coming to me and I . . ."

"Gladly gave her what she came for."

". . . made a mistake." He searched my face. "Okay, two mistakes."

A thought crossed my mind and I pointed behind me to the bed. "Where? And please don't tell me you brought her here, because I swear to God, I will strike a match up in here."

"She came to my school. Five minutes tops, both times. It meant nothing, Anne."

"Meant enough for you to get her pregnant, Smoke."

Suddenly, I was tired. Exhausted, really. I sank down to the bed and let my face fall into my hands. It took me a few minutes to collect my thoughts and set them straight, but I finally managed to calm down enough to accomplish the task. I was too outdone, I mean really thrown for a loop, and it showed on my face as I propped my head up on my fists and stared at Smoke long and hard.

He mistook my silence for acceptance. "It was nothing."

"I changed my whole life for you," I said softly. "I sold a business I built from the ground up and walked away from an entire life for you. And this is what I get?"

"I made some changes, too."

I looked around me with big eyes. "Like what? You sure didn't give up other women, as far as I can tell. You still have your house, your career and all of your friends and family. Hell, you even got another baby out of the deal.

Diana isn't the only one who got screwed here, Smoke, but at least that whore got some good sex out of it." I lifted my hands and let them fall. "I feel like the fool of the century."

"I love you."

"Sure you do," I said as I pushed to my feet and scrubbed my hands across my face. "You have a strange way of showing it. Excuse me." I went to step around him, but he stepped with me and blocked my way. I stared at his chest. "I said, excuse me."

"Say it back to me."

"Oh my God, please don't start this right now. You ought to know I'm not in the damn mood, okay?"

"Say it back to me."

"Get out of my way, Smoke."

"You can't, can you?"

"I don't need this right now."

"What do you need?"

"To pee, first of all," I said, still staring at his chest. "And then I need to get as far away from you as humanly possible."

"So you're leaving?"

"Yep." I took a deep breath and nodded resolutely. "I'm leaving."

"This is convenient as hell for you, isn't it? You've been looking for a way out ever since you came here."

"Was I looking for this mythical way out before or after I sold my house and my business? Or was it before or after I got pregnant? Yeah, that's what I thought. So don't try to run game on me. You did this, not me. Now I'm going to ask you one more time and then I'm going to lose my mind on your ass. Get out of my way."

"You don't even want to know why I did what I did?"

"It's enough just knowing you did it. I don't need to know why."

"Look at me."

I tipped my head back and met his eyes, hopefully for the last time. We breathed in the smell of each other's breath and stared each other down. "What?"

"Do you need me for anything? I mean, other than for taking the trash out and laying the pipe to you when you're in the mood, do you need me for anything else?"

That was actually funny enough to make me laugh. I took a step back, raised my eyebrows at him and . . . laughed. "You have got to be kidding me. You go out and sleep around on me, you get somebody else pregnant and you want to make this about me?"

"It's not just about you, sweetheart. This is about us and what's going on here in this house. About the fact that you don't need anybody for anything, least of all me. You can't even bring yourself to tell me you love me, which tells me that you don't. Either that or you can't."

"What part of washing your damn drawers, cooking your damn meals and cleaning your damn house isn't love? What part of kissing you in the morning before you brush your teeth and massaging your back until my fingers cramp isn't love? What part, Smoke?" I bent over at the waist and pressed the heels of my hands against my eyes, feeling like I was about pass out. This mess was making me lightheaded. "I swear to God, I don't need this." I slapped at Smoke's chest until he finally stepped aside and let me by.

"That's what was messing with my head, Anne. I had a woman at home that I loved like I ain't never thought about loving a woman who wasn't my damn mama, but I was still thinking all the way to the left. Tripping off of shit like you not being able to look me in my face and tell me you love me. Shit like you not needing me to be or do nothing for you. Shit like the motherfucking wall you have around you, every damn minute of the day and all damn night. A brotha can't break that mug down for shit."

"A brotha exaggerates." I turned on the faucet and splashed cold water on my face. "Kiss my ass, Smoke."

"You're not hearing me, Anne. I think you do that shit on purpose, too. I need you to see if you can dig this, though. You listening?"

I stopped patting my face dry long enough to give him my eyes. "I don't have much of a choice, do I?"

Smoke backed away from the bathroom doorway, chuckling and shaking his head at the same time. Looking at me like I was the one with the problem, like I was slow in comprehending something important.

"I'm feeling like I'm not needed. Some days more than others, but that's beside the point. The point is, I'm feeling like I'm not needed, like whatever it is I'm doing for you ain't shit. How can I help falling for the okey-doke, Anne? I have to get my needs met somewhere."

"And once again, Smoke, it's all about you and what you need, what you want. Well, you know what? You *needed* to mess with Diana, so you must've *wanted* me to leave. Mission accomplished."

"See, this is . . . fuck it. You know what?" He held up a finger and moved out of my line of sight. I heard him rumbling around in the closet and then he was back with my carryall. He tossed it on the floor in front of him and pointed to it. "You want to leave? Go. But trip off of this for a minute, baby. This motherfucker is already packed!" He kicked my carryall so hard it left the floor and slammed into the wall beside the doorway. "I wonder why?"

Without missing a beat, I said, "This is why."

CHAPTER SEVEN

ALEC

"Where are you going?"

To be such a little thing, damned if Anne didn't move like a speed demon. She raced down the hallway, zigzagged through the den and skidded into the living room, looking around like she was seriously considering jumping out of the nearest window to get away from me. She saw me coming after her and spun on her heels, heading for the kitchen. I jumped over the coffee table and almost managed to grab a handful of the silky tank top she was wearing before she kicked it into overdrive.

We faced off across the kitchen table, both of us breathing hard. "I asked you where you were going, woman."

"I'm leaving your castle, king Smoke."

"What?"

"You heard me, negro."

She went to pressing on her chest and sucking in mouthfuls of air, turning on the dramatics. I rolled my eyes to the ceiling. "Don't start hyperventilating. This is not the time for you to be . . ."

"See, there you go again, telling me what to do. I don't think you should do this, Anne. And that doesn't sound like a good idea, Anne. Or I don't want Zay doing this or that. You don't stop to ask me anything, Smoke. You just hand down your decision and expect me to go along with it. You're talking this shit about me not needing you, but you haven't stopped to think about the fact that you don't need me to need you. You don't give me time to tell you I need you before you come charging in and taking care of everything."

"Oh, so now I'm wrong for handling my business, running my household and being a man for you?" This was getting better and better. More and more, I was convinced that women didn't know what the hell they wanted from men. At least, the one standing in front of me didn't. "If I was one of those brothas who sat around on their asses all day and couldn't keep a job, you'd be whining about that. If I didn't come to the door and run those damn Jehovah's Witnesses off, you'd be saying I don't have any balls. If you had to tell me to take the trash out or when to take your car in for servicing, you'd be telling everybody you know that you have three kids, instead of two. What do you want from me?"

"I want you to stop stomping around here, issuing orders and giving commands," she had the nerve to say. "I was perfectly capable of thinking for myself and making sound decisions before we started doing whatever this is we're doing and believe it or not, I can still manage to do it now. Plus, I don't know where the hell my daddy is, but you're not him."

"Your daddy?"

"Yeah, my daddy."

I thought about that for a minute while I looked out the kitchen window and chewed on my bottom lip. I had a sudden urge for some water, so I took a glass down from a cabinet and filled it with tap water. I stared at her over the rim of the glass as I drank every last drop. Then, I set the glass in the sink, scratched the back of my neck and took the gloves off. They came off calmly and in a rational voice, but they still came off. I figured it was time.

"Maybe if your ass wasn't forever moping around, depressed about every damn thing under the sun and feeling victimized every time somebody raises their voice, I'd come to you about things. Shit, by the time I wake you up from one of your psychotic episodes, the crisis is long over with. Am I supposed to wait for the Prozac to kick in and make you normal before I take the initiative and handle the situation?"

The way Anne narrowed her eyes to slits and hissed at me told me that I had hit a sore spot. Giant tears popped out of her eyes and rolled down her face without her even realizing they were there. She was too busy wishing me dead to take notice. Now, I thought, now we're getting somewhere.

"Fuck you, Smoke," she sobbed. "Fuck you, okay? I don't take Prozac and you know it. I refused the prescription for an anti depressant because I'm not depressed. I . . ."

"The hell you're not. You sleep too much, you're anti-social and you stopped enjoying life months ago," I cut her off, my voice large and in charge.

"So what?"

"So you need to deal with your past and quit thinking up ways to avoid it. You can sleep forty days and forty nights, but when you wake up, Laverne and Alice are still going to be there."

"And so is Diana, because for some odd reason you can't shake that whore to save your life." She snatched a set of keys off the hook by the door and pointed a shaky finger at me. "You and the rest of these mixed up negro men out here, with your high-yellow women and your self hatred. You make me sick."

I took two steps back and fainted against the refrigerator, wondering if I had heard her right. My eyes stretched big with shock. "And ain't nothing wrong with black women?" She got quiet and offended. "Yeah, that's what I thought. You and the rest of your big, strong black women. The ones that claim they don't need a man, but have vibrators in every shape, size and color up under the bed. Keeping the Energizer bunny in business like a motherfucker. What you sistas need to do is recognize when you have good men and sit your asses down and let your men be men. You can't run every damn thing and I don't even know why you would want to. Then, the minute a brotha walks out, you want to cry about not being able to find a good man. Now that's what makes me sick. Hell, if God meant for a woman to do everything by herself, he would've given her balls, too. But he didn't and here's the catch baby, this is one brotha who ain't giving his up."

"So it's your way or the highway, right?"

"In a pink Cadillac," I said and had to laugh.

She twirled her melodramatic ass out the door and left it standing wide open. It took me a minute of staring at the key hook to realize that something was out of order about it. Took me another ten seconds to figure out exactly what that something was.

"Shit!" I felt shock waves coursing through my body as I watched Anne almost sideswipe my new truck. She was backing it out of the garage and not looking where the hell she was going. Too busy flipping me the bird and gunning the motor like she had lost her mind. I didn't even drive my truck like that. "Woman, if you fuck up my truck, I swear to God . . ."

"God ain't got shit to do with the fact that you lie, Smoke." She took off down the street, screaming out the window. "You lie, you lie, you lie . . ."

I took off running after my truck. "This shit ain't over, Anne!"

I was standing in the middle of the street in silk boxers and nothing else, screaming after a truck and a lunatic woman that I couldn't even see anymore. "This shit ain't over! You hear me?!"

"How you doing, Mr. Avery?"

I looked at the little chump who lived across the street from me—Kenny something or other. Isaiah ran around with him sometimes, when he was home from school. The idiot didn't have the sense God gave a goose. Working three minimum wage jobs when he needed to be in somebody's college. At the very least, in trade school, learning how to do something besides flip burgers and throw boxes into the backs of trucks. And he had the nerve to be cheesing at me like I was the one with the problem.

"Boy, don't you have a dead end job you need to be at?" I sucked my teeth all the way back inside the house and slammed the door behind me. Goddamn kids.

Iris was awake and standing up in her crib when I stuck my head in her room to check on her. She saw me and gave me one of her heart-stealing grins, knowing that I was about to rescue her from her prison like I always did. I changed her diaper and stole about ten kisses worth of sugar while I was at it.

"Looking like your nutty mama," I said as I pushed my face into the curve of her neck and blew air bubbles. I wasn't the least bit surprised when she slapped the shit out of me and then followed the slap up with a wet and sloppy kiss. Just like a damn woman. Give with one hand

and take back with the other. "Alright little girl, you're not that cute. Keep slapping me if you're bad." Now she wanted to love me up, drooling all over the place and cooing. "Yeah, that's what I thought."

I sat Iris in the middle of my bed with an assortment of toys, popped a *Dora the Explorer* DVD in for her to have a one-sided conversation with, and snatched up the cordless phone from the nightstand.

Diana answered on the fifth ring. "You're not pregnant, so what the hell were you trying to do?" She had called me three days ago, crying wolf and then straight clowning when I had damn near caught the Holy Ghost with relief.

"Exactly what I did." She laughed. "I saw Anne burning rubber down the street a minute ago and you running after that bitch like a little *beeootchhh*. That was funny."

"Why am I just now seeing how messed up in the head you are, Dee? This shit stops here, you hear me? From here on out, I need you to leave me and my household the hell alone. Go find some other brotha to terrorize."

"But I like terrorizing you, Alec. I like that you can't do anything but sit back and take it, too."

"Yeah I can, trust me on that. The next time I catch you tripping, Dee, I'ma stick a fork in your ass, because you are done."

ISAIAH

Erica was reminding me of my mama, more and more. They were both actresses like a mug. Tell them something slightly disturbing and all of a sudden, they wanted to call in the National Guard. Five seconds after they promised to stay calm and hear you out, they were bouncing all over the place, screaming your business at the tops of their lungs and wanting to call in Abraham, Martin and John, to back up the National Guard. Couldn't hold water on their stomachs.

The crying was the worst though. I always thought my mama had cornered the market on the crying to make a brotha feel guilty and get her way routine, but I hadn't met Erica yet. She wasn't quite as skilled as my mama, but she was running a close second. Half a box of tissue later and she was still going at it long and strong. Looking at me with those big, wet eyes, knowing a brotha had no defense.

I needed to go ahead and admit to myself that she had me sprung. Against my will, but sprung nonetheless. I was in love with her and my head was still spinning from hearing her tell me that she felt the same way. Putting it out there just so I'd know, she said.

I soaked in what she said slowly and weighed my options. I could pretend I hadn't heard her say what she had just said and keep staring up at the ceiling like I was in deep thought, which I wasn't because she had basically just thrown a brotha off his game. I could charge what she had just said to the game, since we were in the middle of a pretty serious conversation and in the middle of serious conversations was usually when people's emotions ran away from them and they said things they didn't really mean. Or I could take this opportunity to make a nice clean exit from the relationship, tell her that I wasn't ready for the noise she was talking and that I thought we should chill for a minute.

Or I could excuse myself and go into the bathroom, call my old dude and ask him what the hell I was supposed to do. The more I thought about that option, the better it sounded. But there was one big problem. The bathroom was all the way down the hallway and no telling who I'd run into while I was making my way there. And it was a public bathroom, so no telling who might hear my conversation once I got there and made the call.

Either way, I was jacked, so I went with the flow and came right back at her with: "I love you, too." She didn't react anything like I was expecting her to react. Instead of falling all over me and smothering me with kisses, she hopped out of bed butt naked and slapped her hands on her hips, glaring at me like I had pulled a Jared with one of her so-called friends. What the hell?

"I know you do," she told me. "That's why you can't do what Marion asked you to do, Isaiah. For one thing, it's illegal and for another it's just plain old wrong."

"Oh, you know I do, huh?"

"Hell yeah, I know and don't try to change the subject. Why does he want you to do it? Why can't he ask one of the other players? Why you?"

"Because he tripped and bet on the wrong game. He knows I'll be on the court from start to finish, so I could get it done if I wanted to."

Saying Marion's silly ass had bet on the wrong game was putting it mildly. That fool had put some serious cash down on tomorrow night's game, thinking that KSU had a win in the bag and that he was going to walk away with fat pockets. Now he was shaking in his boots and looking at me cross-eyed. Wanting me to do something that was so far over the top that I still couldn't believe he had fixed his mouth to utter the words. I knew he had been betting on some of the games, but I never knew who he was betting with or against and I never gave a damn, either. My job was to hit the court and kick some ass for my team and that's exactly what I did, bet or no bet.

"Do you want to?"

I looked at her like she was crazy. "Hell naw, girl. What kind of question is that?"

She exhaled like somebody had stuck a pin in her and

let out all of her air. Relief was all over her face. "I'm so glad you said that, Isaiah, because I couldn't love somebody who would do something like that to somebody else."

"And you don't."

"I never did like that Marion person, anyway," she chirped, sounding like my mama for real. "You remember I told you something was off about him? You remember that?"

As if I could forget. "Yes, Erica."

I threw the covers back and scooted back to the wall, so she could come back to bed. We were sharing a twin bed, but there was plenty of room, if you asked me. I didn't mind letting her use me as her pillow, not even a little bit, and I liked her letting me use her as my pillow even more.

I laid my head between her breasts and closed my eyes.

"Now I know why he damn near lives on campus."

"De son of de bitch." There was that accent again.

She hadn't never lied. Marion was a son of a bitch and a stupid one at that. If he thought I was running out on the court tomorrow night during a divisional finals game, hell, any kind of game, and doing some shit like the shit he had asked me to do.

He had tried to sway me by reminding me of all the money he had given me, telling me that it was my share of the winnings from all the games I'd won that he had bet on. But I wasn't trying to hear that. I hurried up and told him that I had saved every last dime, in case he required a refund. Hell, it wasn't my fault the NCU Bluejackets had pulled out of the tournament at the last minute and threw a monkey wrench in his plans.

He didn't need a refund though. He needed me to accidentally cause St. Louis University's seven-foot tall starter to have an unfortunate slip and fall. Dude's name was Chung Li and he was supposedly unstoppable on the court—supposedly the ninth wonder of the world. Well, I was six-four myself and I wasn't nothing nice on the court either. Chung Li and St. Louis University hadn't ever run up on KSU and Isaiah Phillips before.

I told Marion that KSU was going to win tomorrow night's game, but not because I was planning on playing with somebody's livelihood. If Chung Li felt anything close to the way I felt about basketball, then we would meet on the court and go toe-to-toe, fair and square. Then, I told Marion to kiss my ass. As soon as I got done schooling Chung Li on the game of basketball, I was going straight to the bank. Marion Witherspoon needed to be repaid in full with a quickness. I was so glad spring break was around the corner that I could've slapped somebody. Me and KSU needed a break from each other and me and Marion needed to break, period.

Me and Erica? Well, we would see.

Sleep was picking a fight with me when my cell phone chirped and then started blasting the bridge from Public Enemy's "911 Is A Joke." That woke me right up. I knew off top who was ringing my bell, so I didn't even indulge Erica in the staring contest that she wanted to start. She was thinking that some chick was tracking me down and I was thinking: *Don't tell me Doolittle called him again.*

I reached down and grabbed my jeans from the floor. Flipped my cell open and put it to my ear. "What's up, da?"

"Have you talked to your mother, Zay?"

"Today?"

"No, two weeks ago, boy. Pull your drawers up and pay attention, okay? Has Anne called you today?"

"Nah," I said, scratching my head. "Why? Something wrong?"

"She ran off with my goddamn truck, that's what's wrong."

By the time I finished laughing, my old dude had hung up on me and I was wiping tears from my eyes. Nobody had to tell me what the deal was, because I already knew. My parents were at it again and suddenly, I had an urge to be back home, watching them clown in person. There was nothing like a front row seat to one of their performances. They could keep a brotha laughing for days—hell— months.

I scrolled through my contact list and found the entry logged under the cartoon image of a pitchfork, pressed send and put the phone to my ear. A few seconds later: "Where are you?"

"At the movies," my mama said. "Why? Who wants to know?"

"You know who."

"Don't tell him you talked to me." Her voice changed directions. "One for the matinee, please." She came back. "He called you looking for me?"

"Wanted to know if I had talked to you today. He sounded worried." I slipped my thumb inside Erica's mouth and watched her suck it softly. She moaned and I tried to cover it up by clearing my throat.

"You mean he sounded worried about his truck. Hell, if I had known the damn thing rode so smoothly I would've taken off with it a month ago. Have you driven it?"

"Mama, please. You going back home after the movie?"

"I haven't decided. What are you doing?"

"Um . . . little bit of studying," I lied. "Mid-terms coming up next week." I heard her ordering a small bag of pop- corn and a large soda and laughing at something the dude behind the counter said to her. "You need me to let you go?"

"No, but you probably need me to let you go, don't you? Sounds like somebody is getting restless."

Damn, she heard that? I gave Erica a pop-eyed look and took my hand away from her hot spot. "Okay . . . so, um . . . I'ma talk to you later, okay?"

"Hhmm," she said and hung up.

"Your parents are fighting?"

"I guess it's time I told you something very important about my family," I told Erica, serious as a heart attack. "You might want to take what I'm about to say into consideration if you think you want to keep being with me, because some things are not for everybody."

She sat up in bed, worried and anxious looking about the face. Touched my arm softly. "What is it, Isaiah?"

"It's like this, I guess." I took a deep breath, trying to come up with a way to break the news to her gently, so that it was less traumatic. "Okay here goes. My people are crazy. Every last one of them and if you hang around for any length of time, it's bound to rub off on you. Are you prepared for that?"

CHAPTER EIGHT

ANNE

I sat through a musical, a family drama and a comedy, in that order. I finally left the movie theater with a numb butt, ringing ears and empty pockets. But there was no way in hell I was going home, not tonight anyway. I didn't think I could stand to look at Smoke's face for more than five minutes without wanting to run to the kitchen and start some grits to boiling. I was absolutely livid and nothing but time and space would calm me down.

Lorena Bobbitt was my new hero and that's all there was to it. Sistas everywhere needed to take a page from her book and put something on their men's minds. Or else we needed to get behind the wheels of two-ton cars and roll over a man or two. Throw it into reverse and roll over their asses again, just for the hell of it. Betcha they'd learn how to keep it zipped up then. I mean, enough was enough.

Turn about was fair play though, wasn't it? I was swallowing the same bitter pill that Diana had swallowed four years ago and I don't know why I was surprised to find that I didn't care for the taste. In the back of my mind, I had been waiting for something like this to happen—waiting for Smoke to go wandering into someone else's backyard, sniffing around like a dog in heat the way men had a tendency to do. But I had Diana pegged for being yesterday's news, so I hadn't anticipated the bag she had come out of. She got me good, I had to give her that. She and Smoke had both gotten me good, come to think of it. I'd never admit it to anyone, but I could get over Diana's tired behind. She was nothing more than a woman and women had been doing this kind of mess to each other for centuries. No surprises there. Smoke, though . . .

I slowed to a stop at a red light and switched on Smoke's expensive satellite stereo system. I needed something to keep me focused, because driving this damn truck right into that tree over there was sounding mighty good right about now. It took me a few seconds to redirect.

There was my cell phone again, vibrating so tough that my entire right side was dancing a jig. Smoke was blowing me up, as the kids say. He had been calling in five-minute increments ever since five minutes after I drove off in his precious truck. According to my cell, I had seventeen voicemail messages and twenty-five text messages. Curious to hear what he could possibly have left to say to me, I pulled into a McDonald's parking lot and dialed into my voicemail.

Message number one: "Anne, you know who this is, so call me back." Delete.

Message number two: "Look, baby, I know you're pissed off, but you need to get on back home and see about your man, okay? Call me. No, better yet, come home." Delete.

Message number three began with Iris babbling into the phone. Then: "You hear that? Your child wants to know where the hell her runaway mother is and frankly, so do I. Baby, just . . . where . . . look, come home. I don't care about the truck, you know that. Zay thinks this shit is funny, but it's not, is it?" Delete.

Message number four went something like this: "You know what, Anne? This is really fucked up. Somebody could be over here dying and you won't even answer your damn phone. I knew you were cold, but damn. I'ma put it to you like this though. Bring my damn truck home right damn now and have your ass in it when it gets here. Comprende?" Delete.

And then message number five: "It's bed time, baby, and you know I can't sleep without you. You know that, so why are you doing this? I get it now, okay? I messed up. I get that. I need you to come home now. Got a brotha worrying and shit." Ten seconds of static silence. "I love you."

And that's a wrap, I thought as I threw the phone into the passenger seat and pulled out into traffic. Love should've brought his ass home, but it didn't, did it?

I busted a U-turn and swerved into a Goodwill parking lot, dialing my cell and narrowly avoiding a head-on collision with a light pole. I was crying so hard that I didn't see the damn pole until it was almost too late.

"Stop calling me!" I screamed at Smoke. "You hear me? Stop calling me!"

"Anne . . ."

"No! Don't give me that *Anne* shit. You shut up and listen to me, alright? You shut up and listen, that's what you do. I love you, you got that? So don't you ever fix your lips to tell me that I don't, because if I hear you say that shit again, I swear to God they're going to find your body."

"Baby, can I talk?"

"Shut! Up!" My lungs felt like they were collapsing, my chest caving in on itself. I struggled for air and wiped snot from my top lip with the back of my hand. Sobs were coming out hard and fast now. I could hear Smoke crooning to me, telling me to calm down, To come home to him, so we could talk about this. "You fucked another woman, Smoke. Do you know how that feels to me?"

"Tell me how it feels to you, Anne. Talk to me."

"It feels like I can't breathe." I slapped my chest and sobbed. "Like tomorrow doesn't mean anything, because today is the end of my world. It feels like it shouldn't matter this much to me, but it does. Like I'm not safe anymore."

Smoke breathed long and hard in my ear. "Baby, come home. Please."

"I don't have a home anymore," I said and hung up. I turned my cell off and kept driving.

"Vern?"

I searched Laverne's face in the darkness and tried to see what she was thinking, but I couldn't. It was way past one in the morning and I was tired, hungry and sleepy. Standing on my sister's doorstep, looking like who done it and what the hell for. I was praying she didn't slam the door in my face, because I had nowhere else to go and no money or identification to go there with.

Laverne's house was the last place I wanted to break down and run to and the look on her face told me that she knew it. "Bree?"

We stared at each other.

When I got tired of staring, I took a deep breath and pushed a hand through my tangled locks. I looked out at the street and said, "I didn't have anywhere else to go, Vern. I know you don't want me here, but . . . can I come in anyway?"

"I don't want you here . . . what . . . girl, get your behind in this house." I stepped inside and she ran around the living room turning on lamps. "What happened to you? Are you hurt?"

"No, I'm not hurt," I said as I sank down to the couch and curled in on myself. "I like this couch. Is it new?"

"Got it last month," she said and lit a cigarette. She inhaled deeply and looked me from head to toe, blowing a thin stream of gray smoke in my direction.

"When did you start smoking?"

"You came all the way over here at one in the morning to ask me about my bad habits?"

I passed her an ashtray when she reached for it and waved smoke from in front of my face. "Those things will kill you, you know."

"So will stress. Are you sleeping on my couch tonight or what?"

"Or what," I said. She brought me a blanket and a pillow, stared at me while she finished smoking her cigarette and then she went back to bed. I was asleep almost as soon as my head hit the pillow.

Sometime during the night, a weight landed at the other end of the couch on top of my feet, and scared me right out of sleep. I came awake faster than the speed of light and snatched the blanket that I was mummified in from over my face. "Who is that?"

I saw a pair of eyes and a hot pink nightgown in the darkness, and that was all. Everything else was chocolate brown and cloaked by darkness. She should've been fast asleep, counting sheep or Barbies or ice cream cones or whatever six year old little girls counted while they were asleep; but apparently, she was wide awake. Sitting her chubby butt smack dab on my feet and staring at me like it was nearly four o'clock in the afternoon instead of in the morning.

I thought I knew why she wasn't in bed. "Do you have to use the bathroom or something?"

"No, ma'am."

Laverne's daughter was the complete and total opposite of her mother. Tracey was toasty brown where Laverne was sweet cream yellow; robustly featured where Laverne's features were thin and angular. She could've easily been mistaken for my child. "Then, what is it? Why are you out here instead of in bed?"

We weren't all that familiar with each other, so I didn't want to start yelling at her little behind straight out of the gate. The last thing I wanted to have to do was kick Laverne's butt in her own house, because her daughter had interrupted good and much needed sleep. But I was incredibly tired and my patience was all of two inches long.

"Well?" I prodded her impatiently.

"It's a monster in my closet."

Oh, for the love of all that was good and holy, I thought. "What kind of monster?"

"A big one," was all she said. Damn kids.

"Did you tell your mom or dad about this monster?"

"Yeah and mama looked, but she couldn't see it. I know it's still there though, 'cause I can hear it breathing when I'm tryin' to sleep."

I started to ask her if she'd been drinking, she was slurring her S's and T's. Then, I remembered that she didn't have front teeth to help her out with that. "You came out of your room and all the way down the hallway in the dark, and you're scared of a monster in your closet? Sounds like you have it all backward to me." I sat up, found her face and tugged on her bare foot. "When I was your age, running around in the dark was scarier than little wimpy-ass closet monsters." She gasped and slapped a hand over her mouth. "Oh, damn, I cursed, didn't I?"

She giggled. "I make my daddy give me a quarter every time he says a cuss word, Auntie Anne."

"Yeah, well, I'm not your daddy. Now get your butt off my feet and take me to this monster. I need to get some sleep tonight."

I followed her down the hallway to her room and flipped the overhead light on, squinting as I looked around at the *Sponge Bob* décor. I pointed at the closed closet door. "He's in here?" She nodded enthusiastically and I went charging toward the closet like I really meant business. Then I had a thought. I stepped back and looked at her. "Open the door for me."

"What if the monster eats me?"

"Little girl, do you really think I would stand here and do nothing while a monster ate my niece alive? Please. Open the door and then move back, so I can kick some butt." She ran over to the door, flung it open and then made a mad dash for the bed, leaping over the footboard like Flo Jo.

"Get him, Auntie Anne!"

I knew it was the middle of the night, but I didn't give a damn. I had to handle my business and handle it correctly; if I hoped to get back to sleep before the sun came up. Something told me that Tracey wouldn't leave me alone until her monster had been demolished.

I started acting a fool two seconds before I stepped all the way inside the closet. Started talking loud and calling the monster out to fight me, woman to monster. I talked much shit about it, called it ugly and booger nosed, said his mama hung her drawers on a rusty nail and dared it to take me on. Behind me, Tracey fell across the bed in a fit of giggles and kicked her feet in the air.

I slapped my palms against the inside wall to make it sound like I was really tussling with the monster and then I threw two empty hangers out into the bedroom, so Tracey could see that I was throwing down. I growled low in my throat, being the monster for a minute, and then I broke out yelling again.

"What in the world is going on in here?" Laverne asked. "Bree, what are you doing?"

"Auntie Anne is killing the monster, mommy! She's killing it for me!"

I gave Tracey a minute or so more of clowning. Then, I stepped out of the closet, closed the door behind me and took a deep breath. "Okay, now the monster is dead. He told me to tell you that he's sorry he ever messed with you. He didn't know you had a crazy auntie and everything. And I'm telling you, after the way I whipped his butt in there, he won't be back anytime soon."

Tracey bounced up and down on the bed, pumping her fists in the air and laughing like only a child can. She came running down the mattress toward me and jumped across empty space into my arms. "Is he really dead?"

"He is *sooo* dead." I set her on her feet. "Go look for yourself." I went into the closet with her and pushed clothes hangers back and forth for her viewing pleasure. "You see him? No? I didn't think so. You think you can get some sleep now?"

"I think so. Put me to bed, Auntie Anne."

"You're pushing it now, little girl." I frowned at her. But I helped her climb into bed anyway. I smoothed out the covers for her and handed her a stuffed white elephant when she ordered me to do so. She puckered her lips and I planted a big, smacking kiss on them and then another one on her forehead. "Goodnight, little one."

"G'night."

Laverne and my mother jumped back from the doorway and looked at me like I was crazy as I slid past them and went back to the couch.

As a child, my relationship with my mother went something like this: I ran around trying to think up ways to get her attention and approval, and she walked around trying to think up new ways and new things to say to make me feel two inches tall. I wanted her to love me so badly that

I was a glutton for punishment. Where a more sane person would have given up on her long ago, I kept plugging away. Fighting the good fight and getting stomped on like a roach.

I thought getting stoned and strolling into our apartment with pupils the size of dinner plates and smelling like a walking crack pipe would get her attention. But even that went right over her head. I did everything I could to make her see me, but she never did. Once I realized that my efforts were in vain, I stopped thinking, period. I let the crack teach me how to stop caring about what she thought, felt or said.

But without crack in my life, I was a creature of habit. I became a child again, seeking her attention and wanting her to see me for who and what I was. I wanted her to look at me one good time, I mean really look at me, and tell me that she knew she'd done me wrong. I was shocked by how badly I suddenly needed her to acknowledge the part that she played in the way my life had turned out. And then again, I was shocked to find that I was still trying to make her see me.

"You want some breakfast?" I said as she strolled into the kitchen and made a beeline for the coffee maker. Her eyes lingered on the plate of bacon, eggs and toast that I had just set in front of Tracey, but she didn't say anything.

I'd made myself at home in Laverne's kitchen hours ago, while everyone else was still asleep and oblivious to my presence. Despite trying to get back to sleeping the way I had been sleeping before Tracey's monster madness, I hadn't been able to. Instead, I drifted into the kitchen and turned on the countertop television to keep me company. I was plowing through my third bowl of Cap'n Crunch and watching vintage episodes of *Bugs Bunny* when Tracey slid into the chair across from me.

Together, we finished off an entire box of cereal while we watched the sun come up. Then, she announced that she was still hungry, which made me realize that I was, too. So I started cooking.

"Mama?" She stopped measuring coffee long enough to look at me. "I asked you if you wanted some breakfast."

"It's good, grandma," Tracey told her. She stuffed her mouth with clouds of eggs and talked with her mouth full. "You better get some, 'fore I eat it all up."

"Grandma ain't hungry right now, baby." She smiled at Tracey and then went right back to making coffee—like I hadn't even spoken. "Can't do nothing without a cup of coffee first."

"No, thank you, Anne. I don't want any breakfast, but that was nice of you to offer," I mumbled under my breath as I turned away and rolled my eyes. I started filling the sink with dishwater and resolved to tune her out. The least I could do was put Laverne's kitchen back like I had found it before I got my stuff and got the hell out of here.

"I guess I don't deserve an answer, huh?" I said before I knew I was angry enough to want to say it. It just popped out. I had opened my mouth to take a breath and there it was. "I guess I'm invisible or something, right? I know you heard me talking to you."

"I think you better lower your voice."

"Or what, mama? Are you going to actually remember that I exist and do something about it?" I paused in the middle of scrubbing the non-stick off of a non-stick skillet and turned to glare at her. "What else can you do to me?"

The coffee maker beeped and drew her eyes away from my face. She pushed up from her seat at the table and took a mug down from the cabinet over her head. "There you go again with that poor, poor Breanne mess. Somebody kicked me, somebody said something mean to me, somebody blah, blah, blah. If you'd stop whining for a minute, you would see that nobody don't owe you nothing, girl. You act like I don't exist, don't you?"

"You don't think you owe me something?"

"Apparently you seem to think I do, so why don't you tell me what I owe you?"

"An apology for one thing." I slapped the dish towel down on the counter and dropped my hands on my hips. "You could start by apologizing for all the horrible things you said to me and for the way you treated me." She opened her mouth to say something, but I waved a disgusted hand and cut her off. "Like shit. You treated me like shit."

"Nobody has time to listen to this mess," my mama snapped. "Least I know I don't. Tracey, you come and get grandma when this one here is gone, okay?"

I couldn't let her walk past me like I was nothing and no one to her. She was shoulder to shoulder with me, eye to eye, and I didn't have enough sense to let her go. I grabbed her arm and caught her off guard, forced her to face me with only inches between us. I narrowed my eyes and tried to see into her soul, tried to find something inside of her that I could reach out and touch. Several seconds passed with us facing off and not saying anything—barely breathing—and then she snatched her arm from my grip and woke me up.

"Mama, why do you hate me? Will you at least tell me that much?" I stared at her back as she walked out of the kitchen and disappeared around a corner.

"Auntie Anne?" I had forgotten that Tracey was in the room. "Auntie Anne?" I looked at her. "Don't cry, please? I don't hate you."

CHAPTER NINE

ALEC

Anne finally came home after nine in the morning and I breathed a long sigh of relief. I had been holding my breath all night long, waiting for her to call me again or to at least answer her cell, but she never did. I had no idea where she'd slept, if she'd eaten or who she had been with. I hadn't slept two winks, worrying about some lunatic grabbing her and dragging her off somewhere. I hadn't been able to convince Iris to sleep for more than an hour at a time, either.

We were both worried silly. Me pacing from one room to the other and her riding in the curve of my arm, sucking on her pacifier and rubbing my head. We kept a vigil going, hoping her mother would come home, so we could relax.

Iris was in the middle of one of her power naps when Anne walked into the bedroom and dropped her shoes on the floor in front of the closet. She stepped out of her skirt and unhooked her garter belt and stockings, rolling first one and then the other down her legs until she held them in her hands. She tossed them on the dresser and pulled her shirt over her head. It landed on the floor on top of her skirt. A little red lacy excuse for a bra was added to the pile and then matching red bikini panties. Naked, she pushed her locks back from her face and headed to the bathroom.

"Where have you been?"

"Out," she said and kept walking. I didn't even merit a glance. She stepped into the shower, closed the door behind her and turned the water on full blast.

After a while, I got up and went to stand in the bathroom doorway. Getting my thrills by watching her soap herself through the frosted glass and feeling my dick stand and salute, even as I cursed viciously under my breath. Don't ask me how I knew that the water had gone from hot to cold, but I knew it. Just like I knew that she wasn't shaking inside the shower because she was cold. She probably didn't even feel the water anymore.

Anne was in there crying so hard that no sound passed her lips. My mother called it soul-crying. She said only a woman could cry like that because women felt things all the way down to the tips of their toes, right down to the bottom of their souls and sound didn't do the feelings justice.

I stripped, stepped inside the shower and reached for her. "Come here."

Her lips came to me first, before the rest of her body followed and after that it was all about the energy we created. The kissing was indescribable. So much tongue being given and taken it was impossible to know where hers ended and mine began. And she tasted so damn good to me that I didn't want to let her breathe without sharing breath with her—didn't want her to make a sound if I couldn't swallow it. I licked and sucked on her breasts until she was calling for me. Then I backed her against the wall and went downtown, licking and sucking her clit until she was screaming for me and cumming at the same time.

It was a beautiful thing, the way Anne looked as I began the slip and slide that had me buried inside her one second and then introducing myself to her all over again the next. I turned the water off, so that it was just her and me in surround sound, loving each other long and strong and committing to it. I came long and hard, calling out like a drunken lumberjack.

I brought Iris into the room with us and laid her on Anne's chest. Between the three of us, she was the only one wearing anything and that was just a diaper. I climbed in bed and pressed against my woman, skin to skin and head to toe, and took her under with me. We slept for six hours straight.

"Marry me, Anne," I walked up behind her at the stove and said. She had Iris perched on her hip and a small pot with formula in it warming on the burner. She glanced over her shoulder at me and then kissed Iris's lips. She said nothing. "Is that a no? Again?" This made ten times that I had asked Anne to marry me and I hadn't managed to get a yes, yet. She had an arsenal of excuses.

"Where did that come from, all of a sudden?"

"It's time." Been damn time, as far as I was concerned.

She turned the burner off and carried the pot over to the sink, where a bottle was waiting. A flick of her wrist had formula flowing neatly into the bottle without so much as a drop going to waste. She screwed on a nipple and put the bottle in Iris's waiting hands. Anne turned to face me and gave me all of her eyes.

"Is it?"

I blinked and she was gone from the kitchen just that quickly. Okay, so probably not the best time or place, right? Wrong. Anne's little ass was going to take my ring

and take it like she meant it, if that was the last thing I accomplished in this lifetime. And whether she knew it or
not, time was running out for her. The more I thought
about it, the more I was not above dragging her off to
Vegas, conning her into one of those instant wedding
chapels and threatening her life like it hadn't ever been
threatened before, if she didn't open her mouth on cue
and say goddamn 'I do.'

Two hours later, the last thing I needed was Don looking me upside my head, trying in vain to get my attention.
I passed Jake a beer and kept on ignoring him. My son
was playing ball on national television and I wasn't about
to miss a millisecond of it, messing around with Don's
wannabe preacher man crap. Plus, I was not in the mood
for a replay of the many ways that I had fucked up, seeing
as how I was perfectly aware of how, why, when and
where, all by my damn self. So he could just go right
ahead and kiss a brotha's natural black ass.

I should've told him to mind his business when he and
Jake showed up on my doorstep a minute ago. He was
here to watch the game, not to play peacemaker. But
Anne was flouncing around in those stilettos she couldn't
live without, snatching stuff and switching so hard that
her titties shook every time she took a step, leaving no
doubt about the fact that she was pissed with numero
uno. His antenae had raised a little more as the seconds
passed.

Jake, on the other hand, knew enough to keep his
mouth shut. Not that he was all that skilled at reading
women anyway, because if he was he would've never
fallen for the okey-doke with the likes of Kee-Kee. The
nigga was an electrician and he wasn't getting any
younger. He needed to be looking for a good woman to
settle down with. Give me a few nieces and nephews be-

fore he was too old to talk some poor women into putting up with him.

And another thing . . .

I had to throw myself a lifesaver and float back to shore. My thoughts were all over the place and I was getting completely off the subject. I took a deep breath, swallowed a mouthful of beer and circled back around to the point at hand, still ignoring Don's attempts at getting my attention.

Anyway, where was I? Oh yeah, Anne. So she was gansta—walking around the house, drawing attention to herself, even though she thought she was being discreet. She spoke to my brothers in passing, on her way to grabbing her purse and keys. Told me that she had made us some sandwiches and threw together some potato salad, and reminded Jake that there was half of a chocolate cake in the kitchen that desperately needed to be eaten. Finally, she cut her eyes at me and told me not to forget to tape the game so she could watch it later. Never mind the fact that she never missed one of Isaiah's games and she was probably going someplace else to watch it by herself. And all the while, Don was staring her down and reading her like a book.

He claimed that he was so in tune with women because he had been married for years and had a teenage daughter, but I wasn't buying it even if he was selling it half off. If you asked me, my brother was a little too in tune with my woman and he always had been. Every now and again, a brotha caught him watching Anne when he didn't think anybody was watching him. And he was always the first one to jump to Anne's defense whenever it looked like somebody might be getting ready to say something to her about anything under the sun. You didn't have to actually say anything, just look like you were getting ready to and there he was.

Don't get me wrong though, I wasn't under any kind of impression that my brother would push up on my woman. But I knew he was hardly joking when he told me that he would probably have given me a run for my money where Anne was concerned if he wasn't already happily married. He told me that shit four years ago, just before he threw in a little side order of 'I'm just joking, man.' Yeah, right.

Nah, I didn't think I'd have to pull him to the side the way I had to do with Jeff's hyper-horny ass. That little nigga was something else with his tittie-staring, eye-winking mack game. Always moving in a little too close when he was reaching for something near where Anne happened to be standing, sitting or just breathing, and forever hanging his head over her shoulder, whispering silly words in her ear to make her laugh. He knew what he was doing. Just like I made sure, in a "your uncle loves you and would do anything for you" kind of way, that he knew I would most assuredly fuck his young world up and make him wish he was a newborn baby again, by the time I was done tossing his ass from wall to wall about my woman. I didn't look nothing like Brother Carlton, for real.

Yeah, Jeff and me had a tacit hands-off understanding. But Don and me were still negotiating a specialized peace treaty, whereby he stayed the hell out of my business and I let him.

Half a second after Anne flounced out the door, he was sliding up to me, beer in hand. "You and Anne having . . . problems?" Left unsaid was the "again" part that I knew he was itching to add on, but had enough sense not to.

"One problem, anyway." My bigmouth ass. Now that I thought about it, I needed to help him mind his own business by being a little more secretive about mine. Old habits were hard to break though. Besides being my big brother, he was my best friend in the whole damn universe. Motherfucker that he was.

"And that one problem is?"

I aimed the remote at the big screen plasma and stole a look over my shoulder, checking to make sure that Jake was still in the kitchen. I caught Don's eyes and said simply, "Diana Daniels." He choked on his beer, spraying all over the coffee table glass and down the front of his shirt. "It's under control."

"Smoke . . ."

"I said it's under control, Don, damn. Are we watching the game or having church?"

"It ain't like you can't use some God in your life," he had the nerve to say. I sucked my teeth and turned up the television volume. He tapped me on my arm as I was watching an interview with Zay and the other captain of the basketball team. I told him to shut up so I could hear what my son was saying to the world. I told him to shut up, period.

ISAIAH

The locker room was like a graveyard. Everybody was lined up on the benches, looking at the floor like zombies, some near tears. Me, I was cool under the circumstances. Okay, so we had lost, but we had only lost by one point and we still kicked some ass. St. Louis University hadn't lost a game by such a slim margin for the last three seasons. Usually, they stomped out onto the court, hiding behind Chung Li, and came away with at least a twenty-point lead. But tonight, them chumps had barely scraped by with the winning point and that was only because my boy, Keshawn, had lost his head a little bit and fouled a player from the opposing team. The free throw they'd been given as a result was what broke the bank.

Nobody was really mad at Keshawn, though. Hell, we

were all tense and playing like our lives depended on it—
sweating buckets and tearing the court up. If my boy hadn't
fouled that chump, I probably would have. Even SLU's
players knew they had barely walked away with a win.
Their coach had shaken our coach's hand like they were
long lost brothers and their team had looked every last
one of us in the eye when we shook for the last time.
There was none of the customary smirks and snide re-
marks, either. One of them niggas even had the nerve to
tell me that SLU could use me, if I was interested. Yeah,
them chumps knew we had brought it to them in a very
special way, no doubt about it.

I jumped in the shower and damn near drowned myself,
trying to wash away hours of sweat and funk. I guessed
the rest of them fools finally got tired of smelling themselves too, because I looked around and suds were flying
in every direction.

"KSU, you know!" somebody called out.

"KSU, what's up!" we all called back. Then somebody
starting reciting one of our cheerleaders' favorite cheers
and we all joined in, sounding like fools for real. "K—S—
U, here we go, here we go! K—S—U, on the flo', on the
flo'! Don't act like you don't know! Breds in the house and
it's about to be *ooooonnnnn!*"

Next thing I knew, fools were running around the
shower room, zapping brothas on the asses with wet towels and leaving welts. I took three zaps and dished out two
myself before Coach Hedowski came to the doorway to
see what all the whooping and clowning was about. And
what did he do that for?

We picked him up and brought him into the shower
with us, two-piece suit, wingtips and all. He tried to act
like he was put out, but we all knew that all of the water
on his face wasn't from the shower.

Erica was waiting for me when I walked out of the

locker room with my duffel slung over my shoulder. I glided right into her open arms and took her tongue all the way down my throat. She was just what a brotha needed after a long, sweaty game. I was thinking of ways to talk her into giving me a full body massage when I heard somebody call my name.

"Yo, Zay!"

It took me a minute to figure out that Marion was coming at me from the end of the corridor. Marion and his little entourage of thugs walking tall, with their short asses. I let them niggas get as close as six feet away, then I looked in Marion's face and said, "What's up?"

"You, nigga. What happened on the court tonight? You was supposed to be having a brotha's back. I told you I had some bank riding on the game, didn't I?"

"And I told you, you were on your own with the bullshit, didn't I?"

"Oh, you talking smart and all that, right? You a big man now, right?" He started walking toward me like he was really about to do something.

I pulled Erica's arms from around my neck and nudged her off to the side, out of the way. "Isaiah," she said, sounding worried. She tried to pull my face around to hers, but I wasn't taking my eyes off of Marion's shady ass. "Isaiah, baby, let's go, okay?"

"Give me a minute," I told her. "What the fuck is your problem, dude?"

"You know what my motherfucking problem is, Zay. Because of your ass, I done lost some straight up dollars. That's some serious shit, don't you think?"

"I think you need to carry your delusional ass back to your hotel room and sleep it off. I don't owe you shit and it ain't my fault you make stupid bets, either."

"Nigga . . ."

"What up, Zay? You a'ight?"

I looked over my shoulder at Keshawn. He was standing in the locker room doorway with five or six of my teammates right behind him. "Yeah, I'm cool. I was just explaining to Marion here that . . ."

"Isaiah!" Erica screamed and cut me off.

I turned my head just in time to catch a right hook from Marion's bitch ass. That shit snapped my head back on my neck and made me lose my mind. It took me back four years to the night of the senior prom and a bathroom on the second floor of the hotel where the prom was being held. A chump named Hood and some of his flunkies had caught me pissing and jumped me over some bullshit.

"Much shit as I done laced your ass with, you got the nerve to play me like a motherfucking fool, Zay? Standing here trying to front me in front of your bitch?"

My bitch? Oh, okay. I saw where this was headed real quick. Not only was I going to have to stomp this nigga but I was going to have to put my foot in his mouth, too. Damn, and all I was really in the mood to do was lay some pipe to my girl and get some sleep.

"Isaiah," Erica hissed nervously.

But I wasn't listening. I stepped up to Marion and got in his face. "Nigga, did you just put your hands on me?" He tried to push me off of him, but I caught his arms and pushed him back so hard that his boys had to catch him before he hit the floor. "And what did you say about my woman?"

"Man, fuck you and that black-ass bitch you fucking. She ain't shit and you ain't either."

He stood up and I knocked him right back down. Stood over him. "Say what?"

I was staring at Marion so hard that I had tunnel vision. That's why I didn't see one of his flunkies coming at me from my right side. I felt what he brought with him though. My head snapped back on my neck for the second and last time, because after that it was on and popping.

My teammates came flying out of the locker room behind me, Marion and his chumps came flying at me head on and we all met somewhere in the middle, trying to crack some heads open. I hoped Erica was out of the way, because the situation got out of control real quick. I lost track of who and what I was hitting. All I knew was that me and my boys were swinging haymakers like there was no tomorrow. On the court wasn't the only place we could kick some ass. It didn't help matters any that we had lost tonight's game. A good fight was just what we needed to work off some frustration.

How did I always find myself in the middle of these fucked up situations?

CHAPTER TEN

DIANA

I saw that little dark bitch long before she saw me, so I had plenty of time to check her out and see what the hell she had that Alec couldn't seem to live without. All he ever talked about was Anne. Anne this and Anne that. Like Anne had sat at Jesus's feet or something. I mean, really. I was woman enough to admit that she was attractive, if you liked the petite, seaweed and kelp, smoothie-drinking type, but she wasn't better looking than I was.

For one thing, she had a head full of dread locks and everybody knew that didn't no man want no nappy headed woman. Her locks were well cared for, but still. Nappy was nappy, power to the people be damned. She had a cute enough face though. It was just a shame that she was so damn dark, because she could've really been somebody's competition if it wasn't for the color of her skin. Another thing everybody knew: out of a big-ass bag of Hershey's Miniatures, the Special Darks were always the last ones left in the bag.

When I was coming up, men preferred light skinned women and if you asked me, they still did. More than a few brothas had taken it a step too far and started running after white women, but that was neither here nor there, and it proved my point. A sista with Crayola brown skin didn't have anything coming most of the time. Every now and again, they hooked up with one of the fat ass boys nobody else wanted or else they ended up with the boys who habitually walked around with visible plaque on their teeth and untied shoelaces. In other words, they weren't competition and nobody worried a lick about any of them taking their men.

Until now, that is.

I was still trying to figure out how Anne's little no-breast having ass had moved in on Alec and snatched him right out from under me. My hair was long and hung straight down my back, I had handfuls of titties for him and her butt was no bigger than mine was. So what the hell was it?

Okay, I thought. I'll go ahead and admit it. The bitch had her shit together a little bit. I followed her around the mall and checked out the way she strutted in one store and out another one in stilettos, like she was wearing sneakers. I wasn't into women in the least, but I noticed the way the muscles in her thighs and calves rotated and flexed, I saw men looking and looking some more, and I had to give her props for having a little something-something. After all, like recognized like.

She stopped at a rack of satin thongs in Victoria's Secret and pushed her blazer back to prop a hand on her hip, and I saw that Santa Claus had brought her some more titties for Christmas. Must've been leftover baby fat. She looked up at a male salesman who made his way over to her so quickly that even I hadn't seen him coming and smiled a crinkled nose smile. That little boy couldn't have been a day over eighteen, if that. What business did he have going wide-eyed and then narrowing his eyes on that

bitch's face like he was looking at the Mona Lisa? And
when did they start hiring men to work in Victoria's Secret, anyway?

I felt a tap on my arm and looked to my left.

"Who is this heifer we're following around?" asked my
girl, Tammy. I had forgotten all about her, I was so busy
watching Anne think she was cute.

I slung my purse higher on my shoulder and smirked.
"That's the bitch Alec left me for." I pointed at Anne
through the glass wall separating us. "His baby's mama.
Bitch."

Tammy took her time looking Anne from head to toe.
Then she said, "Regular bitch," and we cracked up. Sistah
Souljah had coined the term in her book *The Coldest Win-
ter Ever*, but it fit Anne perfectly. She might've had a little
something-something, but when it was all said and done,
she didn't have shit on me.

"She must've put some drugs in Alec's food," I said.
Super salesman trailed Anne over to a rack of push-up
bras that matched the four pairs of thongs she had se-
lected and kept up a steady stream of conversation that
had her crinkling her nose left and right. I rolled my eyes
to the ceiling and looked at Tammy. She was staring at
Anne like she'd seen a ghost. "What's up with you?"

"I know her, Dee."

"From where?" The look on her face was starting to
make me nervous. "Don't tell me she fucked your man,
too."

"Please." Tammy flapped a hand and slanted me a look.
"You're the only one with that particular problem. When I
knew the chick she wasn't looking nothing like she looks
now, trust. Last time I saw her, she was cracked out."

"Wh*aaaat?*" All thoughts of informing Tammy that her
man wasn't as faithful as she had tricked herself into be-
lieving fled my mind. I even forgot that I had been about

to tell her that her man couldn't eat pussy worth shit. "What did you just say?"

"You heard me." She laughed behind her hand. "She was a crackhead. You remember I told you about my brother Sean? The one with the drug problem?"

"Yeah, but I thought you said he was a heroin addict?"

"He is now, but he used to be a crackhead. That's how I know her. A couple of times, I had to track him down over on the south side in those projects over there. That's where I saw her a few times and believe me, she wasn't no prom queen back then, either. Ask Sean, he knows her. I think they smoked together a couple of times, if I'm not mistaken."

I was seeing precious Anne through new and enlightened eyes. "Well, I'll be damned," I said as I folded my arms across my chest and shifted my weight to one side. "I'll just be damned. I wonder if Alec knows his woman is a crackhead?"

"She doesn't look too much like a crackhead now though."

"Don't matter. Once a crackhead, always a crackhead and I'll bet you any money Alec doesn't have a clue." I winked at Tammy. "Yet. I knew there was more to that bitch than met the eye."

I took off walking with Tammy trotting along behind me and pulling on my purse strap. "Where are you going? Girl, I know you ain't about to start some shit, are you?"

ANNE

Diana was just stupid enough to think that I hadn't spotted her and her partner in crime standing at the glass staring in at me like I was a cute little puppy they wanted to take home. She was amusing to me, so I let her think she was really doing something and kept on about my business.

I hadn't gone into Victoria's Secret looking for anything in particular, but I bought undies anyway. Giving myself time to get my thoughts together and come up with a plan of action. Of all the days to run into Diana, this was the worst one of all. I still had visions of Smoke screwing her running around in my head and I did not need to be looking in her face right now—adding insult to an injury that I was trying my hardest to shake off. Sometime during all that monster killing I had done at Laverne's, I came to the conclusion that I loved Smoke more than I hated him, so I was trying to deal with the cards I had been dealt. But that didn't mean my decision to be diplomatic extended to ·Diana Daniels. That whore could kiss the crack of my black ass and tell me how it tasted after the fact.

I walked out of Victoria's Secret and swiftly came to the conclusion that not only was Diana stupid, but she was so abundantly stupid that she wasn't smart enough to leave well enough alone. Lord save the world from empty-headed women and their faithful sidekicks, I thought as she came stomping up to me with a sour look on her face.

Here we go. "Something I can help you with?" I tried to sound civil.

"I wanted to introduce you to my friend, Tammy," Diana said with a smug look on her face. She pointed to the woman beside her and raised her eyebrows like I should've known who the woman was.

I shifted my attention and studied the woman for long seconds, coming up with blanks. "Am I supposed to know you?" Tammy looked uncomfortable and she couldn't hold my eyes for more than a second at a time.

"Indirectly," she finally said. "I think you might know my brother, Sean, way better than you know me." I was still confused and it showed on my face. "Sean Taylor."

"Sean Taylor." I rolled the name around on my tongue for a minute and then I shook my head. "Never heard of him. Sorry." I stepped around them and walked off.

"Her brother is a crackhead," Diana called after me. "Just like you are, Anne. Think about it some more, girl. I'm sure you'll remember smoking with him if you think hard enough."

"What did you just say to me?" I turned back around and looked first at Tammy and then at Diana. Tammy appeared to be waiting for the floor to open up and swallow her whole but Diana was triumphant.

"I didn't stutter, did I? I wonder what Alec would say about you being a crackhead?"

I let her walk up on me, refusing to be the first to break eye contact. When she was close enough to smell my breath I tilted my head to one side, put a thoughtful expression on my face and said, "How do you know that he doesn't already know, you brainless, second rate, trussed up strumpet?"

"Your mama's a strumpet."

"She probably is, but we're talking about you right now. Why is it that you can't seem to move on with your life, Diana? Why can't you get on about your whorish business and stay out of my face?"

"Maybe I could get on with my life if your so-called man would stay out of my panties."

"Hell, if I was a man and a whore kept offering me free pussy, I guess I'd take it, too." Tammy slapped a hand over her mouth to hide the grin on her face. "You know what your problem is? You're angry, because you're not me and you're angry, because you can never be me. You're angry, because your looks, which aren't all that to begin with, are starting to fade and when they're gone, all you'll be is a washed-up whore with a vagina stretched so wide a tractor trailer could run through it. It must really suck to be you, Diana, because you are one silly sista."

"I ain't your damn sista, okay? You need to be asking yourself why your man can't get enough of what I got and why whatever it is you got ain't enough to keep him at home."

Oh, no—this bitch didn't just put her finger in my face. I just knew she hadn't gone and done that. I thought I was imagining things until I caught the look on Tammy's face, which was a cross between awe and fear.

My eyes followed Diana's scarlet red acrylic nail everywhere it went. It came a little too close to my nose and I sucked in a sharp breath. "Get your finger out of my face before I bite it off and spit it in your flat face."

"You might as well get used to looking at this flat face, bitch. Because when I have Alec's baby, it's . . ."

Tammy grabbed Diana's arm and spun her around, interrupting her flow. "Girl, you're pregnant?"

"She wishes she was," I said. "She wants to be so badly that it's killing her fake ass. But you can't be me, can you, Diana? All you can be is a convenient pit stop. Did you know that's what Alec told me you were? Convenient. Right before he got on his knees and begged me to take him back. It must be killing you, knowing all you have to offer a man is that worn out garbage diposal between your legs."

"My ass is worn out?" Diana screeched, eyes wide. "My ass is worn out, Anne? Tell me this then, how many men did you fuck for a crack rock?"

"Just Smoke," I said, sounding Shirley Temple '*Good Ship Lollipop*' innocent. "And his dick was extra good back then too, in case you were wondering. Hopped up and down on it so much we ended up with Isaiah."

"Crackhead bitches having crack babies," she mumbled and had me narrowing my eyes.

"What did you just say?"

"I said, crackhead bitches don't have any business bringing crack babies into the world." Diana gave me a shitty grin and started writing a check with her mouth. "Was Isaiah a crack baby, Anne?"

"Don't bring my babies into this."

"Oh, that's right, you have two crack babies." A check that her ass couldn't possibly cash. "No wonder little Iris had to stay in the hospital after she was born. They had to clean all of the drugs from her little system. Poor baby."

Iris had an ear infection, but that was beside the point. Diana was way over the line. "I just told you not to talk about my babies."

"Fuck you and your kids. Hell, they probably ain't even Alec's kids anyway. You crack bitches will fuck anything for a rock. If Isaiah didn't look just like Alec, I'd have to wonder." She looked over at Tammy with a lopsided grin on her face. "That little one? Now she makes you wonder, because she doesn't look like anybody I know. I'll bet . . ."

I stopped her flow before I had time to think about what I was doing. My fist plowed through her teeth like the tractor trailer I had mentioned a few minutes ago.

One thing I never forgot was how to take a woman down. I'd had more than enough practice tussling with Laverne. Diana was even less of a challenge than my sister had ever been. She was too cute to fight me off with any real strength. Too worried about breaking a nail and getting her hair rearranged to even think about the fact that I was shorter than she was and lighter by at least twenty pounds. The amazon bitch could've probably picked me up and tossed me somewhere if she had any brains in her head, but she didn't.

Her face was important to her, so she bent at the waist and windmilled me to death. Diana put herself in a prime position for me to punch her in her head and knock her

sideways. She went stumbling and almost fell into a water
fountain but I came to her rescue just in time. I wrapped
one arm around her neck and used the other one to plow
nonstop uppercuts into her face.

"I. Told. You. Not. To. Talk. About. My. Damn. Babies.
Didn't. I?" Each word was accompanied by a punch. "You.
Don't. Listen. Do. You? Told. You. To. Leave. Me. And. Mine.
The. Fuck. Alone. Didn't. I?"

"Let me go!" she was screaming and swinging her arms
in the air. Pulling on my blazer and dancing around better
than the Godfather of Soul ever did. "Let me go, you crazy
bitch!" I would've laughed if I wasn't in the middle of acting like I was twelve years old and spanking that ass for
all I was worth.

Mall security came from all directions, pushing through
the crowd that had gathered around us, and insinuating
themselves between Diana and me. I thought I slapped
somebody in the face before I was dragged backward and
my arms were pinned to my sides. I dropped the track of
weave I had come away with on the floor.

"Weave wearing whore," I spat out.

"Crazy bitch!" Diana spat back. I'd busted her nose and
blood was everywhere.

"Remember that the next time you come running up on
me, running your mouth."

"I don't think she's gon' forget it anytime soon," Tammy
said and scratched her head.

"Victoria's Secret isn't all that cheap," I told the security
guard who was walking off with me in his arms. "Bring my
bag along with me, if you don't mind."

Jail cell lighting was harsh as hell, I thought as I stared
out of my cell and into the cell where Diana was being
held. Somebody with a warped sense of humor had the
bright idea to put us in cells facing each other, so I had a

clear view of every move she made and vice versa. We had stared each other down for a while, but then that got old really quick, especially since one of her eyes was swollen shut. I watched her squat over the toilet and pee, and then she watched me do the same, both of us sucking our teeth and looking out for something we could make fun of.

If she had holes in her panties, I was all set to drive her into the ground about it, but she didn't. She was one of those cotton panty wearing chicks though. I lifted my skirt and squatted like a queen sitting on a throne and let her see my royal blue silk garter belt and matching bikini panties. No holes here, baby. And no cotton, either.

On to the next order of business, which was using the pay phones in our cells to call somebody to come and bail our silly behinds out. They had given us each enough money for one phone call and we had both wasted them calling somebody who wasn't home. I listened to her curse up a blue streak when she couldn't reach whoever she had called. Then, I let her listen to me curse when Smoke's missing in action butt didn't answer. We caught each other's eyes, counted to ten and rolled them at each other.

"This is all your damn fault," Diana walked up to the bars and said.

"This is your mama's fault for having your ignorant ass," I replied.

"Bitch."

"Whore."

"I would've never pegged you for a crackhead." She shook her head sadly. "I thought Alec had better taste than that."

"He does, that's why he's with me and not you."

"Seems like you should've had enough sense not to get strung out."

"Well, I didn't and so what? I'm over twenty years clean

though. I had enough sense to do that much. You can call me fifty different kinds of crackheads, Diana, but if you think you're hurting me by saying it, you're not. Whores like you don't phase me."

"Did I ever tell you how delicious Alec's cum is?"

I flagged down an oncoming guard and pointed across the aisle into Diana's cell. "Put me in there with her, please, Mr. Officer." I was serious as a heart attack, but he just laughed and kept walking. "I think maybe I didn't kick your ass good enough, since you're still running off at the mouth."

"Speaking of which, you owe me a hundred dollars, too. Thanks to you I have to get my weave done over again."

"I owe you another ass whipping, that's what I owe you," I said. "Let me know when you're ready to collect."

We backed away from the bars and retreated to our respective corners.

A little while later, I turned my back to her and pulled a folded dollar bill from my bra. We hadn't been searched very thoroughly, because there happened to be no female officers available to perform the task when they brought us in. I always kept a few dollars in my bra—a habit I started back when I was smoking and had never managed to break. Just goes to show that not all habits were bad habits and out of bad always comes some good. The pay phone ate my money and I picked up the receiver. I lifted a hand to start dialing.

"What are you doing over there? Where did you get more money?"

"Shut your trap," I said over my shoulder. "I told you, you talk too much, didn't I? Duh.

I'm making a call." I listened to the phone ring endlessly on the other end. "Goddamn it!" Where was Isaiah when I needed him?

"Bring your ass over here and loan me a dollar."

"I'm not loaning you shit." We met at the bars again, me gripping mine like I was a seasoned criminal and her gripping hers like she had been in prison long enough to become somebody's bitch. "You've borrowed enough of what belongs to me to last a lifetime."

"I had him first and you know it."

I thought about it. "You're right and I wasn't trying to take him, either. I came looking for him to help me with my son. That's all."

"Yeah, right."

"Believe it or not, I don't care. Isaiah was trying to be a thug and I wasn't having it and you know yourself, boys need strong men in their lives."

"So why wait sixteen years to come looking then?"

"I wasn't ever planning on looking for Smoke again, but I was desperate. Isaiah was experimenting with drugs. He was messing around in school and scaring the shit out of me every other day. It didn't take me long to figure out that he was showing his ass, because he was angry with me. Every time he asked about his father, I gave him an excuse. A lie, really. Got to the place where he stopped buying the lies."

"Like mother, like son."

"See?" I pushed my locks back from my face and blew out a stream of calming air. "See, that's what I'm talking about right there. Your nonstop, clueless mouth. But you're right about one thing and that's the fact that my son could've ruined his life like I almost did mine. You don't have kids, even if you do fantasize about having them, so you can't really relate to what I'm saying. I wasn't about to stand by and let that happen. I worked too hard to pull myself up to let him fall down."

"How did you do it?"

"Do what?"

"Pull yourself up?"

"Had an aunt who took me to live with her when I was seventeen," I said after a minute.

I was debating on how much to reveal because something told me that trusting her with too much information would be a huge mistake I'd live to regret even more than I regretted getting myself locked up for the first time in my life. This was surreal.

"I was clean when I gave birth to my son and I've been clean ever since, not that I owe you any explanations."

"And Alec knows about all this?"

"Alec was the one I bought drugs from," I said and watched her eyes pop out. God, she was stupid.

She eventually tapped into my thought process. "Smoke?"

"Smoke," I confirmed. "Now do you understand?" I left her at the bars and went to sit on my bunk. A few seconds later, she did the same thing. "I wasn't plotting on him, Diana. As a matter of fact, I told him time after time to take his behind back to you, but he wouldn't listen. He kept chasing after me."

"You stopped running too, didn't you?"

"Did I have a choice? You know how he can be when his mind is made up about something."

"I suppose that dick of his rendered you helpless, too."

"It is persuasive," I said and we cracked up. Then, we came to our senses and fell silent, sliding each other sideways looks and rolling our eyes. I went back to the phone and fed it another dollar. I listened to Laverne's cell phone ring and ring and ring. "Where the hell is everybody?"

"I don't have the slightest idea where your folks are, but I do know one thing. I might have to sit here all night, because, unlike your ghetto ass, I don't keep money in my bra and I'm flat broke."

I stopped pacing and looked at her like she was crazy. "Pays to be ghetto now, doesn't it? And I promise you, when I get bailed out, I won't tell a soul you're in here, so you can rot right here in cell block H."

"You are one cruel bitch."

"Must be the crack," I said and squatted over the toilet again to pee.

"What the hell made you start smoking that shit anyway?"

"I'll introduce you to my mother and my sister sometime. They're color struck just like you are, so you'll probably become fast friends. Couldn't do nothing but zone out to get away from them."

"And you were, what, ten when you starting smoking?"

"None of your business," I said over my shoulder as I washed my hands. I snatched a couple of paper towels from the dispenser and dried my hands. "Fourteen when I took my first hit and seventeen when I took my last. Sorry I don't have a more tragic, disgusting history for you to salivate over."

Diana suddenly had to pee, too. Midstream, she looked up from her squat and caught my eyes. "You wouldn't happen to have a tampon stuffed in your teeny tiny bra, would you?"

"Nope. I do have ten more dollars though."

She wiped herself, washed her hands and then came stumbling over to the bars, wild-eyed and desperate sounding. "Help! Let me out of here! Somebody help!"

Five minutes passed with her screaming at the top of her lungs like an idiot. Calling for help that wasn't coming. When I felt a migraine coming on, I decided to take pity on her pitiful butt.

"Here." I stretched a creased dollar bill as far as I could across the aisle toward her. "Just so you can shut up and you better make the most of it, because I'm not giving you another one. With your cry baby ass."

She looked at the dollar and sniffed up a tear. "Thank you, bitch."

"You're welcome, whore."

"I'll bet I get out of here before you do."

"I'll bet I knocked part of your brain out and its still back at the mall. That's why you're talking crazy."

"I have a crisp hundred dollar bill in my purse. Put some money on it."

"Make it fifty, because that's all I have."

"You mean Alec doesn't give you money?"

"Are you betting or what, whore?"

We raced over to the pay phones and started dialing.

I tried Smoke again and then Isaiah, and still didn't get answers. Smoke's cell phone went straight to voicemail and Isaiah's just rang. Laverne wasn't answering her cell either, dammit. I heard Diana over in her cell, talking fast and begging someone to come and get her, and I tried to pull my locks out by the roots.

I slammed the receiver down and stared at it. I picked it up and slammed it down again. Wasn't this some shit? Ten seconds later, I was dialing again and listening to the phone ring on the other end. She answered on the fourth ring and I squeezed my eyes shut and gritted my teeth. Then I said, "Mama?"

Don's face was the first familiar one I had seen since they had thrown me into a jail cell and tossed away the key. He walked down the aisle and stopped in front of my cell, looking back and forth between me and Diana and shaking his head. "Imagine my surprise when I came to work and found out you'd gotten yourself locked up, Anne."

"Don!" I could've cried, I was so happy to see him. "Get me the hell out of here."

"Sorry, toots," he said. "Can't bail family members out."

"We're not really related, so quit playing and get me out

of here. What the hell? Where did you get my cell phone?" I reached through the bars and snatched it from him. I had seven missed calls and four voicemail messages.

"No fair," Diana butted in. "Listen, Dan, you can't be showing her special attention. They have rules about that."

"It's Don and I'm well aware of the rules. Smoke's been calling all over the city looking for you," he told me. "Call him back right now."

I pressed a button and put the phone to my ear. "Smoke?" I said as soon as he picked up. "Don said you were looking for me."

"Where the hell have you been? I've been calling all over the place, trying to hunt you down and why does Don know how to reach you and I don't?" He was yelling so loudly that I'm sure Diana heard him clearly all the way over in her cell. Damn sure Don did, if the knowing smirk on his face was any indication.

I looked at him, saw something that I didn't need to see and took my eyes to the wall. "I'm in jail."

"Jail? Jail, Anne? Is that what you just said? Jail?"

"Would you lower your voice, please? Yes, that's right, jail."

"For what?" Smoke's voice had gone soprano on me.

"For beating the shit out of Diana, that's what."

"You wish," Diana yelled. Don and me turned to stare at her and she closed her mouth.

"Will you shut up?" I yelled back. "I should've busted your lip instead of your nose." I put the phone to my ear again. "Anyway, why are you looking for me?"

"As much as I'm dying to hear the story, it'll have to wait. We need to get up to KSU quick, fast and in a hurry," Smoke said. "Isaiah is in the middle of some shit again and they're talking about kicking him out of school. I'm headed there now."

"You're going without me?" Now my voice was soprano. "What kind of mess is that?"

"I've been looking for you for hours, woman. This is time sensitive shit we're dealing with. Nobody told you to get yourself arrested. Put Don on the phone, while I'm thinking about it."

"Where are you now?"

"About an hour and a half outside of the city. Let me speak to Don."

I held the phone out to Don. "He wants to speak to you."

"I'll pass on listening to his ranting and raving." Don pushed the phone back in my direction. "Tell him I'll drive you down to KSU as soon as you make bail."

"What?" Smoke shouted in my ear. "What did that chump just say? He was driving you down to KSU? Oh, hell no, I don't hardly think so." I heard him burning rubber. "I'm turning around now, so wait on me."

"My mother is supposed to be coming to bail me out, so pick me up at the house," I said and hung up. "Don, you need to quit playing and bail a sista up out of here, for real."

"What about her?" He hooked a thumb toward Diana and raised his eyebrows.

"To hell with her."

"Fifty big ones, bitch," Diana reminded me.

"I haven't forgotten, whore. It's still on and popping, believe that."

She opened her mouth to respond, but I waved to her to be quiet when Don's walkie-talkie crackled on. "Detective Avery, I have someone here to make bail for Breanne Phillips," a staticky voice said.

I did a victory dance. "Thank God! For once in my life, she comes when I need her. There is a God. And I get fifty dollars out of the deal, too? This must be my lucky day."

"Sir, there's someone here for Diana Daniels, too." She went to acting like a fool in her cell, making silly faces and sticking her tongue out at me. Don was looking at us like he didn't know who we were.

"I'm on my way out," Don spoke into his walkie-talkie.

I froze. "Wait a minute," I caught Don's arm. "Ask him what time we got bailed out, Don."

"Anne, please."

"There's money riding on this and you know there's two things I don't play about. My babies and my money. Ask him!" When he finished laughing, he asked.

We were released from our cells at the same time and in our rush to make it to the door, we almost collided with each other. Every last one of the guards sucked in their breaths and waited for the inevitable explosion, but there was none. I simply stepped back and motioned for her to go ahead of me.

"Thank you, bitch."

"Just saving the best for last, whore, so after you."

"I don't have any change." She tried to play me after we had collected our property and it was time for her to pay up.

"I will go to jail again, okay? Be a woman and honor your debts, Diana. Hell, it was your idea to bet, anyway. I should've known you'd pull some mess."

"Oh, I pay my debts all right." She looked around the police station. "Does anyone have change for a hundred dollar bill?"

"You have jokes, right? You're in a police station, so what do you think?" I ignored the look Don shot me and found my wallet. "Here." I passed her my fifty and took the hundred she passed me back. She watched me fold it neatly and slip it inside my bra, shaking her head. "It would behoove you to take a few lessons, because the money in my bra saved your life."

"Whatever, you ghetto bitch."

"Whatever right back at you, you worn out strumpet whore. Stay away from my man."

"And you stay away from me."

"Then, we understand each other."

Don touched my arm and cleared his throat loudly. "Anne . . ."

"I'm coming," I snapped. "Give me a second, Don."

As much mess as I had talked back at the police station with Diana, I couldn't think of a thing to say to my mother when it was just her and I in the backseat of the cab she had waiting at the curb for us. I could tell she was embarrassed about having to bail me out of jail, because she kept sending me admonishing glances and looking away when I met her eyes. After a while, I got tired of seeing the shame in her eyes and turned my face to the window.

"Aren't you a little old to be fighting and carrying on?"

"Isn't it a little late to be lecturing me?" I shot back and kept looking out the window.

She reached out and put her hands on me and I almost choked on my tongue. I tried to remember the last time she had struck me and couldn't. All the more reason why I lifted a hand and rubbed the back of my head, staring at her through crossed eyes. "Excuse me?"

"Excuse me?" she parroted and rolled her eyes. "I'm still your mother and that smart mouth of yours is really starting to get on my nerves. I didn't come all the way across town and spend my money bailing your behind out of jail, just to hear your lip, so shut it up."

"I'm paying you back every red cent just as soon as I can get to the bank, too, because if you think I'm about to start listening to you telling me what I owe you every other minute you can forget that."

"You don't owe me nothing."

"You got that right."

"Just like I don't owe you nothing."

"You got that wrong," I said as I leaned forward and touched the cab driver's shoulder. "Make a left up here at the light and then another left at the third stop sign. I'll let you know from there. And why are you driving ten miles an hour?"

"I'm going the speed limit, ma'am."

"Could've fooled me. We've been passing the same house for the last fifteen minutes."

"Will you sit back and let the man drive?"

"Can I help it if I'm anxious to be home?"

"Anxious to be away from me, you mean."

"Can I help that either?"

"You act like I was the worst mother in the world, Breanne. You need to stop that mess.

Make people think I abused you or something."

"Black ass," I said in a singsong voice that sounded just like she had sounded all those years ago. "Nappy headed ass. And then after *The Color Purple* came out, 'You sho is ugly,' ha, ha, ha. Gal, you so black I don't think you can get no blacker. Make sure you get an education, because damn sure ain't no man gon' want your ashy ass. Maybe they switched my baby for you at the hospital. And my personal favorite, mama. If abortion had'a been legal when I got pregnant with you, you wouldn't be here."

"I was just talking mess, girl."

"Breanne, bring your black ass here," I kept talking. "Get your black ass out of my house. I'm gon' turn out the lights, so I can't see your black ass. Sick of looking at you, anyway. Here, here, black gal. Here, here . . ." I caught my breath and stared down at the hand she wrapped around my forearm. She was squeezing my flesh so tightly that I tried to jerk away and couldn't loosen her grip.

"I said, I was just talking mess. Now, stop it right now, girl."

The struggle over possession of my arm was brief and I eventually reclaimed it. "I'm not too black for you not to leave a hand print," I said as I rubbed my arm. "How about that?"

"Bobbi told me you had grown into a sweet young woman, but I can't tell it by listening to the way you talk to me."

"Aunt Bobbi didn't tell you anything." She started to say something else, but I held up a hand to stop her. I shifted in my seat and went back to my window. "Fourth house on the left," I told the cab driver.

"I called down there twice a week, every week, to check on you, girl. I caught the bus and came to see you get your GED, came to both of your college graduations, too. Bet you didn't know that, did you? I sat in the back, so you wouldn't see me 'cause I knew you didn't want me there."

"I figured you didn't care about being there."

"You didn't ask me to find out, did you?"

"You were part of the reason I was in the situation I was in, in the first place. I took that first hit of crack to drown out your voice. Bet you didn't know that, did you? Oh my God, if we ever get to my house it will be a miracle!" I couldn't believe how slowly we were rolling. "Right here!" I reached for the door handle as soon as the cab rolled to a stop in the driveway.

"I'm not the same person I used to be, Breanne."

"That's good then, isn't it?" I opened the door and dropped a foot to the pavement. "Because if I thought you were doing the same thing to Tracey that you did to me, you'd have more than old age to worry about. How much do I owe you, mama? Oh, wait, I almost forgot." I took the hundred-dollar bill from my bra and tossed it over Father Time's ancient shoulder, told him to take my mama home and to keep the change. "I'll bring the rest to you first thing next week. He should have you home by then."

"Why are so you hateful, Breanne?"

"Why do you hate me, mama?" I waited for an answer, but she didn't offer one. "That's what I thought. When you answer my question, I'll answer yours."

I let myself in my house and made a conscious effort to wipe my mama from my mind. I had more important things to deal with right now and I didn't need her voice creeping out of the corner that I had banished it to all those years ago and messing with my thought process. Didn't need anything distracting me from seeing about my son and handling my business. And where the hell was Smoke? What the hell was taking him so long?

After I scrubbed the smell of imprisonment off of my skin and jumped into some traveling clothes, I packed a bag and sat on the living room couch facing the door to wait. Hateful, my ass.

CHAPTER ELEVEN

ALEC

The deal was like this: Isaiah and some of his teammates were in deep shit. End of story. Apparently, my son had been running around with a shady dude named Marion Witherspoon, thinking he was cool people when he really wasn't. According to the dean, Zay was mixed up in some kind of plot to hurt another player that had gone wrong. There was something like ten sides to the story, so the dean was kind of shaky on all of the details, but that was the gist of it. And, oh yeah, Marion Witherspoon was accusing Zay of running marijuana for him. Far be it for me to leave that little detail out.

Oh my God, I couldn't wait to sink my foot so far up that boy's ass he'd be walking like he wore pink panties for the next twenty years. I was going to be like Beyoncé, ringing the motherfucking alarm, because KSU hadn't yet seen a fire like the one I was about to start.

Not that I was under the impression that Zay was running drugs. I just knew that sometimes he wasn't the sharpest tool in the shed when it came to the company he kept. First, Hood, and now, this Marion nigga. The first thing I was going to tell him when I saw him, after I slapped him upside his head, that is, was to bring his ass out of the Land of Oz and pay a—fucking—tention. Not everybody was happy to see him coming and at twenty-one years old, he should know that by now.

Zay's problem was that he was a nice person. Too damn nice, if you asked me. One of those "*I* forgive you" people, which irritated me no end. Sometimes, there was no forgiveness. Sometimes, you had to slit a motherfucker's throat, wipe his blood on his shirt and walk the hell away so he could die in peace. Shit, sometimes you had to stand over a motherfucker and watch him die, just to make sure he was really gone and out of your hair.

Zay's other problem? He fainted at the sight of blood. Which was something I wished I had been around long before he was sixteen years old to put a stop to. The nigga who concluded that women didn't have any business raising men by themselves hadn't never lied. Now, if somebody could just do something about sorry ass brothas who didn't stick around to make a difference, I'd be all right. But, I was digressing.

I took my eyes off of the road long enough to glance over in the passenger seat at Anne. There was nothing that could be done about women who ran off and hid to have brothas' sons and then kept them hidden for sixteen years, was there?

"How in the hell did you manage to get arrested?" I asked her for the fifth time. "Explain it to me again, because I'm still a little fuzzy."

"You heard me the first four times, Smoke. You just like to hear me say it."

"It is kind of funny, if you think about it."

"There is nothing funny about me getting arrested for whipping your woman's ass." She pushed a button to crack her window.

"I thought you were my woman."

"Your dick tells a different story, now doesn't it? It's the next exit. Slow down, before you miss the turnoff."

"I know where I'm going, Anne. Please don't make me pull over and put you out, okay? How many times have we made this drive?"

"About a hundred and I have to remind you about the exit every time." I laid a hand on her thigh and she pushed it off. "That whore was with some woman who supposedly knew me back in the day," she said. "Next thing I knew, she was in my face, calling me a crackhead and talking mess about my children being crack babies, saying that they probably weren't yours. So, I punched her in her mouth. It really wasn't about you at all. Nobody talks about my babies and gets away with it. Old as I am, I tried to hurt that yellow whore."

"Don said you busted her nose and gave her a black eye," I recalled incredulously.

"I should've stomped her face in, that's what I should've done."

Anne slapped my hand away again and whipped her cell phone out at the same time. I listened to her check in with Big Mama on how Iris was doing and then check her messages.

"*Hands* just made me a formal job offer," she said as she closed the phone and dropped it back in her purse. "I guess I can forget about taking it now that I'm a convicted felon, huh?"

"Don got the charges dropped to traffic violations," I told her. She was exaggerating and she knew it. The original charge had only been misdemeanor peace disturbance. Diana had backed away from filing assault charges when Anne hit her with a counter assault charge. As usual, she was being dramatic. "Just make sure you pay the court costs and fines on time."

"No, you make sure *you* pay the court costs and fines on time. This is all your fault, anyway."

"Hold up, I thought you just said you were fighting over your babies?" I eased my hand back to her thigh and squeezed. She ignored my question and my hand. "Anne?"

"Shut up, Smoke."

"You know you love me. You need to stop acting hard and admit it." The smile on my face slipped sideways when I saw the expression on hers. A cross between intense anger and child-like vulnerability.

"What's important to note here is that you now know that *I* love *you*, right Smoke? Why else would my damn near forty year old behind be fighting in the middle of a shopping mall, where anybody could've seen me, if not for my family? Or over my man?"

I understood that it was a rhetorical question, so I kept my trap shut.

"That's what I thought," she said. "And slow down, before we miss the turn off that I always have to remind you not to miss."

I slowed down.

"Let me do the talking," I said as I shifted into park and looked through the windshield at the administration building in front of us. I got out of the car and went around to the passenger side to help my woman do the same.

"Whatever you say." She wasn't sounding very convincing.

"I'm serious, Anne." I watched her ass jiggle inside her skirt as she walked down the corridor in front of me. Wound up or not, I could still find some attention to pay to my woman's ass.

"I am, too. Stop it." I slid my hand up her thigh and she giggled. "Come on now, Smoke. This is neither the time nor the place." Then, "Smoke, I swear to God."

We jumped apart at the sound of a throat clearing nearby. We looked at each other, then at what I assumed was Doolittle and his cat.

"You must be Isaiah's parents," Doolittle said with a smirk on his face.

I had a responding smirk ready for his cat carrying ass. "How did you know?"

"Family resemblance. Why don't I show you to the dean's office?"

"Yes, why don't you?" I suggested easily and earned an eye roll from Anne behind Doolittle's back.

We followed Doolittle into the inner sanctum and met with a tall brotha named Hester Grandberry, the Dean of Student Affairs and the same dude who was trying to side-track my son's academic career. I took one look at his balding head and pinched face and automatically went into defense mode. Something about his looks screamed uptight, unyielding and totally unnecessary. I decided I didn't like him just on GP.

Doolittle and his cat sat off to the side on a wrinkled leather couch, leaving the two chairs positioned across from Grandberry's desk for me and Anne. I waited for Anne to sit and cross her legs, and then I sat down and got right to the point.

"Where is my son?" Anne shot me a quelling look that I politely pretended not to see. This was not the time for ass kissing and glad-handing. I was here to straighten things out and keep my son in school, not to chitchat about the weather.

"We've sent word for him to report here shortly," Doolittle spoke up in fake British accent as he straight-ened his tie, cleared his throat and carried on. "Before he arrives, I'd like to go over the specifics of the situation, so we'll all be aware of what's at stake here."

I rolled my eyes to the ceiling, looked around and ran

right into Anne's narrowed gaze. I did a double take and raised my eyebrows like, what?

Grandberry picked up the tale in a rusty southern accent. "As you know, the charges against Isaiah are fairly serious. Aside from the fighting . . ."

Anne sat up in her chair. "Fighting? What fighting?"

"Isaiah and some of his teammates were removed from Exum Center for fighting, which is where all the confusion started. There have been some allegations of drug trafficking on Isaiah's part and then there is the possibility of a formal complaint being brought against Isaiah for taking part in a plan to injure another player."

"Drug trafficking?" Anne was too outdone. She whipped around in her chair, staring at me with her mouth hanging open and her eyes wide. "Did you know about this?"

"No, baby, I didn't." What else could I say? I rubbed her back and coaxed her into sitting back in her chair and chilling out. The last thing I needed was for her to flip out and start throwing stuff around Grandberry's office. Anne was off the chain when she got started.

But, of course, I did know about some of the shit going on down here at KSU. Quiet as it was kept, Doolittle was the one who put a bug in my ear just a few minutes before I got the call from good old Hester. I wasn't planning on mentioning that to anyone though, because I was pretty sure that Doolittle wasn't supposed to do that and I appreciated the brotha looking out, even if he was a little, shall we say, strange.

According to Doolittle, Zay had gotten mixed up with a scout for the Colorado Mountaineers who also happened to be Marion Witherspoon. If I knew my son, he was probably thinking that Witherspoon was going to pave the way for him to be picked up in the NBA draft, which was why he didn't quite see everything there was to see about Witherspoon. He never questioned why, if the chump was supposed to be all that and a bag of chips, he was living in an efficiency hotel room. Nor had he ever stopped to wonder why Witherspoon was doing more partying than scouting.

Doolittle had questioned a few things though, and this was what he had come up with: Witherspoon was on indefinite suspension, because of illegal gambling. He had come to KSU's campus before the basketball season started, intending to snag a few players for the Mountaineers, and had somehow become sidetracked by all the gambling he was doing. Probably some of the scouts from other teams had reported him, because he was a fool and he had ended up being suspended. And then one had to factor in the drugs, which was where Dino came in. I had received a callback from Dino just before all the bullshit popped off between Diana and Anne and I was just now working my way around to processing what I had learned and adding it into the scenario playing out right now.

Witherspoon was a weed head, plain and simple. Put him in close proximity to a campus full of rowdy coeds and he was in hog heaven. Dino had put me on to the fact that Witherspoon maintained a decent little income by selling weed, which was probably where all the money Zay had suddenly come up with had most likely originated. The question was whether or not Zay was aware of that.

Not, I decided as I tuned back into the conversation. I couldn't see Zay knowingly running weed back and forth across the campus, but that did still leave the question as to why he had saved the money he had been given, instead of spending it like any other twenty-one year old would've done. He might not have known about every little thing that was going on, but he damn sure knew something.

"So what happens now?" Anne was asking Grandberry.

"The case will go before the Student Conduct Committee and they'll have the final vote on whether Isaiah will be allowed to remain in school or be expelled."

"And what are the charges against Isaiah? Specifically?"

"Conduct unbecoming of a student athlete and allegations of drug trafficking."

"Allegations, you said." Anne went into lawyer mode, whipping out a pen and a small notepad from her purse to take notes. "So nothing has been proven, he's just been accused?"

"Yes," Doolittle said.

"He can't lose his scholarship because of allegations, can he?"

"That's where it could get tricky, Ms. Phillips. In some cases, simply being accused of this kind of behavior is enough to have lasting repercussions. And the issue with the fighting has already been confirmed. Isaiah admits to taking part in the brawl, so that's one strike there."

"Self defense?" she suggested and then waved a hand. "You know what, forget about that right now. Who are the other teammates involved?"

Grandberry cleared his throat and glanced at Doolittle. "I'm really not at liberty to disclose the identities of the other students, since they will each have to be disciplined, as well.

We're doing our best to keep this situation under wraps for as long as we can. The last thing we need is for the media to get hold to something like this and blow it out of proportion."

"This situation is that serious?" I asked.

"It's that serious. Anytime there are allegations of drug trafficking on a college campus, we must tread lightly, Mr. Avery. Throw the co-captain of the basketball team into the mix and things really get interesting. This is a very unfortunate situation."

"Unfortunate doesn't even begin to describe this situation," Anne said. She shifted in her seat and turned toward Doolittle and his cat, pen poised. "What are their names?" Doolittle hesitated and she narrowed her eyes on his face. "You might as well go on and tell me, because I'm not leaving this campus until I find out."

I thought I saw Doolittle bite down on a smile, but I couldn't be sure. He had the kind of look about him that made it impossible to figure out exactly what he was thinking. A smile could've really been a frown and vice versa or he could've been having a bowel movement. Who knew? But there was no mistaking the seriousness of his voice when he finally parted his lips and started rambling off first and last names. I made a mental note to remind Isaiah that allies sometimes came in strange, cat carrying packages. Doolittle wasn't as crazy as he let everybody think he was and neither was I, really.

But I was about to show my ass, nonetheless.

The door to Grandberry's office creaked open and Isaiah stepped inside, looking everywhere but at Anne and me. That alone told me that he knew what time it was between me and him, but in case he was even a little bit confused, I was getting ready to set it off.

Anne and I stood up at the same time, but for completely different reasons. Instead of approaching Isaiah, she turned toward me with her palms out and a nervous expression on her face. I slung a chair out of my path and almost slung Anne right with it. I was shaking my head, telling Anne not even bother trying to diffuse the situation, before my mouth finally opened and I came out with what inquiring minds wanted to know.

"You want to tell me just what the fuck is going on here, Zay?"

"Da, look . . ." he said and unknowingly flipped a switch inside my head.

I think I sprouted wings and flew across the room at his ass.

ISAIAH

That whole scene in Grandberry's office was embarrassing as hell. My old dude taking flight and slamming a brotha against the wall, breaking up three of Grandberry's picture frames and scaring the shit out of Doolittle's cat. My mama slinging snot east, west, north and south, while trying to wrestle my old dude off of me. Grandberry threatening to call security if my crazy parents didn't settle down and my old dude telling him to sit his cross-eyed ass down before he wrapped the phone cord around his head like a rubber band. Doolittle crawling around on the floor, trying to convince his cat that it was safe to come out from under Grandberry's desk. And my mama in her stilettos, accidentally stepping on the cat's tail when the little ugly thing finally did come out.

I could've broken out speaking in tongues when my old dude's cell phone rang and sent him out into the hallway to take the call. My mama went skipping out behind him and I thought peace had finally been restored. Until they started shouting at each other in the hallway, that is. I prayed for an earthquake to suddenly hit, a volcano to erupt, anything to shut my parents up. I didn't have no problem admitting to people that my folks were special, but this was straight ridiculous.

By the time we left Grandberry's office, nothing had been decided, but one thing was for sure, Grandberry and Doolittle were happy to see the doorknob hitting our asses, for real. After all the clowning and acting black my parents had done, there still wasn't anything that could be done to stop the inevitable. My disciplinary hearing was scheduled for two weeks from now and I had to wait until then to find out if I was going to lose everything I had worked so hard for. Plus, I was being suspended until then.

I probably should've killed Marion when I had the chance. I could survive my old dude's neck choking and hollering like a fool, but my mama's doe-eyed, little girl lost looks was a different story. A brotha would happily bust a cap in somebody's ass and go sit down for a bid, just to keep from getting one of those looks. I think my old dude knew just what the hell he was doing when he mumbled something about having some runs to make real quick and jetted, leaving me alone with her.

"Mama," I said for the third time.

We were in my dorm room supposedly packing up the rest of my stuff, but she was doing more pouting and I was doing more explaining than anything else. I tossed the last of my clothes in the super-size duffel bag lying open on the bed and dropped down to my haunches in front of her. She had plopped down on the bed and refused to move—acting like a little kid.

I squeezed her thighs and made her look at me. "I can't even lie and say I wasn't fighting, because I was. But that other shit—I mean stuff—I'm not good for it. I know you don't believe me, but . . ."

She waved a hand in front of my face and sighed like she had the weight of the world on her shoulders. "I know that, Isaiah. I just can't believe this is happening again. I can't get you out of school safely for nothing, can I? Tell me where I went wrong as a mother."

"You didn't go wrong anywhere, mama."

"I had to. I mean, you always seem to find the craziest folks to befriend and I just know that's my fault somehow." She went to picking lint that wasn't there off my shirt. "Maybe if I had put you in some boxing or karate classes, instead of making you take that etiquette class."

"Mama, please."

"Was it the Boy Scout troop I made you join?"

Now that I had to think about for a minute. "Maybe," I said and cracked a smile. She moaned and covered her face, which made me laugh. "Would you stop being so dramatic? Look." I took her hands away from her face. "You didn't do anything wrong, okay?"

"Those story times at the library couldn't have been very helpful, come to think of it. Making you sit by that one boy with the tangly eyes and that other one who ate his own boogers. I swear to God, if I could do it all over again, I would turn you loose in the middle of the ghetto and let you learn some street sense."

I should've been insulted, but since it was my mama talking crazy to me, I took her words in the spirit that they were meant. Plus, I knew she had a few screws loose. "Oh, so I'm street stupid, right?"

"You were the only little black boy running around with a skateboard in one hand and a can of Ensure in the other, Isaiah. That tells the story right there."

My head snapped back on my neck, eyes got big. "That's what that was? You told me that was chocolate milk. No wonder the kids were always laughing at me."

She threw her head back and cracked up. "See?"

"Oh, now see you gone have to pay for that." I stuck my fingers in her armpits and tickled her up from the bed. She went from laughing like a lady to screaming like a baby hyena.

"Stop it, boy! I mean it now. Stop it, before you make me pee on myself!"

"Had me being the butt of everybody's jokes," I said and kept tickling. "Uh-uh, don't try to slide to the floor now." I caught my mama around the waist and brought her back to her feet, caught her when she tried to make a run for the door and lifted her clean off the floor like she was a ten pound weight. I started in on her sides, where she was really ticklish and had her begging for mercy. "Tell me about the Ensure now. Come on, mama, tell me." She wiggled around in my arms, half laughing and half screaming, until she had an arm wrapped around my neck, a leg wrapped around my waist and a knee up in my chest.

And then, Erica walked into my dorm room and caught me tripping with my other woman. My first love. My mama. Everybody froze and damned if I wasn't standing there looking like I had been cold busted.

CHAPTER TWELVE

ERICA

Here I was, coming to surprise my man and see him off properly and he was up in his dorm room love tapping and play wrestling with some other hoochie? I didn't think I had seen her around campus, but there was a community college down the street and around the corner, so she could've found her way over here from there. And judging from the nervous look on Isaiah's face, they had known each other for longer than ten minutes, too.

She was staring at me and I was staring at her. She looked like she might've been thinking about getting froggy and jumping. I already knew I was thinking about getting froggy and jumping—right on top of her locked up head. Isaiah was first though.

I circled around the two of them and crossed my arms under my breasts. *Okay*, I thought. Time to see exactly what I was up against. Isaiah had the good sense to turn her loose and set her on her feet, which gave me a clear view of exactly how much ass I was probably going to have to spank about my man.

I looked her from head to toe. She was way shorter

than I was and she had the nerve to be kind of cute with it. Wearing low rise, hip hugging jeans on her little bubble butt and stilettos that weren't doing a damn thing about adding some height. Since I had on my Nikes and some track pants, I already had the advantage. Now, all I needed was some Vaseline and a safe place to drop my diamond studs until I was done doing what I had to do.

"Isaiah?" the little Betty Boop-looking chocolate drop said. She laid a possessive hand on his chest which sent me straight into second gear. She was strong enough with her game to touch my man right in front of me? Oh, hell no.

"Yeh, Isaiah." I tilted my head to one side and reached up to make sure my ponytail was tight. "Who dis be?"

"Oh my God, do you see what I'm saying about the company you keep?" She flapped a dismissive hand at me and rolled her eyes to the ceiling. "This one can't even speak English, for Christ's sake."

What? Did she just . . . ? "Dat's it, now I'm 'bout to kick your ass!"

"Isaiah, you had better get this amazon, boy. I just got out of jail and I will go right back. You know I don't play this kind of mess."

"Bring it on, den. Les' see what 'cha got."

"Erica . . ."

I wasn't interested in hearing a damn thing Isaiah had to say to me right now. He tried to block me, but I was too quick for him. I faked him out and whirled around him, heading straight for the itty-bitty one with all the mouth. She drew her right fist back and I drew back my left. One of us was going down today and my money was on her.

"Erica!"

I saw stars for a minute and then Isaiah's face was in my face. He had taken me back against the wall so fast that I was winded from the trip. With one hand in the middle of my chest, he held me there and stared at me like I had lost my last mind and he was ready to help me find it.

"What is dis?" Angry tears rolled down my cheeks. Not only was he manhandling me in front of her, but he was defending her, too. I slapped his hand away from my chest and gave him a look of my own. "You choose this bi . . ."

He put a finger to my lips. "Watch out now, girl. I love you and all that, but you can't be talking about my mama like that."

"Can I put my switchblade away now?"

Isaiah glanced over his shoulder and did a doubletake. "Mama please, okay? Where did you get that?"

"A big nosed, bubble-eyed bitch named Bubba gave it to me while I was in the joint," she said, lying through her teeth with a straight face. "I was going to take this bad boy for a test drive, too. Ease up on her Isaiah, I taught you better than that."

She was his mama? A man walked in the room and I didn't have to wonder who he was.

"Zay, bring your ass. I'm ready to . . . what the hell? Anne, give me my blade. I was looking for the damn thing last week."

I thought I was seeing double. Two fine ass, gray-eyed specimens for the price of one. Looking at Isaiah's daddy, I could see exactly what Isaiah would look like in twenty years and I decided right then and there that I wanted Isaiah's babies in my belly. Well, I had kind of already decided that, but still. Here was indisputable proof that my decision making process was for the most part, sound.

Oh, my damn.

"You cool?" Isaiah asked me. I shook my head, because I needed a few minutes to find my voice. "All right then, meet my parents. Think you already met my mama, so this is my da."

"Alec is fine," dreamboat told me as I slipped my hand

inside of his and forgot to shake. He read the expression on my face and cracked a knowing smile. "Erica, right?"

"Um . . . right." Alec sure was fine, he was telling the truth about that.

He had to know he was fine, the same way Isaiah had to know it. They had the same creamy caramel skin, the same soft wavy hair, and the same sleepy, gray eyes and cleft chins. The same everything, right down to sexy little moles at the sides of their noses.

I took my eyes off of his face and put them on Isaiah's. "Baby, I'm sorry. I thought . . ."

"Thought you were going to have to throw down for your man?"

"Thought she was going to get her throat slit, that's what she thought."

"Da." Isaiah sighed and looked at his father.

Da scratched the back of his neck and sucked his teeth while he came up with a game plan. "Okay, so . . . Anne, let's go get a soda or something. Give Zay and his friend a few minutes alone."

She let herself be led out of the room, but not before she shot me a death look. "Always with the crazy ass women," she was saying on her way down the hall.

"Told you your mama was going to hate my guts," I said when the door was closed behind them.

"Well, at least now you know it's not because of the color of your skin."

"I have to think long and hard about how I'm going to make this up to you, boo."

A shiver ran down my spine as Isaiah pushed his hands down inside the back of my track pants and gripped my ass. "I think I know a way . . ."

But I wasn't quite done. "Damn, how is your mama so cute?"

"She is kind of fly, ain't she?"

He started sucking on my neck and my eyes rolled to the back of my head. Still, though. "Looking all perky and petite, and young and ripe."

"You switching teams in the middle of the game, or what?"

"Boy, don't play with me." I reached down and pulled my T-shirt over my head.

"I'm just saying. I saw you looking at her ass."

"I was looking at that switchblade she whipped out on me. Was she really going to cut me?"

"Gut your ass like a fish. I told you, she don't play about her special baby boy. You thought I was lying?"

"And she was really in prison?"

"Did ten years standing on her head."

He saw the horrified look on my face, took two steps back and howled. Me? I suddenly had to pee. Badly.

Walking the green mile had to be a cakewalk compared to walking the yellow brick road that led to Isaiah's parents. Now that the smoke had cleared, his mama looked harmless enough, but now that I knew who she was, I was even more intimidated than I had been when I walked in and thought I was catching Isaiah with another woman. In truth, I had caught him with another woman, just not the average run of the mill hoochie, like I first thought. This was the queen hoochie, the hoochie who topped all other hoochies. Not a hoochie at all, really, but a petite female version of Moses, from what I had been told. The way Isaiah described his mama to me, the woman could part water, walk on it and boil it better than anybody else in the world.

I would've been hard pressed to describe the way his face lit up when he talked about his mama. He got this gleam in his eye and a smile on his face that could've easily evoked some fierce jealousy in me if I didn't know he was talking about the woman who had birthed him. My own mama had always told me that a man who loved his mama and treated her well was a good man, so I thought the way Isaiah got all googly eyed over his mama was adorable. Thought I had finally picked a winner after that whole debacle with Jared and his wandering dick.

Fast forward to the here and now, and I didn't know what to think. He didn't appear to be too upset about me almost cold cocking his mama, but you never could tell. The way he had tossed me against the wall quick, fast and in a hurry, let me know that there was a line there and I had almost crossed the hell out of it. He could joke all he wanted, but I knew the real deal. One word from his mama and I was out of there. Hell, one wrong move toward his mama, not counting the one I'd already made, and he would show me the door without the slightest problem.

I knew Isaiah loved me, but the boy was insanely crazy about his mama, which was cute, but it was also frightening, too. I hadn't known a woman to wield so much power over men since the days of Helen of Troy. I figured some serious ass kissing was in order if I ever hoped to sit down and smoke a peace pipe with her—with her little stiletto wearing self. I don't know why I was expecting a heavy-set matronly looking woman, but I was. Anne Phillips was about as far from my vision of Isaiah's mama as she could get. A Foxy Brown in fly dreads, snug fitting jeans and stilettos hadn't even occurred to me.

I took the last few steps toward the table where his parents were sitting and stood there looking everywhere but at his mama. Ten silent seconds passed with me wringing my sweaty hands and trying to come up with something sensible to say. She already thought I was crazy, as it was. Isaiah poked me in my back and tipped his head toward his mama, waiting for me to put my money where my mouth was. His daddy had been in the process of raising a glass to his mouth and even he froze, eyeing me warily and waiting to see how I would redeem myself. It felt like every eye in the student lounge was on me and every ear tuned in.

Now what?

I couldn't seem to remember the little speech that I had been rehearsing in my head during the walk over here. Couldn't remember anything other than the shiny switchblade she had snapped open on me. So I cleared my throat and said the first thing that came to my mind.

"My name is Erica and I love your son," I said.

CHAPTER THIRTEEN

ANNE

I was loving the basket of crispy fries soaked with ketchup sitting in front of me and I kept right on eating after Miss Erica's declaration of love for my son. I popped another fry in my mouth and chewed slowly, licked ketchup off of my thumb and forefinger and reached for another one. I swallowed a mouthful of raspberry-peach iced tea and went back to my fries. I hadn't so much as glanced at her dizzy behind since she'd walked up.

Smoke liked to make it seem like I was living in a fantasy world, like I didn't have sense enough to know my twenty-one year old son was sexually active. Like I was sitting at the bottom of the denial bucket, refusing to accept the inevitable. But the fact of the matter was that neither scenario was exactly true. I mean, what mother wanted to know every little detail of her son's sex life? What mother wanted to envision her baby getting his rocks off? I sure as hell didn't, but I wasn't crazy, either. Hell, I had bought my son his first box of condoms and laid down the rules of the road to him myself. At the end of the day, I couldn't do a damn thing about it when he decided he was ready to start having sex, so I had focused my energies on lecturing about safe sex and on threatening his life if he brought me grandbabies before I was ready to have them.

Like any good and diligent mother, I was on my job. I wasn't proud of it, but I had snooped around Isaiah's room every time the opportunity presented itself when he was living under my roof. Besides the fact that I wasn't having any Columbine slash Branch Davidian mess going on in my house, I had read all of the silly little love letters and smoochie cards he had always carelessly left lying around, and I hadn't felt one iota of guilt about doing it. Plus, I washed his funky drawers, so nobody knew like I knew.

He was fifteen when he had sex for the first time, which was a one-time deal, and seventeen when he had sex for the second time, at the beginning of his senior year in high school. Back then, he was dating a little girl named Aisha, who had graduated from high school a couple of years before and was a sophomore in college. I know he hadn't thought he was fooling me with all those late evening study sessions they'd had. I hadn't been particularly fond of Miss Aisha but Isaiah saw something in her that floated his boat, so I kept my mouth shut, made sure he had plenty of condoms and drilled safe sex into his hard head like I was searching for crude oil.

By now, my job was just about done, wasn't it? That's right, I said it. Just about. There were still a few things that I intended to attend to, but, unfortunately, Miss Erica wasn't one of them. At this point, Isaiah was at least capable of choosing his own girlfriends. Not that I wouldn't continue to be on hand in case he ever tried to get stupid with his selections, but he had the basics down well enough. Good hygiene, home training and table manners; common sense and goals; and finally due respect for the one who had made it all possible—me.

I ran down the checklist in no particular order as I chewed on one fry after another. Her hygiene appeared to be in order, as far as I could see. And according to Smoke, who had heard it straight from the horse's mouth, her daddy was a preacher man and her mama was a social worker, so she probably had good home training and table manners; even if they weren't immediately evident. Common sense? The jury was still out on that one. Smoke was just now filling me in on Doolittle's house call a little while back and I was still rolling that information around in my head. I'd have to revisit that "oh so important" area later. I was, however, feeling her in the goals department. She planned on becoming a doctor, which was A-Okay with me. If it ever came to that, she would be an asset rather than a liability to my son.

I was just a little shaky on the whole due respect issue where Miss Erica was concerned, seeing as how she had almost made me cut her amazon behind. But I could see where she was coming from and quiet as it was kept, I could appreciate her spunk. Just not so much when it was directed at me. My son was definitely a keeper, because I hadn't half-stepped on seeing to that and if she was willing to go to the floor for his scrawny butt and he was okay with her going to the floor, then whatever.

I had to keep playing the role though, had to keep letting her think I was helter-skelter come back to life in live and living color. At least for a hot little minute, anyway, because I was still checking her out. I ate my way to the bottom of the basket and reached for more ketchup.

"Anne."

I tried the top and couldn't get it to open. "What?" I said as I passed the bottle to Smoke for him to open. He thought the innocent and clueless expression on my face was funny.

"You need to quit." He swiped ketchup from my bottom lip with his thumb and stuck it in his mouth. "I believe Erica was saying something to you."

"Oh, really?" I looked at her like I hadn't noticed her walking up, with my eyebrows raised expectantly. Damn, I was a good actress. "I'm sorry, did you say something to me?" I dumped ketchup on the remaining few fries and waited.

"Um . . . yes, yes I did." She took a deep, fortifying breath and squared her shoulders. "Isaiah and I have been dating, and when I walked in his room and saw him picking you up and everything, I thought . . ."

"You thought?"

"Well, it's not like you look old enough to be his mother, so I was thinking you were somebody he was messing around on me with."

"Ah." I shifted my attention to Isaiah. "Did you finish packing?" He responded in the affirmative and I shifted back to Miss Erica. "You love my son?"

"Yes, ma'am."

"Then that's one thing we have in common, isn't it? Because you know I would've cut you, right?"

"Isaiah told me about the ten years you spent in prison," Erica pointed over her shoulder at Isaiah and said with a straight face. She really thought I had been to prison, which was absolutely hilarious to me.

I threw my head back and laughed long and hard. When I could talk, I removed my feet from the chair across the table from me and pushed it out toward her. "Sit down, girl."

ERICA

I thought I heard the entire student lounge population release one big relieved breath, but maybe it was just me and Isaiah who were breathing a little easier. I couldn't be sure and I didn't really care. The important thing was that I had apparently made the first round draft cut. I sat my butt in a chair and was glad about it, too.

I was glad for a couple of different reasons, the first one being that I wanted to spend as much time with Isaiah as I could before we both left campus. I was leaving in the morning to do an independent study. After that, I had promised my daddy that I would go with him to Alabama for a two-week teen Bible Camp he was hosting down there. He seemed to think I would be a great role model for the kids and I wasn't about to argue with him, even though his judgment was arguably questionable. After that though, I was going to be on the first flight headed to Indiana and my boo. One of my sorors was from Indianapolis and I had talked her into talking her parents into letting me visit with them for Christmas break.

The other reason I was glad was because, what with all the confusion surrounding Isaiah and his possible expulsion from school, everyone seemed to have forgotten that I was there when the confusion started. I told Isaiah that I wanted to go and speak with Dean Grandberry about what I had seen and heard the night of the fight, but he refused, saying he didn't want me getting mixed up in his problems. But, the way I saw it, I was already mixed up in them by default. They were trying to kick him out of school and revoke his scholarship and I was scared to death for him. If I knew something that might help him, I had to let somebody know.

I sat there and had lunch with Isaiah and his parents,

and observed the dynamics of their relationship. When they asked me questions about my family and where I grew up, I answered as completely as I could, giving them as much information as I thought they wanted, but I couldn't help being relieved when the attention shifted away from me and back onto one of them. Watching them was very telling.

It didn't take me long to figure out that Isaiah and his father were so alike it was uncanny. Aside from the fact that they could've been identical twins, they finished each other's sentences and shared looks that only they could decipher. They had a shorthand type of language that they spoke with each other and that only they understood. I sensed that they were more than father and son—they were best friends.

If Isaiah had gotten his gentle touch and sensitive nature from his mother, which I still hadn't confirmed, he had learned how to be a man from his father. His daddy was hands-on, always touching him in some way, either with his hands or with his eyes, and his manners were atrocious when it came to whispering in mixed company. If he wanted to share a private thought or observation with Isaiah, he did so without apology. Sometimes Isaiah listened intently and nodded his head gravely in response while other times he blushed and they chuckled together the way men do. I guessed they were talking about me then and I wondered what his daddy was saying to him.

Talk soon turned to Isaiah's situation and I had my first glimpse into the mind of Isaiah's mother. Up till now, she had kept the hard as nails façade going strong. Not that she wasn't polite and interesting to talk to, because she was. But for Isaiah, her special baby boy, she was wide open. All pretense of being unfeeling vanished. The woman loved her son so much that she would probably go toe-to-toe with Jesus himself, if she felt she needed to. She let her hands tremble and her eyes water, let her mouth tell her son that she loved him, believed in him and supported him to the fullest, without hesitation. I saw her words wash over Isaiah like a balm and knew that they were what he had been waiting to hear—from her. She was so important to him that she could render him speechless with a look and puff his chest out with a word.

Did he have room in his heart for me? I couldn't answer that right now, but when Isaiah reached out and pulled me and my chair closer to him, then laid a hand on my thigh, I thought that maybe I could venture an educated guess. Damn, I loved that boy. I hadn't finished the thought when my eyes were meeting hers across the table and locking in. The looks women shared were something else.

Isaiah's daddy and his mama were so in love with each other that it was cute. My parents shared a special kind of love too, but this was new to me and slightly embarrassing. Where my daddy would run and find some tissue to give my mama for her tears, Isaiah's daddy took care of his mama's tears with his mouth. My daddy kissed my mama on her forehead in mixed company and folded her hand inside of his for comfort, and I had always thought his shows of affection sweet. I had always wanted that same kind of affection for myself. Now I was thinking that I wouldn't mind a little bit of a different kind of show of affection every now and again, too.

Was there a such thing as making love in public, fully clothed? As I watched Isaiah's daddy run a hand up and down his mama's back and push his hand deep into the midst of her locks to massage her scalp, I decided that there definitely was. Her eyes went from blinking to sort of gliding open and closed. If she were a cat, she'd be purring so loudly right about now that they'd have to ask her to please keep it down. She liked the way he rubbed her neck and shoulders. She loved the way he turned her head when he wanted to and stole a kiss just because he could. She concentrated on the words he whispered in her ear, just before he pressed a soft kiss to that same spot. She couldn't play hard through all of that even if she wanted to.

One thing for sure, though. She had her men wrapped around her pinkie finger. They catered to her, listened to her when she decided she had something to say; and they took her seriously. If so much as a wrinkle appeared on her forehead, they were both like, what? What's wrong?

I brought my water glass to my lips to hide a smile and soaked it all in. Meanwhile, I had come to a decision about who I needed to talk to. Right here was the center of it all. The men, they were large and in charge, but nothing was going down if the woman of the house didn't want it to go down. Or if it did, they knew enough to be slick about it and keep it from her. She knew she was in control, but she was gracious enough to pretend that it really was a man's world. That was the first lesson any woman learned, myself included.

"Do you have pictures?" I perked up when I heard Iris' name. Isaiah had one measly picture of his baby sister and it was from when she was first born. I was anxious to see what she looked like now. Anne pulled out her wallet, unsnapped it and passed it to me. "Oh, she's so cute and juicy. I love juicy babies. So much sweet meat to chew on."

"She's a mess," Anne said as she snapped her wallet closed and dropped it back in her purse. "Eight pounds when she was born and about thirty now. If Smoke would stop stuffing her mouth with all the junk he eats, the poor child might have a fighting chance."

"Smoke?"

"That would be me," Smoke said and did that thing with

his eyes that I had seen Isaiah do so many times before. "Childhood nickname."

"Oh . . . the eyes." Another mystery solved. If my babies didn't inherit those gorgeous eyes I was going to give up on God altogether. Hell, no justice, no peace.

"Lethal, aren't they?" Anne wiped her hands on a napkin and pushed away from the table. "I have to visit the little girl's room. Be right back."

I watched her strut off and grabbed my purse. It was now or never. "I need to go, too."

ANNE

Erica scared the mess out of me, running up behind me the way she did. My thoughts were so consumed with my son and what was happening to him that I didn't hear her following me. I bent over the sink and splashed cold water on my face, stood up and looked in the mirror, and damn near screamed. She moved like a cat, which could be an asset, as well as a problem—especially when I was the one she was sneaking up on. I had to stand still and wait for my heart to stop racing.

She offered me a handful of paper towels and smiled an apology. "I didn't mean to scare you, but I was hoping to get you alone for a minute, so we could talk."

"Please don't tell me you're pregnant, because I don't think I could handle that right now," I said as I patted my face dry. I searched her eyes in the mirror. "You're not, are you?"

"No. I like babies, but I have medical school to get through first." She smiled and touched my arm. "I like you."

"I like your answer." I tossed the paper towels in the direction of the trash can and fished a tube of lip gloss from the depths of my purse. "What did you want to talk to me about?"

"It's really more like a question that I need to ask you." Erica glanced back at the door and then walked up behind me at the vanity. "I don't know if you know, but I was with Isaiah the night he and his teammates got into the fight with that so-called scout and his thugs."

"Did you tell the dean what you saw?"

"Isaiah wouldn't let me," she said. "That's why I was hoping to have a chance to speak with you about it. Ever since that night, I've been feeling like something is off, you know?"

I froze and caught her eyes in the mirror. I stared her down and caught her vibe. Slowly, I recapped the lip gloss and turned to face her. "How so?"

"I don't really know, specifically. I just feel it. Isaiah probably didn't mention it, but my people are from the islands and folks say my nana had the sight." She saw skepticism circle around my head and land on my face, and then she put out a hand. "Don't get me wrong, I don't have it. I need glasses to see twenty feet in front of me. I'm just saying . . . the more I think about it, the funnier I feel . . . and it's probably nothing. But if it is something and I don't say something, I'll never forgive myself."

Just what I needed, a rambler. "Spit it out, Erica."

"Okay, but don't laugh."

"I won't," I lied. If it was funny I was going to be the first one cracking up. "If you think it might help my son, tell me. Let me decide if it's nothing."

"It's just that . . ." She shuffled around and looked back at the door again. "Does something or somebody called Hood mean anything to you? During the fight, when they were pulling everybody apart, I heard one of the guys say something about letting Hood know how the shit had gone down. Excuse me for cursing, but that's what he said."

I heard my purse hit the floor, but I was too shocked to give a damn. Erica bent down to get it for me and I stopped her with a hand on her arm. "You dropped your . . ."

"Forget the purse." I pulled her into a corner away from the door. "Tell me everything you know."

I guess somebody on my family tree had the sight too, because I felt a shiver running down my spine. All along I had felt like something was off too, like this thing with Isaiah was somehow too far-fetched and impossible to believe. But this . . . this I could believe.

Isaiah took up with that fool Hood during his "I hate the world" phase. It was Smoke who finally disabused him of the notion that Hood was somebody that Isaiah needed to be affiliated with. All the preaching and, yes, nagging I had done about Hood the hoodlum had gone in one ear and out the other, but one word from Smoke and Isaiah had finally seen the light. Suddenly, he decided that smoking weed and drinking forty ounces was beneath him, when I had been trying to tell him that all along.

Smoke had a different way of communicating with Isaiah though. He was more of an *I can show you better than I can tell you* type of person and what he had shown Isaiah was that Hood wasn't the one Isaiah needed to fear—Smoke was. Smoke had used his, shall we say, disreputable sources to track Hood's drug dealing behind down. Then he proceeded to beat the boy's behind like he had stolen something.

After Hood had seen to it that my son had ended up in a near coma and Smoke had tried to break a bone in his behind, we thought we'd seen the last of him. But it was never that straight forward and simple, was it?

Hood was like a fly. The more you swatted him away, the more he kept coming back. Four years later, and he was still stalking my son, wanting to exact revenge for a nonexistent wrong that he perceived Isaiah to be guilty of committing against him. And it looked like he wasn't planning on resting until everything Isaiah touched turned to dust.

Oh, but if he thought that either me or Smoke had relaxed our guard even a little bit since then, he had another thing coming. I just had to think about the situation a little more and come up with a way to deal with him, for once and for all. I was getting too old to be worrying the way I was. Plus, I needed to be preserving my energy for when Iris started getting up there, because everybody knew that raising girls was ten times more aggravating than raising boys. Isaiah was a grown man and he needed to get on out of my hair, damn him.

My Aunt Bobbi had always told me that hindsight was the best sight and Lord, was she right. If I had known then what an incredible pain in my ass raising children was going to be, I might've seriously considered joining a convent and praying my way through life instead.

Yeah, right. My kids *were* my life; which brought me back around to my original dilemma—what to do about Hood the hoodlum. If you asked me, the boy's mama had failed to do what she was supposed to do and don't even get me started on his daddy. Folks weren't raising their children anymore. Nowadays, they were just letting them grow up and sadly, more and more Hoods were running the streets than would-be scientists and senators. More black kids were in penitentiaries than in classrooms.

Well, here was one mother whose kids weren't going anywhere near anybody's penitentiary. But Hood? Well now, Hood was going somewhere . . . mark my word on that. That boy's days were numbered. R. Kelly had the right idea, singing about when a woman was fed up.

I didn't exactly know how I was going to fulfill my mission of getting Hood off of my son's back, but one thing I did know was that, with Isaiah's disciplinary hearing coming up in two weeks, a sista didn't have but a minute to spare.

Acting purely on instinct, I reached for Smoke's cell phone two seconds after he'd finally carried his behind to sleep and took it into the kitchen with me. I didn't think he was ever going to get through rubbing and sucking on me. I mean, usually I could match his sex drive, dollar for dollar, but tonight I had other things on my mind. He wanted to flow and flow and flow, until I finally had to take control of the situation, hop on top of him and ride him into the sunset. When his eyes rolled to the back of his head, the countdown was on.

I scrolled through Smoke's contact list, politely deleting Diana's name and numbers while I was at it, and pressed SEND when I stumbled upon the person I was looking for. I looked over my shoulder and adjusted the speaker volume just in case Smoke managed to muster up the energy to come looking for me. I seriously doubted it, but still . . .

The phone rang three times and then: "Man, you better have a good reason for interrupting a brotha in the middle of doing his do. Honeys is hot tonight, you heard me?" I didn't respond, because what the hell could I say to that? "Smoke? Nigga, I know you ain't playing on my phone and shit."

"This is Anne," I finally said.

"Oh . . . well, um, Smoke know you got his phone, Miss Anne?"

"No, but Smoke doesn't think I know about those ridiculous diamond earrings you bought my daughter, either. So how do you say it? It's all good? Yes, that's right. It's all good."

"I told that nigga you wasn't no joke." Dino laughed in my ear. "Since we sneaking around behind my boy's back and everything, what can I do for you, Miss Anne?"

"You can stop calling me Miss Anne, for one thing." I propped the phone between my head and shoulder and grabbed a handful of cookies from the cookie jar. Nervous munching. "I know Smoke called you while we were in Kentucky and I'm guessing he went to meet you somewhere. Am I right?"

"Can a brotha plead the fifth?"

I parked a cookie between my back teeth and thought about some milk. "Won't do any good. I heard him talking to you when he didn't know I was listening and I already know your friend, Hood, is still plotting on my son. That's what I called to talk to you about. So do you think you can put the honeys on hold for a minute?"

"For Smoke's woman, anything. But answer me this though, how is my little shorty? I mean, how is Iris?"

"Iris is fine, Ira." He sucked in a surprised breath and let it out in a series of dry coughs. Now, it was my turn to laugh. "Are you feeling me now? Can we meet somewhere and talk in person?"

"Sure we can. Just tell me when and where, so I can let Smoke know."

"No. I need this to be between you and me, for the time being, anyway. I just need a few questions answered and then you can tell Smoke whatever you want to tell him."

"*Daayuumm*, you doing it like that?" His voice changed directions. "Damn shorty, is your husband married?"

Oh, puhleeze. I rolled my eyes to the ceiling and stuffed another cookie in my mouth. "When?"

"I can do a little something-something first thing next week," Dino said.

"Do a little something-something sooner than that," I said right back. "What time are you free tomorrow? I have a business meeting around ten, but I'm free after that."

"Well, shit, since you bossing a brotha around and everything, you can hook me up with some lunch around one. You down?"

"I'm down, all right. One o'clock. Russ' Steak House?"

"Ma, you ain't said nothing but a word. Peace."

I remembered to delete my call before I hooked Smoke's cell phone back up to its charger and eased it back onto the nightstand where I found it. I could probably get some sleep now.

Probably, I said. Because as soon as I was in bed good, Smoke was curling up around me and snoring in my ear like forty going west. But everything about him wasn't quite down for the night. Damn.

CHAPTER FOURTEEN

ALEC

I should've been waking Anne's sneaky ass up and asking her what she thought she was doing, but how had she said it? It was all good. I thought I knew what she was up to, but I wanted to wait and see how her plan was going to play out. Tomorrow at one. Russ' Steak House, indeed.

If I knew my woman, she was about to set some shit off and I was about to let her. I mean, what else could a brotha do? Especially since she was two steps behind Smoke.

I always did like me some Bonnie and Clyde. But check it, who had told her Dino's real name?

ANNE

I was running late, so if Dino was at all punctual he was already here. I stood in the entrance to the dining room and scanned all of the faces in the place, hoping that I'd recognize him right off, but, alas, I didn't. I had seen a few fuzzy pictures of his gigantic behind, but they were old

and not at all helpful to me right now. Truthfully, I didn't
know who the hell I was supposed to be meeting. If he
stood me up, it would take me at least another hour to figure that out. I guessed this was my punishment for not
talking about this with Smoke first.

I made eye contact with several men who could've
been Dino, but they all wore blank expressions. Where
the hell was this dude?

DINO

I decided to stop playing with Miss Anne and make my
presence known. She had looked me in the eyes three
times, but every time our eyes met, I gave her a blank expression. Really though, I was giving myself time to check
her out a little bit before we broke bread and got down to
business. You could tell a lot about a person by taking the
time to study them before it came down to exchanging
pleasantries. And I was all about studying and shit, being
in the line of work that I was in. I hadn't avoided the pen
all these years by being negligent and you know this.

The way Smoke bragged on that ass, I would've thought
she was ten feet tall or something crazy like that. Hell, she
was a little bitty thing, but she was tight with it. Looking
sweet in a classy business suit and some of them "come
fuck me" heels that all women needed to invest in. Just
my humble opinion, but them badboys was pimping out
Miss Anne's legs and I wasn't mad at her, either.

My curiosity was definitely piqued. I couldn't wait to
hear what Miss Anne had to say to me. Couldn't wait to
get an up close and personal look at the woman who had
put the smack down on my boy and turned him into a
house dog. When she met my eyes again, I lifted my eyebrows and smiled. I cracked up when she rolled her eyes

at me and came strutting across the dining room toward the booth that I had chosen in a back corner.

"You're late," I said as soon as she slid in across from me. "Kept a brotha waiting something like twenty minutes. What's up with that?"

"I was picking out my office and meeting my new staff," she told me as she looked around the dining room nervously. "Sorry."

"You got a new job?"

"I start in two weeks, so I guess so. What about your job? Should I be worried about sitting here with you in plain sight?"

She had cute dimples and pretty white teeth. "You been watching too many movies, ma. You think somebody's going to come running through here shooting at me and you?"

"It could happen," she said as she kept looking around.

I took a sip of water and set the glass down slowly. "While you're looking, you see that dude on the other side of the room, right by the door?" She found him and nodded. "Mine. What about the brotha back here in the corner across the room, hugged up with the honey with the luscious titties?" She stopped looking long enough to shoot me a look. "He ain't all that interested in sucking them badboys right about now, believe me. Check it, you see the white boy sitting at the table in the middle of the room, reading the paper?" Her eyebrows raised. "Mine and one of my most good and faithful men. He'll blow your brains out in the middle of dinner and keep right on eating, trust." I lifted a hand and signaled for the waiter, who was also on my payroll and strapped like a sandal at this very moment. "Sit back and relax, Miss Anne. I got you covered like a blanket."

She ordered a steak salad and iced tea. Me? I was starving and not in the mood to play around. I ordered a medium rare T-bone, a loaded baked potato and fresh steamed veggies. Raspberry cheesecake for dessert and a bottle of house red wine to wash it all down with.

I sent the waiter off in search of more bread and folded my hands under my chin. I put my eyes on Anne's face and left them there. "What kind of job did you get?"

"I'll be working for a non-profit organization called *Hands Are Not For Hitting*. It's a . . ."

"Ah." I cut her off with a smile. "Helping women who been abused and shit, right?"

"Right. You're familiar with the organization?"

"I'm familiar with women who let men beat their asses." I sat back and spread a linen napkin across my lap, reached for a roll as soon as the basket hit the table. I broke it in half and offered a piece to Anne, chuckled when she took it and put it to her lips. "My stepfather used to tag my mama's ass on the regular until I got old enough to start tagging his ass, you feel me?"

"She went to a safe house?"

"Nah, she went to his funeral," I said and left it at that. The waiter was back, wanting me to do some wine sniffing and pallet rinsing. I obliged him and then offered the first glass to Anne.

She shook her head and saluted me with her iced tea. "Where is your mother now?"

"Laying her spoiled ass up in a two-story Victorian down in St. Louis. Her and my aunt don't do shit, but sit around knitting and acting like ladies of the manner all day. But, that's cool. As it should be. A woman takes care of her kids, her kids ought to take care of her, right? She picks up the phone and tells me she needs some shit paper and I'ma have a truck unloading the motherfucking Charmin factory on her front porch before she can hang up the phone good."

Anne stared at me for the longest time with a smile on her face. "You love your mama's dirty drawers, don't you?"

"I'm supposed to, ain't I? She worked all kinds of crazy jobs, feeding my ass and putting clothes on my back. I watched her sew her own panties up and then turn around and buy me brand new Fruit of the Looms. For a long time, we lived in a one-bedroom apartment over in Robinwood and check it, she slept on the couch and gave me the bedroom. Now, she's got seven motherfucking bedrooms to choose from. Can sleep in a different one every night, if she gets a wild hair up her ass. Let a nigga beat her ass? Shit, don't sleep, Anne. I made his ass say her name a hundred times, so he would never forget. Then I made him say mine." I caught the look on her face and looked out the window for a minute. I got myself together and slowed my tongue down. "I see you know what I'm saying."

"How old were you?"

"Fifteen," I said and gave her a disarming smile. "So, you Smoke's lady, huh? Think I remember seeing you around the way a time or two . . . back in the day."

"Back in the day, you probably did. I was out there a little bit." Our food came and gave her something to do with her hands. She drizzled dressing over her salad and passed me the salt and pepper shakers when I reached for them. "I bought a little bit of that shit you and Smoke were selling."

"Life has been good to you, I see. Am I right, sista?"

"Very good, brotha. What about you?"

"Good enough. I'm thinking about retiring in a little bit and getting the fuck out of dodge. What do you think about that?"

"I think a cat only has nine lives. How many have you used up?"

" 'Bout as many as you have, I guess. Tell me what's up with my godson? He done got himself mixed up in some more shit, I hear."

"Little bit," she said around a mouthful of salad.

I chewed steak and waited for her to tell me more. Didn't have to wait long. I listened to her like I hadn't already heard the low-low from Smoke and gave her my full attention. Something about the sound of her voice demanded nothing less. When women who loved their children talked, you just had to listen.

"Hood is involved," she finished. "But you already know that."

"Somebody put a bug in my ear."

"He has to be stopped."

"And he will be." She started to say something else and I waved a hand. "Let me enjoy my lunch first. I like to talk business on a full stomach. What you been doing all day around the house if you ain't been working?"

"Taking care of Iris . . ."

"With her cute ass. That's my heart there. Looks just like her Uncle Dino, don't she?"

Anne laughed and indulged me. "Just like him. But you know she can't wear those earrings until she's like, sixty, right?"

"Shit, that little girl is already rich, 'cause you know I'm looking out. Love me some babies and Smoke's babies is like my babies, trust."

"Do you have children?"

"A couple," I told her. "But they mamas scared to let 'em be around me too much. You know how that is. They ain't got a problem taking my money, though."

"You should be able to see your kids."

"You think I don't? I see my shorties each and every day. They old enough that they don't run off at the mouth about shit, so it's cool. What they mamas don't know won't make me hurt 'em."

"Now you just got done talking about somebody putting their hands on your mother, Dino."

"You're right, but now we talking about my kids. You love your kids, don't you? Won't you hurt a motherfucker about your kids?"

"That's not the same thing as what you're talking about."

"And didn't you just do a bid for beating somebody's ass about your kids?" She damn near choked on her food and had to cough it off. "That's what I thought. You gotta get yours and I gotta get mine. What else you been doing at home all day?"

"Watching television, cooking and cleaning. The usual. You probably think a woman's place is in the kitchen, barefoot and pregnant."

"You probably think I'm stupid enough to answer that question, don't you?" We laughed together. "You been keeping up with the *Young and the Restless*?"

"Here and there."

"What is that damn Victor Newman up to? Last time I had a chance to sit down and check his ass out, he was fucking around with Diane . . . again. That nigga ain't gon' never learn."

She pushed the dregs of her salad away and slid my cheesecake in front of her. "You ain't never lied. I'm trying to figure out what he sees in her. Plus, she's like a revolving door. First, Victor, then Jack, then Paul and now back to Victor."

"Wait a minute, didn't she do John Abbott, too?" I used my fork to slice the cheesecake in half and took a bite from my half.

"Ugh. Don't remind me."

She caught me tripping and got me to talking about

soap operas and shit. A brotha looked around and we had
eaten every damn thing on our plates. And we was still
talking about *Y&R*. I drank a third glass of wine and then
switched back to water.

"You need to tell your woman to start taping the shows
for you," she suggested.

"Which one of them? They'll be fighting over who gets
to do it."

"You ain't right."

"Ain't trying to be." The waiter slid the check onto the
table and tiptoed on to the next table. I snatched it up and
passed it back to him along with a few c-notes, while
Anne was digging around in her purse for her wallet.

She looked up and showed me her credit card. "The
deal was that I was treating."

"That ain't how it goes down between me and Smoke.
His people is my people, always and forever, baby, believe
that." When the table was cleared and I had elbow room, I
leaned forward and braced my elbows on the table. I
stared her down, checking her heart and reading her
mind. "A'ight now, Miss Anne. This is what a brotha needs
you to do. You listening?"

"I hear you."

"Good. Then lean your sexy ass across this table and
get up in my face, real close like. That's right, just like
that. Talk real softly and explain it to me, okay?"

"What am I supposed to be explaining?"

Baby girl was a flirt, for real. She batted them big eyes
at me and licked her lips like a pro. Had me smelling steak
on her breath and wishing my name was Smoke or some
shit. I brought my water glass between us and took a sip.
Tipped the glass in her direction and watched her take a
sip, too.

"I think so."

"A'ight, so tell me then."

"Tell you what?"

"Tell me what you want to do about your boy Hood."

I watched Anne's sweet little ride pull out into traffic and shook my head. Smoke eased up on me on my left and I turned my head in his direction. "Please tell a brotha you through fucking around with dirty Diana."

"Been through," he said. "You see that?"

"In live and living color, boy. What the fuck are you smoking that you can't see it for yourself?"

"I jumped stupid for a minute, you're right. She's got a brotha on lock though. Handling her business."

"Better be making sure you handling yours. I wasn't two seconds off of fading that ass out, you feeling me? It's room in my stable, f'sho."

"You got a bunch of work horses in that motherfucker, chump. My woman ain't nothing like that."

"Shit, it's about time for a stallion, don't you think?"

"You trying to fuck with my head?"

"Nah, but did a nigga learn his lesson?"

"You think you my daddy or something?"

"I'm one of them motherfuckers, son. Go ask your mama, she'll tell you. Shit where you lay your head and you know what a happen. Told you that shit a long time ago. Did you forget?"

"Did you forgot why we're here?"

"Hardly." My car stopped at the curb and my driver got out. I waited until she came around and opened the back door for me, and motioned for Smoke to follow me. "Come sit in my ride with me, son. Let me hip you to some shit real quick."

My baby, Charmaine was on her job. Looking special as hell, just the way I liked for my women to look. Titties popping out of her suit jacket, suit pants hugging that ass right and proper and "come fuck me" heels on them pretty ass feet. She caught Smoke before he could slide past me and get in my ride, ready to frisk him from head to toe. He intercepted her hands and looked at her like she was crazy and then he looked at me like I was crazy. His eyebrows raised and his eyes went from hazel to gray right quick. A storm was brewing.

"Don't mind Char, Smoke. She new and shit." I reached out and brushed a lock of her silky hair away from her face. Smiled like I wanted to sniff her pussy. "This here is my right hand, baby. I cut that motherfucker off and gave it to him for safekeeping, you heard me? You see his ass out somewhere, you make sure motherfuckers give him whatever the fuck he wants and some shit he wasn't even thinking about wanting, a'ight? This like my firstborn." I had her smiling at him like we was about to have a threesome in the back of my ride.

"How long you been fucking this one?" Smoke asked when we was laid back against luxurious leather, chilling.

"Char?" I laughed and put some fire to the end of a blunt. "Shit, she sucks more pussy than I do. Ain't *thanking* about no dick, for real." I offered the blunt to Smoke and cracked up when he raised one eyebrow and stared at me. Char slid into the driver's seat and pushed a button to raise the privacy glass. "You gon' let your woman run the show this time around?"

"I'm going to let her *think* she's running the show. What's the plan?"

"Time to put some heads to bed, son. Your woman got some heart. I like that shit. Your boy Hood is about to cease to be a problem, trust."

"Think you said that shit the last time," Smoke said and waved smoke from in front of his face. "And lookie-lookie here."

"Well, last time I didn't have the pleasure of looking down your woman's shirt, now did I? She's all upset and shit, and you know big daddy can't have that. She you and you me. Hood? He ain't shit. Tell me this though, how the fuck did she know my name is Ira?"

"I think Iris told her," Smoke said sarcastically. I could see that he didn't have a clue."You know women stick together."

"You ain't never lied." I pressed the intercom button. "Char, let's take a little ride right quick."

CHAPTER FIFTEEN

ISAIAH

Big Mama was planning on making every brotha in the family work their asses off today, for real. It was barely nine o'clock in the morning and we were on the prowl, all of us yawning and cursing under our breaths from lack of sleep. We had been over to Big Mama's house since six this morning and at the rate she was going, we weren't going home until six o'clock tomorrow morning. Damn, her little butt was worrisome.

"This is all your fault for being such a pussy," Smoke spat in Don's ear. "Told you to tell her we didn't have time for this shit today, but *nooooo* . . . ."

"And speaking of pussy," my Uncle Don whispered back, "I smell it on your breath, so back up." I laid my head back and hollered.

Smoke popped me on the back of my head and slapped a piece of paper against my chest.

"Boy, go over there and get the screws we need. This is your half of the shopping list." He handed Jeff the other half of the list. "Don't get lost, either."

"What ya'll 'bout to do?"

"We 'bout to sit our old asses down and wait for you two to come back with the supplies we need," my Uncle Jake said as he sat his lazy ass down on a bench by the automatic doors. Smoke and my Uncle Don joined him.

Me and Jeff sucked our teeth and eyed them with malice. "Ya'll ain't right, Da. You told Big Mama you was gon' make sure everything was right before we left the store, so how you gon' make us do all the shopping?"

"I know what I told my mama, boy. That's why I'ma check everything before we leave the store. And you ain't slow, you can read. Go get the stuff and get on back here. I'm trying to be back home before the game comes on tonight."

I threw a cart in front of me and walked off.

I'll be damned if Big Mama didn't have us working around her house like a bunch of runaway slaves. What had started off as simple back and front lawn mowing had quickly turned into my Uncle Jake having to replace a few circuit breakers and then rewire two lamps. Smoke had been assigned to the basement steps, where four of the boards needed replacing and the banister was loose. And my Uncle Don was going to have to figure out why the bathtub was leaking down on the livingroom ceiling quick, fast and in a hurry. She hadn't asked anybody anything; rather just started pointing and barking instructions as soon as me and Jeff had put the lawnmower back in the garage. I was like, what? Didn't nobody feel like running around Home Depot at nine o'clock in the morning, especially since I hadn't crawled into bed until after three A.M. in the first place.

Shit.

Me and Jeff split up and grabbed all of the stuff on our lists in twenty minutes flat. We met back up in the aisle where the plywood was and picked out four planks of white oak for the dude to saw into two-foot slabs. Then we pushed our carts to the front of the store and looked around for those lazy ass old dudes of ours. I came around a corner and stopped so quick Jeff's basket jumped up on my heels. What the hell was this?

That's probably what my eyes were asking Smoke when he turned around and saw me standing there. I looked from him to Diana and back to him. "What's up?"

She slid her arms down from around my old dude's neck and stepped back. "Hey, Isaiah. How you doing?"

"I'm all right, Diana," I said, still looking at Smoke. I could feel my eyes going from hazel to gray in a matter of seconds. "You all right?"

"I'm good. Alec has been telling me about how well you're doing in college."

"Funny, 'cause he hasn't said anything to me about you, Diana. I wonder why?"

"Chill out, Zay," Smoke said and put a hand to my chest. I swiped it away real respectful like and shook my head. "This isn't what it looks like, okay?" He looked past me at Jeff and raised his eyebrows. "Take the baskets on up front and meet your dad by the registers, okay?"

I watched Jeff roll off. "What does it look like?"

"Don't get smart."

Diana was standing there, trying to look innocent, but I was old enough to know when a woman wanted some dick and she wanted some of my old dude's dick like a mug. She wanted them boots knocked badly. And what was she doing in Home Depot, coincidentally at the same time that we were here, anyway? Chance encounter? I didn't think so.

Quiet as it was kept, this was the second time I had run up on this Smoke and Diana saga. I'd heard him arguing with her on his cell phone once before, when he thought he was being discreet. My mama tended to sleep late, but I didn't.

"I'm not getting smart, but tell me this though. How did she know we were coming here, da?"

"Look, I'm not about to get into this with you right now, Zay. Go find Jeff and I'll be with you in a minute, okay?"

"Your father and I were just talking, Isaiah," Diana said. "We do that from time to time."

He sighed like he was tired."Dee, you're not helping."

"Yeah," I nodded my head. "That's what it looked like." I caught Smoke's eyes. "Like you were just talking." My head was shaking as I walked off.

If he hadn't been my daddy, I would've lit his ass up. I didn't appreciate being disrespected. Not even a little bit. It was one thing for him to do his dirt in the dark, but to be hooking up with his little honey on the side right in front of my face and expecting me to be cool with it? Say what? Not that the issue was simply discretion, because it wasn't. I didn't play about my mama and, daddy or no daddy, I wasn't going to stand for him to be taking her through some bullshit that I was aware of. I just knew he didn't think I was going to be all chill about the situation. The expression on both of my uncles' faces as I walked up to them told me they had seen Diana too, and they already knew what was up. I had walked up on the tail end of the situation and caught Diana with her arms around my old dude's neck, but no telling what I missed while I was shopping.

Wasn't this some shit?

I saw Diana prance out of the store and then Smoke was moving up behind me, reaching for his wallet and motioning for the cashier to start ringing stuff up. I told myself to wait until we were out of the store, even until it was just me and him, but I couldn't do it.

"I'm not down with you disrespecting my mama right in front of my face," I said as I dumped the items the cashier had already scanned back in the cart.

Smoke slapped down a fifty-dollar bill on top of the bills Don and Jake had already slapped down. "I told you this isn't what it looks like, Zay. And you can watch how you talk to me, too."

"She's got her hands up around your neck and her titties all up in your chest and the shit isn't what it looked like?"

"That ain't what you saw and you know it. Oh, and you cursing me now?" He had the nerve to be getting loud with me, causing a scene.

"My mama's going to be doing way more than that after I tell her you're up in Home Depot with your piece on the side."

"Anne isn't going to be doing a damn thing, boy, because you ain't telling her shit."

"Oh, I'm not?"

"Nah, you're not. I'm in control of what goes on in my house, not you, okay?" He snatched the change from the cashier and stuffed it in his pocket. Then, he caught the look on my Uncle Jake's face and yanked it back out to stuff in his hand, instead. "Diana is an issue that me and Anne are dealing with right now and you're going to stay out of it. The last thing I need is you running off at the mouth like a little kid."

"The last thing I need is you running around on my mama and thinking I'm stupid while you're at it."

"You finally got some steady pussy in your diet and suddenly you're a relationship expert?"

"Um . . . excuse me," my Uncle Don butted in. He was looking around us with embarrassed eyes. "Can we move this to the truck?" I grabbed a cart and rolled it outside.

We tossed everything in the bed of the truck and hopped up in the cab, none of us looking at each other. Smoke adjusted the rearview mirror and stared at me, trying to catch my eyes, but I wouldn't look at him. "Zay."

Then, "Boy, I know you hear me talking to you. Do I need to pull this truck over?"

"Aw, shit," Jeff groaned under his breath. Beside him, Jake started whistling lightly.

"Yeah, go ahead and pull over, because one way or the other you're going to stop calling me *boy*, like I'm ten years old."

The truck swerved to the side of the road and Smoke went to climb out. My Uncle Don's hand shot out from the passenger seat and grabbed his arm. "What are you doing?"

"What does it look like I'm doing? My son obviously thinks he can kick my ass, so I'ma show him that he can't." He glanced at Don's hand and raised his eyebrows. "Do you mind?"

"So, you're going to fight the boy, because your shit is out of order?"

"My shit is not out of order. Diana . . ."

"Apparently doesn't take rejection very well or else you're not rejecting her the right way." Smoke was glaring at Don. "What, nigga? You know I'm telling the truth. A woman can't do no more than you let her do. If you were telling her the right way, she wouldn't be following you around the city, stalking you. I'm like Zay now. Exactly what the hell *are* you doing?"

I sat back in my seat and smiled, though there wasn't a damn thing funny. "Yeah, Da." I finally met his eyes in the rearview mirror. "Exactly what *are* you doing?"

We stared at each other in the rearview mirror all the way back to Big Mama's house.

Smoke gray on smoke gray and both of us mad as a mutha. I was surprised that he didn't drive us into a tree or something, hard as he was staring at me and I was staring at him.

* * *

Smoke walked in the bathroom while I was standing over the toilet and closed the door behind him. He came so close to a brotha that I thought he thought I needed him to help me keep my dick moving in the right direction. I finished peeing and zipped my jeans up.

"Can I help you with something, Smoke?"

"Oh, it's Smoke now, huh? Acting like a little bitch."

"Whatever." I stepped around him and turned the faucet on, pumped some Lavender Essence hand soap in my palm and looked at him in the mirror. "How long have you been slipping with Diana? Since my mama moved here?"

"I'm not slipping with Diana and your little production in Home Depot was all the way unnecessary. You best not even think about coming at me like that again, Zay—ever in your life, you feel me?"

"Then you best keep your little secret honeys out of my face. What did you think I was going to do? Slap you on your back and ask you how I could be down? That's my mama you're playing with."

"Nothing about what me and your mother have is play time, boy. Diana is having a few problems getting that through her head, that's all."

"Heard you arguing with her on your cell," I said and dried my hands on Big Mama's good towels. For a split second, his face told me that he was worried about exactly what I'd heard, so I let my face tell him that I'd heard enough.

"I'm not running around on Anne, Zay."

"But you were?"

"I'm not answering that, because it's none of your business. All you need to know is that I'm with Anne and not Diana. The situation is under control."

"Ask me why I don't quite believe you, Smoke." I reached for the doorknob and came face-to-face with him. "That's why my mama got arrested, isn't it? Clowning with Diana over you, right?"

"Like I said, Diana is still showing her ass."

"But the situation is under control."

"The situation is under control."

"I think it better be," I said and left the bathroom. He was right on my heels.

"Are you threatening me, boy?"

"There you go with that boy stuff again." I stopped walking and looked at him over my shoulder. "Nah, I ain't threatening you, Da. All I'm saying is that I love my mama, a'ight?"

"I love Anne too, and none of this shit is what it looks like, so let me handle my business, all right?"

I walked off and left him standing there, wondering if I was going to honor his request.

ANNE

I had to face two facts. One, enlisting Dino's assistance with doing something about that hoodlum Hood wasn't only part of what needed to be done to make this situation right. And two, Isaiah would still have to go before a disciplinary panel to decide his academic fate at KSU. The two events were connected, but still so separate that I got a headache just thinking about them. Hood had started enough mess to cause my son some serious problems, which was undoubtedly his intent, and it could be years before Isaiah lived this mess down.

Even if the press never got hold to the story, which thank God they hadn't so far, having his scholarship revoked would be bad enough. No matter how good Isaiah's grades were, that would be on his transcripts from now until doomsday and any way you wanted to spin it, potential employers would see it and want to know what the deal was. Hood could disappear from the face of the earth, but his trifling legacy would live on.

If my Aunt Bobbi were still alive, she'd be running around waving her old torn up Bible in the air, telling me to fall on my knees and pray. Let her tell it, prayer changed things, God was always there to listen to folks who hadn't ever stopped to talk to him before, and He was standing at the ready to dispatch one of his angels to be a wingman. One of those peacemaking angels like Gabriel with the light of the world in his heart.

Well, no sense in me faking the funk. Going to God begging and carrying on, when I knew good and well that me and him had some other, more extensive mess to discuss before I would even think about falling on my knees, was out. I hadn't stepped foot in anybody's church since Aunt Bobbi was alive. I was never one of those folks who called on God only when it was convenient. So you know, strutting up in church for Easter and Christmas services just to see the fashion shows was out.

Don't get me wrong, I had certainly sent up little reminders over the years, just like any other mother had. I knew He or She or Somebody was up there, checking things out and keeping tabs and I wasn't above making my presence known. But I had always been more direct and straight to the point with mine. I had put it down something like this: Lord, keep my son safe or I will lose what little piece of my mind I have left. You know, the piece that the crack didn't fry. Or, Jesus please . . . I'm trying not to go to prison tonight. Help a sista out, would you? And my personal favorite: You want to see me at the pearly gates? Then, take my son away from me and I will make that a reality—after I start a few fires and incite a few riots, of course.

He thought I was a certified lunatic, I knew He did.

That's probably why He had let me go this long without striking me down or plaguing me with a terminal illness to test my faith. He probably knew that I didn't have but a little bit to start with. Rock the boat and I was liable to make a deal with the devil to calm the waters. See, me and Isaiah had a pact that even Isaiah didn't know about. He had saved my life just by choosing my belly to make his home in and I took that seriously. I put the crack pipe down and picked up motherhood. I chose life, with all of its trials and tribulations, and told the world to kiss my black ass. I had my son's back the same way that he had mine, so messing with him was just like messing with me. Messing with him meant that it was all the way on.

Oh my God, was it on.

Nobody could make me fall on my knees like my son could. And Iris, she had the power too, she just didn't know it yet. But we were talking about Isaiah right now. That boy could make me do things that I had sworn up and down I'd never do. Isaiah could make me drop the stack of mail that I had just gotten from the mail carrier, the one who flirted with me each and every day, and fall to my knees beside the bed. That boy had me remembering how to pray and meaning every word, too.

But, I was still a heathen.

"Lord," I prayed, "I don't need any of your poo-butt angels, you hear me? I need you to send me the Archangel Michael—the one who kicks ass and takes names later. You know who I'm talking about, so don't play. My Aunt Bobbi told me all about him, okay? So let's get busy here. How about that?"

I slid an envelope across the mattress toward me and looked at it again. I pulled out the letter it had brought with it and unfolded it. Smoke hadn't seen it yet and neither had Isaiah, but I had read it three times already: Isaiah's hearing summons. As I reached for the phone, I thought of something else my Aunt Bobbi would be telling me if she were here right now. God helps those who help themselves.

Dino was capable of doing something about Hood, but there was someone else who could take the game to a whole new level. Someone else who could help me save my son and I needed all the help I could get. I dialed a number I knew by heart with a trembling hand.

"Hello." I held the phone and listened to him breathe, searching for my voice. "This is Anne."

"I know who this is. How are you, love?"

I broke down crying then. I tried to talk through my tears and did a jacked up job of it all around. I was surprised that he caught anything I said, but he had known me when I had much more to cry about. He'd learned a long time ago how to make sense out of no sense. When I talked and cried at the same time, I made no sense.

I told him I was fine and then I gave him the short version of Isaiah's saga. I finished with, "So . . . how are you?"

"Anne?"

"Yes?"

"Do you need me to come?"

I sucked in a sharp breath and let it out like this: *"Yeeeees."*

"I'll call you when my plane lands," he said and hung up.

I thought about the fifty different ways that Smoke would kill me when I told him what I had just done. Which was why I wasn't planning on telling him—about what I had just done, I mean.

Ulysses Palmer had won my Aunt Bobbi over with his gentle southern accent and the fact that he never stepped foot inside of her house until he had removed his hat, if he was wearing one. She never had to remind him to wipe his feet on the rug by the door and he was the type of brotha who remained standing until every last woman in the vicinity had been seated. A true gentleman, the likes of which every woman should have the opportunity to bounce up and down on at least once in their lives. Big city life had its perks, but there was something to be said about some of that good old sweet southern hospitality, too.

He was a tenured professor by the time I figured out that I wanted to tackle college and that's where we met. I thought I was hiding way back in the corner of his lecture hall, trying to learn on the sly, but he seemed to always find me with those quiet brown eyes of his. He seemed to always be calling on me to answer a question or to respond to one or another of the controversial thoughts he was fond of putting to his philosophy classes.

It took me a while to come to the conclusion that he was attracted to me. I probably still wouldn't have put two and two together if he hadn't sat himself down at my table in the library and put it out there for me. Dumb as I was, I wasn't trying to read more into the looks he sent me and, at first, he was too much of a gentleman to make me. He was a good fifteen years older than I was and I thought his interest in me was purely paternal.

He created wind around me one day and I looked up from a textbook and saw him folding his long body into the chair across from me. I opened my mouth to speak, but he put a finger to his own lips, motioning for me to be quiet.

"Shhh, this is a library and people are trying to study," he leaned across the table and whispered. He reached for my spiral notebook and I lifted my hand so he could slide it across the table toward him. I waited to see what he was scribbling on the blank page he had turned to.

Have you eaten dinner?

I wrote back. *Why?*

Because I'm hungry.

And then me. *So go eat.*

Come with me. Have dinner with me, Anne.

Probably against the rules. I passed him the notebook and chewed on my thumbnail.

Just dinner.

Promise?

He read what I'd written and smiled with his whole face. Then I read what he wrote back and smiled, too. *No.*

For weeks and weeks, we shared meals and talked about philosophy. We watched movies together that sparked some heated debates about integrity and morals and values. I could feel my brain expanding and stretching itself around things that I hadn't ever stopped to consider before. I let him teach me how I was supposed to use my tongue in a kiss and I told him about who and what I used to be. I let him meet my son and my Aunt Bobbi and I told him *why* I used to be who and what I used to be. He never balked, never even blinked twice when I said what I said, so I kept talking.

Ulysses had books all over his house, everywhere, in every room. I ran here, there and everywhere, trying to inhale as many of them as I could. I was hungry for knowledge and he opened his home and his head up to me, and let me have my way with them. I had no idea that I was hungry for his touch until the day he walked up behind me at the bookshelf in his study, swept my locks away from my neck and put his mouth there.

"What are you doing?" I had asked him.

He licked my lips and then opened his mouth on the ball of my shoulder and licked there too. He looked at me long and hard. "You don't know?"

"No." All I knew was Smoke and being with Ulysses was nothing like being with Smoke. It didn't take me long to figure out that what I thought I knew was nothing. And I do mean nothing.

"Can I show you?"

For the second time in my life, I followed a man to a place where there was something waiting for me that made me feel so damn good that I couldn't believe it. I didn't get lost though. I got found.

Seeing him again after all these years was like stepping back in time. We had always kept in touch via the telephone and sometimes e-mail, but there was nothing like setting eyes on him and being able to reach out and touch my first love. Nothing like licking my lips, swallowing and tasting his scent in the air around me. He stood when he saw me coming and stared at me as I pushed Iris' stroller the last few feet to the bench where he was sitting. I was staring too, taking in both the changes and everything about him that was just as I remembered.

"You grew a beard."

"You grew a baby," he said and we laughed. He spread his arms and I was right there, letting him grab me up off of my feet and swing me around until I was dizzy and giggling like a kid. Then, he set me on the bench and shifted his attention. "So, this is Iris?"

"This is Iris." I rolled the stroller closer to me and folded the sunshade back, so Ulysses could have a closer look at my favorite girl. She had fallen asleep during the walk to the park, but the sun in her face had her eyes blinking and her face creasing into a displeased frown. She opened her eyes and looked at me like, what the hell?

He smiled and laid a hand on my bare thigh. Squeezed. "She's gorgeous, Anne. Give her to me."

CHAPTER SIXTEEN

ALEC

I almost caused a five car pileup, slamming on brakes and stopping dead in the middle of the street like I did. Somebody laid on their horn and somebody else cut real quick and sped past me on my left, flipping me the finger as they went. I waited until everybody was calm again and the coast was clear, and then I pulled into a parking space at the curb and sat back in my seat.

What the hell was this?

Anne had lost her damn mind and lost it for real, too. Here she was in the park right around the corner from our house, hugged up with an unknown man and looking like she was hanging on his every word.

What the fuck was this?

The chump's hands were all over my woman, rubbing her back, squeezing her neck and stroking her face every other second. And his mouth was right behind his hands, dropping kisses on Anne's cheeks and two or three times, on her nose. Too damn close to her mouth. She wasn't fighting him off, so I knew she knew him. Me? I hadn't ever seen the chump a day before in my life. From where

I was sitting, shit was way out of order and suspicious looking as hell. He was holding my baby and slobbering all over her, making her laugh and wrap her little arms around his head like she knew who the hell he was. I watched him take my woman's hand and kiss the back of it. Then, I reached for my cell and dialed Anne's cell.

I saw her unclip her phone from her waist and look at the caller ID. Then I cursed under my breath when she put the motherfucker back on her waist and said something that was apparently funny to the chump whose lap she might as well have been sitting in.

What . . . the fuck . . . was this?

For a minute, I thought she was creeping with old horny-ass Coach Leonard from Isaiah's high school days. Back then, that bull-necked white boy had been trying to give a brotha a run for his money where Anne was concerned, but unless he had lost something like a hundred pounds and grown a beard, this wasn't Leonard.

This white boy was tall, thin and long in the face. One of them oxford shirt, sleeves rolled back from his wrists wearing chumps. Big, nerdy watch that did everything but tell the time, jeans so old they were damn near white washed and Reebok walking shoes on his gigantic feet.

He stood up and almost touched the sun with the top of his head, and took my baby with him. Grinning up into her face like they were shooting a television commercial. Kissing her in her mouth like his blood was running through her veins. I gripped the steering wheel and fantasized about the fifty different ways that I was going to murder Anne.

I was lying in wait for her when she came walking in the house later on, carrying the stroller in one arm and Iris' suddenly sleepy butt in the other.

Fuck that. "Where you been?"

She broke stride long enough to give me a look that I

wasn't even trying to see. "I told you where I was going when I left," she said. "I took Iris to the park."

"You've been at the park for the past four hours." I took the stroller from her and put it in the storage closet. Then, I scooped my baby out of her arms and kissed her cheek. Smelling like Escada and shit. I never did like Escada.

"She was having fun," Anne had the nerve to tell me.

Fun, my ass. "Thought I was going to have to come looking for you." I took Iris to her room and laid her down in her crib. Then, I followed Anne into our bedroom and shut the door behind me. "You going somewhere else?"

"I'm supposed to meet my mother in a little bit," she pulled her T-shirt over her head and said. "Did you remember to stop by the ATM?"

"I stopped." I tossed a wad of cash on the dresser and wondered how much time I would get for murder in the very *first* degree. She unsnapped her bra and I unsnapped my belt. I pulled my shirt over my head and dropped it on the floor on top of her shorts. "You about to take a shower?"

"Yes. What are you doing?" Her eyes dropped down to where my dick was saluting her, so hard that it was bobbing in the air. Straight up ready to explode. She knew what time it was. "Smoke . . ."

"What? *Smoke* . . ." I mimicked her as I backed that ass into the bathroom and offered her my tongue. She took it and I tried to choke her with it.

"Did you hear me say I had to meet my mother in a minute or two?"

"Alice can wait, but big daddy can't. Let me talk to you for a minute, Anne."

"I do not have time to tangle with you right now, okay?"

I bent my knees a little bit and stood back up with my dick between her thighs. I gripped her ass and slid her back and forth on my pole—let her wet it up while I tongued the shit out of her. I looked in the mirror behind her and saw her ass perched on the vanity. Cursed under my breath when Zay tapped on the bedroom door.

"Da?"

With his bad timing having ass. "What?" I shouted over my shoulder.

"Um . . . you busy?"

"Little bit. You need something?"

"Go see what he wants, Smoke," Anne put her face in my face and suggested.

Uh, not. She didn't suggest nothing else after I hooked my hands under her knees and spread her legs east and west. I laid my head back on my neck and gritted my teeth going in, exhaled pulling out. Anne's mouth was already open and her head thrown back, so I went after her tongue. I spread her legs north and south, and started stroking long and soft.

"I need to borrow your truck for a minute." Zay again.

"Smoke," Anne whispered and pushed me back and out. She hopped down from the vanity and gave me her back. Bent over that bad boy and looked back at me over her shoulder.

Some clapping was going on, getting louder and louder, when I said. "Take the fucking truck, Zay, and go away. I took a step back, pulled Anne back with me and lost my mind. Mr. Charlie didn't have shit on Smoke. I tried to put something on Anne's mind. Better yet, I tried to take something off of it.

CHAPTER SEVENTEEN

ALICE

This was my story to tell, so I guessed it was about time I told it. I couldn't do no more wrong to my youngest by taking it to the ground with me, could I? Time to face what I had done and tell the truth about why I had done it. Not that that would make it right, mind you. But at least everybody would know where everybody else was coming from. Breanne was always a nosey little thing, always asking questions and trying to figure out why blood was red and the sky was blue. So maybe she would be analytical or whatever the word was about what I was about to tell her. She was a fully-grown woman now, so maybe she could hear what I was about to say, woman-to-woman, and forgive an old woman the stupidity of her youth.

I never loved one of my babies any more than I loved the other one and that's the truth, but that wasn't saying too much, since I never thought about loving myself too much either. I was a single mother and I came up during a time when mothers were about their business and didn't take mess from anybody. I made sure my girls had clean clothes to wear and a clean place to lay their heads. I thought I was doing the best that I could do. I dragged them to church and pinched them to keep them from sleeping too hard during the sermons and I never let them see me running men in and out of my place. I never did play that mess.

Everybody always commented on how well mannered my girls were and I ate the praise up. Yes, I did. Laverne always had way more mouth than Breanne ever did and Breanne was always looking at the floor when you said something to her, but they were some good girls. I never expected a moment's embarrassment out of either of them, which was why I could've slit my wrists when Breanne started using that mess.

I think I knew the exact minute that I lost her. I knew the second she walked into my house as high as a kite and floating around like a little brown bubble that first time that I had created a monster. And I couldn't do anything, could I? Especially since I might as well have been the one who gave her the mess she was using in the first place. Matter of fact, I was the one. She didn't get it from me, but I gave it to her just the same.

Come on now, I needed to go ahead and tell the truth and shame the devil. Put satan back under my feet.

I probably couldn't pay anybody to believe me, but Breanne was always my favorite. I should've been ashamed to say that, but I wasn't, because nobody else could hear my thoughts and that's how it was going to stay. I knew I wasn't the first mother to think it and Laverne didn't ever have to know. I still loved them the same in my heart, but Breanne was my special baby girl, even though she didn't know it.

That's why I was so crazy about Laverne's girl, Tracey, because she reminded me so much of my Bree before I went and did what I did. Bree was always hopping in my lap, wanting mouth kisses and slobbering in the same glass that I was drinking from. That girl was nothing but love, with her little brown behind, and I loved me some Bree. Let her tell it though, she don't remember none of that.

She don't remember me tagging the old biddy's behind that lived down the way from us in Robinwood, about her oldest girl always picking on my baby. She don't remember me coming into her and Laverne's bedroom after they were asleep and grabbing her up out of bed. Pulling her into my arms and trying to squeeze that mess out of her system, so some love could get squeezed in. She don't remember . . .

I remembered though, and what I remembered was plenty.

Breanne wasn't lying when she accused me of talking badly to her. No, she wasn't lying one bit, even if I wished she was. But it hadn't started out like that. I hadn't always been so bitter about my life and so angry with her for being part of it. I used to know how to be happy. I used to know how to love.

Me and my people were originally from Louisiana and my bloodline was quadroon. From the top to the bottom, we were all some high-yellow folks and honey, when I said the men were running behind us something terrible, I wasn't lying. My mama and daddy were cursed with four girls and all of us were something to look at. I was the youngest, one of those "change of life" babies; so by the time I was ready to start courting, all of my sisters were married off to yellow men and having yellow babies of their own.

I married like I was supposed to do and found myself tied down with a yellow man who liked to use his fists a little too often for my taste. I scandalized my good and proper family when I divorced his demonic behind and moved back home with Laverne in my arms and nothing but the clothes on my back. My mama tried to talk me into going back to him, too. She said a woman's place was with her husband, but my mind was made up. My daddy wanted to go after that red bone man and skin him alive but I wouldn't let him go to jail over my mess. So he sat around smoking his pipe and worrying about me, until he had a heart attack and died. He left Laverne and me alone with my mama, but I still wasn't going back to an abusive man. To hell with that.

I took a job working the makeup counter at Finch's Department Store and got me and Laverne a nice little apartment across town from where my mama was holed up in that mausoleum of a house that she refused to sell after my daddy died. You see, my parents had money and I was raised to appreciate the finer things in life. I was raised up in Jack and Jill and my mama was a member of the Links. Yes, she was. So you know my parents had the old time money that these lottery-winning folks didn't know anything about.

Me working an ordinary, common person's job sent my mama into a tizzy. I was rubbing elbows with the descendant's of slaves, of all things, and bringing disgrace on the Misheaux name. Sending Laverne to public school, where the good Lord only knew what she might be exposed to. I couldn't do anything right, the way my mama saw it.

By the way, that's what my maiden was. Misheaux. I was Benoit after I married, but I took my maiden name back before the ink was dry on my divorce decree.

Alice Fuqua Mischeaux used to speak French fluently. She used to hold court with senators and other high ranking public officials and wouldn't bat an eyelash. I used to do and used to know a lot of useless mess and didn't none of it prepare me for the real world, let me tell you.

I'll never forget the day I got on the wrong train going to work and ended up clear across town instead of at work, where I needed to be. I had snagged my stockings climb-

ing the train steps and spent the entire ride crying about
something silly like that. It never occurred to me that I
could buy more stockings when I got to work, because I
was too worried about being seen out in public not all the
way put together. Mischeaux women just didn't do that.
At least they used to didn't do that. I didn't have the slightest idea what they did these days.

That's how I met Silas Phillips, riding the wrong train
and crying like a fool, and Lord what did I go and do that
for? Silas was everything my family despised. A dark
black Negro man with working man's hands and hardly a
pot to piss in, nor a window to throw it out of without
splashing himself in the process. He was a railroad
worker back then, but I didn't care what he was, to tell
you the truth. All I knew was that he offered me his handkerchief and I looked in his big old brown eyes and forgot
my name.

Whew, that man had some strong shoulders, some big,
strong hands and a smile that wouldn't quit! I have to fan
myself right today, just thinking about him. He could touch
me and make me melt, whisper in my ear and make me
swoon, put some of that good loving on me and make me
speak in tongues. Lord, have mercy, I loved me some Silas!

I fell all the way out with my mama and the rest of my
family and fell all the way in love with Silas. I packed my
mess, grabbed my baby and followed him all the way to
Indiana, because he said the job opportunities were better for black men up north. He put a ring on my finger and
gave Laverne his last name to prove to me that I wasn't
the only one who was seeing stars and that was enough
for me.

He was a good provider too. At the time, there wasn't
too much need for railroad workers in Indiana, but he got
to working real quick driving a city bus and making de-

cent money. We bought us a little tract house on Gary's east side and got down to business making us a family together. He loved him some Laverne and she called him daddy all day long, but he wanted a house full of children and I wanted to give him whatever he wanted. Honey, when I say I was in love, I mean, I was in love. Don't ever doubt that, you hear?

I reached out and turned Bree's face toward mine and raised my eyebrows, so she would know that I meant business. "You hear me, girl?" She nodded and I shifted little Iris on my lap and kept talking. We were having lunch at a little overpriced bistro downtown, but neither one of us had touched our food. She was too busy staring at me and I was too busy looking back into the past.

We were just starting to worry that maybe I couldn't have no more babies, just starting to talk about maybe taking in a couple of negro orphans, when I finally got pregnant with Breanne. Heck, Silas loved me down to the soles of my feet and he didn't care if I couldn't push no more babies out of my belly, just as long as I was going to be the mother of his children and we could raise them together. There were plenty of unwanted colored babies out there, he said, and we had plenty of love to share with one or two of them. Shoot, four or five of them, he had the nerve to say, but I told him to hold on now.

Bree came out looking just like her daddy and you would've thought that man had won the lottery, he was so proud. He would take his daughters everywhere with him, Bree on one hip and Laverne on the other, telling everybody about how one of them was sugar and the other one was spice, but they was both twice as nice. He never made no difference between my girls and if I didn't already love the smell of his breath first thing in the morning, I loved him even more then. They didn't make men like my Silas anymore and that's the truth. My God, if I could just roll over and hear him snoring one more time, I'd die a happy woman.

He was a gentleman through and through. Always offering a handkerchief for a crying eye and a hand to a weary soul. Might even say he was too much of a southerner to know when to hold them and when to fold them, because being a gentleman was what ultimately got him killed.

If I could go back in time, I wouldn't let him out of the house, knowing he was going off and away from me forever. I would do that thing I used to do, the thing that made him late for work sometimes, and keep him with me. All I needed was a good five minute headstart on the fool who had walked on the city bus and started shooting for no good reason. Five skinny minutes and somebody else's husband would've been assigned to that bus and my own husband would still be alive. Somebody else's husband would've been the one who stepped in front of somebody else's child and took a bullet to save that child's life.

Breanne was two when her daddy was killed and me, well, I was just plain old dead after that. Dead in my mind and dead in my spirit. I laid my husband to rest over in Minestone Cemetery and not one member of my family came to see him off—not one of them. So you know I was too through.

I used most of the insurance money to put him away like he deserved to be put away and what was left, I used to pack my babies up and take them back home with me. I couldn't be in Indiana without Silas. My mama had sent word for me to come back home, so I did. I hadn't been in her house ten minutes before she was telling me about her housekeeper and about how the woman could take my littlest one to live with her and her family, and pass Bree off as her own. I could be free again, she told me. I wouldn't have to worry about everybody seeing the evidence of what I had done and knowing that I'd had a dark black Negro man between my thighs. My mama had even picked out the next high-yellow man she wanted me to marry.

I took my babies and ran as far away from her as I could get. We fell all the way out, again, and I ended up laying up on Silas's family for a month or so. But they were poor. They were living in a lopsided little shack on the Bayou and doing bad all by themselves. Plus, they weren't too happy about a near white looking woman running around in their midst, trying to fit in and not doing a very good job of it besides. They offered to keep Bree, because of Silas, but me and Laverne? Well, me and Laverne, we had to go.

I did make friends with Silas's youngest sister, Bobbi Marlene though. We got to be real tight, her and me. We used to walk through the mud barefoot together and have crawfish eating contests and everything like that. I could whip up some gumbo so good that it would make you want to slap your mama, on account of her. She rode the train with me back to Indiana and helped me and my girls get settled in the new housing project in Indianapolis, which was far enough away from Gary that I could sleep at night. She stayed with us in that little two-bedroom apartment for a couple of months and then she left me by myself, heading to Mississippi to make a life for herself.

I sure did hate to see her go, because as long as she was with me it felt like I still had a piece of Silas with me. They had the same smile, the same laugh and the same way of pronouncing some of their words. Yes, indeed, I would look at her and see my man all over her face. I would leave my bed and crawl onto the couch with her, curl up under her like a baby and cry myself to sleep many a night.

I never wanted another man, never wanted anything else if I couldn't have Silas and I ain't had another man since. Young folks didn't know anything 'bout no love like that and that was the truth according every book of the Bible ever written.

Iris went to fussing and I took the juice bottle Breanne passed me. I popped it in her mouth, thought about it and then popped it right back out. She looked at me like I was crazy and then she split up with the grins when I stole me some sweet sugar. She was just as cute as she wanted to be and every bit of her granddaddy, too. Trying to be my heart, with her little fat behind. I kissed the bottom of her foot, gave her back her bottle and looked at her mama. I kept talking, because if I didn't say this last part right now I wasn't ever going to say it.

I was just as bitter as a lemon. I started walking around with my face all twisted up and my eyes looking like slits. I didn't want to have to take a job at the Goodwill, pricing used clothes and mess. I didn't want to have to sew up my babies' panties and undershirts so they would last just a little while longer. I didn't want to have to buy food to feed my babies with food stamps and I sure enough didn't want to have to call my mama every other day from the pay phone in the corner store that was down the street. I had a phone in my place, but I didn't want my babies to hear me begging my mama for help and then have them see me crying, because she laughed in my ear and slammed the phone down on me each and every time. Same thing with my sisters. None of them would help me. I was well and truly on my own.

Got to the place where every time I looked at Bree, I saw her daddy and I got mad. Mad, you hear me? Mad, because he was gone and mad, because I was all alone with two kids I couldn't hardly take care of. The last thing I needed, feeling the way I was feeling, was to have my girls constantly pulling on me. Mama, will you buy me this? Mama, can I have this? Mama, how come we don't have this or that, like so and so does? Mama, give me a hug or a kiss. Mama, give me everything you got and then some. Mama, Mama, Mama.

Lawd, Lawd, Lawd. Ya'll know what I'm talking about. Ya'll know what it's like when a woman is so sick and tired and so tired of being sick and tired that she can't think straight. I didn't love myself, so how could I love my kids the way I was supposed to love them?

I must've started hating Breanne because she looked just like her daddy. He wasn't there for me to be mad with, so I was always mad with her in his place. She took all of my anger and resentment and loneliness on her little shoulders and carried them for so long that she finally broke. I needed to make somebody hurt the way I was hurting and she was it, bless her little heart.

When I called her a little black thang, I was really calling for her daddy to come back to me. When I told her how black and ugly she was, I was really pining for her daddy's dark skin and soft touch. When I talked about her ashy skin, I was remembering how I had oiled my man's back for him every night. Soon as I got done talking about her kinky hair, I would go in my bedroom and touch the puff of coarse hair I had taken from her daddy's head before they put him in the ground. She thought I hated her and I didn't even want to think about what Silas must've been looking down on me and thinking to himself. I figured that was probably why I always seemed to be struggling to make one end touch the other, because he was watching me do what I did and making me suffer his disappointment. I know I deserved much worse.

"Oh, how I loved that man," I told her and wiped a tear from my face. I hadn't let myself cry in I didn't know how many years. "Only me and God knows. And now you."

The little one was asleep now, spread out in my arms like a rag doll and snoring with it. Same way her mama used to do. I stole me some more granny sugar from her sweet little lips.

"She's got her granddaddy's forehead," I said and burst out crying.

ANNE

It had been years since my hands had known the softness of her hair, years since I'd sat next to her and stroked all of that hair on her head. When I was a child, I would crawl up in her lap and get a comb tangled in it. Pull out strands at a time in the name of playing beauty shop. I used to want to be a hairdresser when I grew up and then I wanted to be an ice skater and then, somewhere along the way, I just wanted my mother to love me.

Not once in my life had I ever seen her cry or even give the appearance of being weak in any way. Seeing it now, I couldn't figure out what to do with myself and I just wanted her to go back to being a nemesis that I could deal with on my own terms. The more I thought it, the harder she cried.

I became irrationally angry with her. She was sitting here crying to me about a daddy that she had never bothered to share with me. Most of what I knew about Silas Phillips I had learned from my Aunt Bobbi. Any pictures that I had ever seen of him had been sneaked when my mother hadn't been looking, or else spread out on Aunt Bobbi's kitchen table. She was the one who had taken me to Louisiana one summer and sat Isaiah in his great-grandmother's lap before the woman died, not my mother. My mother had given me nothing but grief on top of grief and made me feel guilty for being born.

I stroked her hair and let her cry, but I was still angry. "How dare you do this to me," I said after a while. We were in a crowded restaurant and people were looking in our direction but I couldn't see any of them. "How . . . dare . . . you." I was so angry that I could only whisper and one word at a time, at that.

"Breanne . . ."

"All these years I thought you hated me, mama. All these years." I stood up and took my baby away from her. I dropped Iris willy-nilly in her stroller and strapped her in while she screamed for me to check myself.

"Bree, let me have her back," my mother said, reaching for Iris and pleading with her eyes. "Don't take her from me like this. Don't be like this, you hear?"

"Here." I snatched the money I owed her from my bra and pushed it in her hands. "You can have this, all right? This is what you can have, because this is all I owe you."

"I'm your mama, girl." She stood up too and faced me. "I love you."

"Do you have any idea how long I have waited for you to say that to me?" I didn't wait around for an answer. I spun Iris's stroller around on two wheels and headed for the door as fast I could.

I made it as far as the corner.

"Hey," I whispered as I stooped down in front of my mother and pulled her hands away from her face. I came back to the restaurant and found her still sitting where I had left her, still crying and causing a scene. "Hey . . . look . . . stop all this, okay? Just stop it."

I pressed a fistful of paper napkins in her hands and

rolled my eyes to the ceiling. It didn't sound like she was planning on slowing down anytime soon. If anything, she was gathering steam. Crying like she had years and years worth of stuff to get off of her chest and all the time in the world to do it in.

I set my purse on the floor by my feet and wrapped my mother in my arms. "Breanne," she sobbed and I held her tighter. I rocked her back and forth.

My lips found her ear. "It's okay, mama. It's okay, now. I'm here . . ."

I found Ulysses sitting at a miniature table in a corner of the hotel's bar. "I shouldn't be here," I said as he stood up to meet me. I squeezed his hand and fell into the chair across from him.

"Rough day?"

I told him about my meeting with my mother. "Life was so simple when I was living in Mississippi. All this drama is crazy."

"Are you happy here, Anne?"

"I made my bed."

"But you don't have to lie in it, if you don't want to."

"Listen to you," I smiled. "The ink isn't even dry on your divorce papers, Ulysses. Are you flirting with me?"

"You know I am. It hasn't been that long."

"Long enough. How are your boys?" Out of what he freely described as a hellacious seven year marriage, he had a pair of adorable six year old twin boys. Both of them mirror images of their daddy. I had a picture of them saved to the desktop of my laptop.

"Beautiful," he said as he took a sip of wine. "They loved the signed basketball you sent them. Isaiah is a king in their eyes."

"Isaiah is a king in my eyes."

"You've done a good job with him. I'm always so proud

when I see him on television, hooping his ass off. Can't believe he's the same little boy that I taught to pee in a straight line."

"He talks about you sometimes," I admitted softly.

"I know. We talk. Mostly we send e-mails and things, but every now again he'll call me to check up on an old man, he says."

"I didn't know that."

"Well, now you do. You didn't think you were the only one missing me, did you?" I was speechless. "He's been my other source of information about you over the years."

"Your other source?"

"I have my ways of finding out what I want to know, Anne. Same as you. I hear you finally stopped running from *Hands*."

"You?" I gasped, shocked.

"I knew they were looking for someone and I knew you'd be perfect. I saw what you did with the *Olive Branch*, so I threw your name into the pot. Now the rest, you did that yourself, so don't look at me like that."

"I should've known. I don't know if I should be pissed with you or what."

"Or what. I just want you to be happy, Anne. Now that I think about it, you never did answer me when I asked you if you were, a few minutes ago."

I thought about the question as I looked around the bar.

"I am, I think."

"You don't know?"

"I think I am."

He sat back in his chair and shook his head as he laughed at me. "Still the same old Anne, I see. As cagey and unpredictable as you want to be." He swallowed a mouthful of wine and stared down into his glass. "You love him?"

"You asked me that before," I said. "When I first told you I was moving here to be with him."

"I did."

"What was my answer then?"

"And it's still the same now?"

"Still the same. Feels funny talking about another man with you like this. Face-to-face."

"You find it hard to do?"

"Hard enough."

"You ever think about us? Wonder what could have been?"

I couldn't look him in his eyes and lie to him. "Sometimes." I took a deep breath and squared my shoulders. "Some of the time, Ulysses, yes, I do. I find myself wondering why I left Mississippi in the first place." A group of people across the room suddenly pumped up the volume, screaming and whooping it up. "Somebody's having a party?"

"I think it's somebody's birthday or something. Should we go somewhere a little less noisy? A little more . . . private?"

"We shouldn't," I said and stared him down every bit as hard as he was staring me down.

CHAPTER EIGHTEEN

ALEC

"So who's the tall glass of white milk your woman is creeping around with behind your back?"

I sat up in bed and looked around the bedroom like I was crazy, trying to find the source of the voice whispering in my ear. I realized that I was holding the cordless phone and snapped the hell out of it. "What did you just say to me?"

"I said, who's the tall glass of white milk your woman is creeping around with behind your back?" Diana breathed into the phone. I heard her suck in a breath and knew she was smoking a cigarette. Drinking too, because that was the only time she smoked. "I didn't think little Miss Perfect had it in her."

"You saw Anne out somewhere?"

"I'm looking at her right now. She doesn't know she's being looked at though. If she did, she'd probably be over here trying to bust my other nostril open. Crazy bitch. So who is he?"

"Where are you?"

"The Cumberland Suites," she said and inhaled. "Hold on, wait a minute, she's . . . Oh shit, Alec. Why is your woman getting on an elevator with him? Going up, up, up, baby. Thirteen floors, if my eyes are telling me right, because you know I've had a few drinks and I don't know where I put my glasses. Oh, hell, here they are . . . right on top of my head. Hello?"

I broke every speed limit in the city, hauling ass downtown to the Embassy Suites.

I walked into the bar and saw Diana leaning up against it with a silly looking birthday hat sitting sideways on her head and a drink dangling from her fingers. I ordered a beer and sat on the stool next to her.

"This better not be some more of your bullshit, Dee." It was just now occurring to me that I had walked right into one of her traps. Still though, Anne *was* missing in action.

"White guy?" she said. "Wavy black hair and one of those Richard Gere noses? Tall and slender, smart looking?" She watched my face fall sideways and nodded slowly. "I see you know what I know. This situation would be a little funny if it wasn't so fucked up."

"And exactly how is that?" I took my beer, passed the bartender a Ben Franklin and told him to cover Diana's tab.

"Well, you can't really blame little Miss Perfect, can you, Alec? It's about time sistas started giving back a little bit of what they get. Your girl is a little bit more than what I gave her credit for and she ain't doing no more than what you did, is she?"

I ran my tongue around my teeth and rolled my eyes at Dee. "Fuck you."

"I can make that happen, too."

I caught her hand on my thigh, two inches away from my dick. "Stop."

"Oh, look, the elevator doors are opening. Might be Anne. Oh, damn, not her, is it?" She glanced at her watch and tossed back half of her martini. "Close to an hour she's been up there, Alec. What do you think she's doing?"

I caught her hand in the process of wrapping itself around my dick and removed it smoothly. "Stop."

"Let me whisper something in your ear real quick," Diana whispered. "I have a room here. We could go upstairs and fuck our brains out."

"You must be out of your mind. Come on now." I squirmed around on my stool and eventually crossed my legs to keep her hands away from my dick. "Seriously, Stop." I set my beer on the bar and looked at her. "Stop."

"No more, Alec? Ever?"

"Not as long as I'm with Anne," I told her.

She went to pouting, stomping around like a big kid and making me laugh even though there wasn't a damn thing funny. "Tell me, what's so special about that bitch?"

"Can't even explain it. It just is what it is. You ever been in love?"

"With you, yeah." She signaled the bartender for another drink and stared at me. "You ever been in love?"

"I'm in love with Anne."

The elevator doors opened and she tipped her head in the direction that she wanted me to look. I turned my head and scanned the lobby, hoping to see Anne and didn't. "Good luck with that," Diana said close to my ear. She picked up her drink and walked off.

I sat there waiting for Anne to show her face for three more hours. She finally stepped off of an elevator and strutted across the lobby. It was after two o'clock in the morning. I sat there after she was gone and drank one more beer for the road.

A brotha had to get his house in order for real.

ANNE

You don't want to know, trust me . . . Just take my word for it that I had stepped back in time and cum, excuse me, *come*, full circle.

I pulled my car to the curb around the corner from home, laid my head on the steering wheel and cried like I hadn't cried in years—like I hadn't cried since I'd left Ulysses in Mississippi.

ISAIAH

For some reason, Tracey thought her little chubby butt was always supposed to be sitting in my lap. She was always wanting me to ride her on my knee like Bill Cosby had done all those kids at Rudy's sleepover, on an episode of *The Cosby Show*. But I was just like him when it came time to ride Peter's little fat butt on his knee, because Tracey hadn't missed a meal, either. She was lucky she was sweet and cute.

I could've shit on myself and happily walked around in a sagging diaper all day when the doorbell rang and saved me from breaking a sweat—or from traction—whichever way you wanted to look at it. I had bounced Tracey on my knee for twenty minutes straight by then and I was starting to really feel it.

Today was Tracey's seventh birthday and we were all over to Laverne's house, eating cake that Laverne had baked a couple of minutes too long and trying to look glad about it. My old dude was playing around with his cake and concentrating on the frosting. My mama had taken one bite and started talking about some nonexistent diet that she was on while my Grandma Alice just wasn't eating any, period. She had said something about watching her sugar, but everybody knew she was as healthy as a horse and nowhere near diabetic. Everybody but Tracey, that is, which I guessed was a good thing.

"Hold up, boo," I said to Tracey and set her on her feet. Nobody else was running to the door, so after the doorbell rang twice, I got up to answer it myself. I couldn't get there fast enough though, because my other little cousin, Brittani, beat me to the door and threw it open like somebody was coming to see her. She had been in her room, yakking on the phone all day and now, all of a sudden, she was at the door. She was something like fourteen going on forty, with her little funny looking self. I rolled my eyes and went back to the kitchen. Let her get shot or snatched and see if I gave a flying shit.

"Who was it, Isaiah?" Grandma Alice asked me. I shrugged and eased my cake down the garbage disposal. I winked at her and clipped her plate on the sly, too. She smiled at me like I was Rick James and she was Teena Marie.

"I know one thing," Aunt Laverne whined. "Ya'll better stop throwing this cake away." My old dude let her see him taking a big bite and she smiled. "Thank you, Alec. At least somebody has some manners."

Then Grandma Alice spoke again, sounding confused. "Um . . . does anybody know this man?" We all turned to the doorway and my mama choked on her punch.

I couldn't help the grin that spread across my face. "What the hell? When did you get in town?" I walked across the kitchen and hugged him like he was my long lost daddy or something. Hell, he almost was my daddy for real, the way him and my mama had been going at it before we moved from Mississippi. I hadn't seen him in a minute, but we kept in touch.

"It's good to see you, Isaiah," Ulysses said and hugged

me again. "Been checking you out on my flat screen, boy. Handling your business and everything, but I told you that the last time we talked, didn't I?" His eyes went from one face to another. "Good afternoon, everyone."

"You could've told a brotha you was coming," I said. "We could've had dinner or something. And what's with the wolverine situation going on round about your face?"

He laughed. "Doing a little something-something. You know how I do it."

"Yeah, I know," I laughed, too, and turned to my mama. "Ma, did you know . . . ?" Anybody could see that she knew, so I shut up. I shot a look at my old dude and cleared my throat. "You ain't never met my Aunt Laverne and my Grandma Alice, have you?"

I thought I heard a sound like "tink" as my Aunt Laverne made her way across the kitchen with her hand out. Must've been the sound of her tits and ass perking up, because I could've sworn she suddenly had a little bit more of both. Touching her hair and carrying on.

"I'm Breanne's sister," she gushed and shook for five seconds. "Laverne. It's a pleasure to meet you."

"The pleasure's all mine, Laverne."

She stood there staring at Ulysses like she hadn't ever seen a man before. "Um . . . mama?"

I cracked up when Grandma Alice rolled her eyes, pushed Laverne out of her way and said, "Go find your husband." She slipped her hand inside of Ulysses's hand and caught his eyes. "I'm Breanne's mother. Alice. You know my girls?"

"Only Anne," Ulysses said and glanced at my mama. "She and I go back a ways. She was one of my star pupils."

Was I tripping or was my mama sitting over there blushing?

"I see," Grandma Alice said. "Well, come on in and make yourself at home, Mister . . . ?"

"Palmer. Ulysses Palmer."

No, she didn't, I thought. She didn't see nothing, but I was seeing everything and thinking, what the hell?

Smoke stood up and took his plate over to the sink. Then, he walked up to me and Ulysses and nudged my grandma right up and out of his way. He stuck his hand out and gripped Ulysses's hand, staring him down with gray eyes. I scratched my head.

"Da," I said just in case he was about to start flexing.

He shook his head. "I'm cool. Come here, Anne. Introduce me to your . . . friend."

"Um . . . Ulysses Palmer," my mama squeaked out, "meet Alec Avery. Isaiah's father."

"Pleasure," Ulysses said and opened his hand inside Smoke's. That was his cue to back up a little bit and give the man his hand back. "The resemblance is very strong."

"I think you already know Iris." Smoke let him have his hand back and I think everybody heard my sigh of relief. Everybody except Smoke and Ulysses looked over at Iris, who was making a mess in her high chair. They kept staring at each other.

"We've met."

"Wait now, where did you say you knew Anne from?"

Aw, shit one time.

"From when she lived in Mississippi. She was . . ."

"One of your star pupils. I got that part." Smoke tapped my mama on her butt and snapped her face up to his. "You been holding out on me, baby?"

"Smoke please, okay?"

"So what brings you all the way to Indiana . . . Ulysses? Interesting name, by the way."

Nobody heard a compliment anywhere in what Smoke said, least of all Ulysses, so he didn't bother thanking my old dude. What he did was cock a brow and put a shitty grin on his face.

Aw, shit two times.

"Anne called me."

"Anne called you, huh? And why did she do that? Ulysses."

"Maybe you should ask Anne."

"Nah, I'm asking you. Ulysses."

"Smoke . . ." My mama looked around the kitchen for some help, but there was none to be had, because everybody was standing around staring. Just like I was.

Ulysses apologized to my mama with his eyes. "She thought that maybe I could do something to help Isaiah out of the situation he's in."

"And why would she think that? Ulysses."

"Probably because I can and I did. Smoke."

Aw shit, three times.

They stared at each other. "That's right, you're a college professor or something like that, right?"

"Or something like that."

"So Anne had to track you down, huh?"

"Anne and I are good friends and she's always known where and how to find me. We've always kept in touch. Haven't we, Anne?"

"Oh, now see, don't do that," Smoke said and put up a hand. "Don't talk to my woman like I'm not standing right here."

"Was I doing that? What? Anne isn't allowed to speak for herself?" He looked at my mama like she was crazy. "This is what you chose?" Not, this is *who*, but, this is *what*.

Aw shit, four times. And here we go.

Everybody moved at once. Smoke came forward and my mama moved in front of him, trying to push him back. I stepped in front of Ulysses and walked him back into the living room. Grandma Alice went to collecting all the knives and Aunt Laverne grabbed up the kids, running them down the hallway and out of the way. I thought about telling her to leave Brittani in the way.

Smoke: "Who let that motherfucker up in here, anyway? Nah Zay, bring that ass back here, boy."

My mama: "Smoke, stop it." About to cry.

Me: "I knew I should've stayed at home like I started to. Let's go outside." I felt like I was having to choose between two daddies.

Ulysses: "Tell your mother to come outside and talk to me, Isaiah."

I didn't have to tell her. She must have had telepathy or something, because she came strutting outside a few minutes later, wiping tears from her face and motioning for me to go back inside the house.

"Ma," I said and caught one of those "do what I told you to do" looks. I raised my eyebrows and looked at Ulysses.

"Isaiah," she sighed.

What else could I do but go back inside the house? That's probably where I needed to be, anyway, since that's where Smoke was. Somebody needed to guard the door, because he would roll right over everybody else without the slightest problem.

"Keep in touch?" Ulysses asked me.

"Don't I always?" We gripped each other in a bear hug. "Thanks for coming and doing what you did for me. And I still got to come down there and shoot some hoops with your boys, too. I haven't forgotten."

"Looking forward to it."

I stepped inside the house and ran right into Smoke. I held him back with one hand and pushed the door closed with the other.

"What the fuck is your problem, Zay? You cloaking for that chump now? Hugging all on him like you all of a sudden lost your motherfucking mind."

I put a finger to my lips and cracked the door a little bit. "Shhh, so I can hear."

He looked at me for a second. "Scoot over so I can hear, too." We huddled by the door, eavesdropping.

"Sorry about that," my mama said.

"Me, too. Are you all right?"

She said something, but we couldn't hear whatever it was. "What the hell did she say?"

Smoke asked me. I shook my head and waved for him to shut up. They were talking again.

"I was stopping by to leave word that I was leaving . . . tried your cell and got the voicemail . . . left you a message. I was hoping you were here, though. If not, I was going to try calling you again . . . thought maybe everyone would be gone and we could meet here and be alone again before I left."

"Again?" Smoke whispered to me.

"I would've loved to, but I haven't had time to check my cell," my mama said. "I could've arranged it again with Laverne . . . Laverne's cake is awful . . . my niece's birthday . . . so you finally got to meet my family . . . what time is your flight?"

". . . I'm going to miss you, Anne. The past few days have been like old . . ."

I started coughing under my breath, drowning Ulysses out and giving my old dude an ear full of fake throat clearing. My mama wasn't crazy for real, not that I ever thought she was, but still. The expression on Smoke's face told me that he knew what time it was, too. I felt a little sorry for him and then I thought about running into Diana in Home Depot and smiled at him. He flipped me the bird.

". . . miss you, too . . . can't thank you enough . . ."

"You sure you love him?"

Me and Smoke stood at attention, listening hard as hell and staring at each other.

"Yeah," my mama finally half said, half breathed. "I love him. He gets to acting like this though and I couldn't tell you why."

"I think you could."

"You're probably right." She laughed and then got quiet for a minute. "You have a safe flight, okay? And call me when you get there, so I'll know you made it safely."

"Give me a hug." Silence for longer than a minute. That was one long hug. "One last kiss for old time's sake?"

And off Smoke went. He knocked me sideways and stepped out onto the porch. "Anne." She pulled away from Ulysses and took two steps toward my old dude.

"Anne." She looked back at Ulysses like Lot's wife.

"Anne, baby, come inside the house."

"You call me if you need me, you hear me?" Ulysses pressed.

"Anne." My mama didn't answer Smoke fast enough. "Anne, I swear to God . . ."

I thought I was looking at an episode of *Good Times*. The one where Penny had to choose between her real mama and Willona. Pacing back and forth between the two women, trying to decide whether to go or to stay. Thinking about who she belonged with and getting all mixed up in the head. Back then, I had cheered when she finally grabbed on to Willona. These days, a brotha was too old to be cheering, but I did walk into the corner behind the door and whistle into my fist when Smoke brought my mama back inside the house with him.

I stood in the doorway and waved, watching Ulysses' rental drive off. Then, I closed the door behind me and snagged Brittani around the neck as she ran past me. "Next time the damn doorbell rings, you leave it the hell alone, okay?"

"Hear, hear," my Grandma Alice said from the kitchen doorway and then she cracked up.

One of these days, I was going to make my way around to writing a book about some of the crazy stuff that went on around here, I thought as I fell onto the couch and stretched out. Nobody would believe me any other way. Or . . . Wait a minute. What about a reality television show?

I followed my mama to the bathroom and nudged her across the threshold so I could close the door behind us. We were looking at each other like we were ready to throw some blows.

"What are you doing?" I asked.

She stepped up to the sink and washed her hands. She looked at me in the mirror as she dried them and said, "Nothing."

Now where had I heard that before?

CHAPTER NINETEEN

ALEC

Anne had a brotha twisted in the head. I wanted to pull her card so badly that I could taste it. I wanted to grab her by the ankles, turn her upside down and just shake, until all the cards she was keeping close to her chest fell out. I was trying to keep my cool, but it was damn hard to do. *Damn* hard. I was so fucking mad that I could hear myself breathing.

After that motherfucker left, she didn't even try to come to a brotha with an explanation. She didn't even step to me like she knew she was wrong—because she was definitely wrong—and try to do a little backpedaling. She had brought another man into our mix and I was supposed to just deal with it? Yeah, right.

I was never the type of brotha, hell, the type of man, to put up with shit like this. I ain't never been about sharing a woman, knowing she was boning some other dude and being cool with it. I ain't never looked a brotha in his face while I was fucking his woman behind his back, so I knew I wasn't going to stand for somebody doing the same shit to me. I didn't know who the fuck Anne thought she was playing with, but she needed to ask somebody to give her the answers to the pop quiz, because her boy Smoke was not about to be tested.

And putting me out on front street? Oh, hell no. Why did I sit up in a hotel bar and wait for my woman to finish rolling around with another dude? When did I start doing that? Add insult to injury and Diana was sitting right next to me, all up in my business and thinking the shit was funny. Then, I looked around and here was good old okey-doke standing in my face grinning and looking at my woman like he could eat her up in two quick bites. Bold motherfucker.

Good thing Zay had walked him outside and given me time to get my thoughts together, because I was about to punch him dead in his grill, for real. All those long teeth just begging me to keep a few of them badboys as souvenirs. Ulysses Palmer. What the fuck ever. Country bumpkin bastard ass nigga.

That's right, I said nigga. Up close and personal, I had a chance to check him out and what I first thought was a white boy had turned out to be a damn brotha. One of them light bright, damn near white brothas, but a brotha just the same. Which brought me around to the other issue that I was suddenly pissed the hell off about. All this time, Anne had been giving me the blues about dating red bone women, accusing me and everybody else of being color struck, when she wasn't any better, really. She couldn't have found a decent brown skinned brotha to chill with while she was in Missa—damn—sippi? You know what? I thought about it. You know what? I was through thinking about that chump. I was through tripping off of Anne and the little games she was trying to play, too.

I parked my truck and got out to open Anne's door for her. I grabbed Iris' good sleeping butt and followed Anne inside the house. As usual, she was looking extra sweet in a tailored skirt suit and CFM heels—like she had been going to a business dinner instead of a kid's last minute birthday dinner. One thing I liked about Anne was that she never left the house half-stepping. I stared at her legs as she climbed the stairs that led to the kitchen and shook my head, thinking about the law somebody needed to pass. No one pair of legs had any business being that damn sexy.

"Here, I'll put her down," Anne said and reached for Iris. I took turned her over to her mother.

And had that chump really stood in my face and called Anne his star pupil? Not once, but twice?

Nobody knew like I knew and that was the damn truth. Anne could work it, twerk it, perk it and all of that. I didn't need him running up in my face acting like his dick was the only one that could make her sing like a bird—like he knew my woman better than I did. He might've started the race, but who was the one finishing that motherfucker? Wait, I didn't hear anything. What was that? You said, who? Oh yeah, that's right. Me. I told myself I wasn't going to say anything, that I was going to let it ride and see what I could see. But, alas, lookie-lookie here.

Anne. Easing in bed and sliding across the mattress in my direction. She draped a leg over mine and pushed her face into the side of my neck. I stared up at the ceiling and let her get good and comfortable. Titties pressed against my side, bush straddling my thigh and fingers tangled up in my armpit hair. I was having a man-to-man conversation with my dick, telling it to go back to sleep and stay that way. The last thing on my mind was breaking my back. Maybe breaking a neck or two, but my back? Uh-uh, not so much right now.

She pulled the covers up over her back and then I pushed them right back down to my waist. I wasn't all that cold myself. She was looking for my arm to be where it usually was, which was wrapped around her waist and holding her close, but it wasn't, because I wouldn't let it be. I wasn't feeling huggy-huggy right about now, either. Damned if I wasn't sniffing her, trying to pick up another man's scent.

A blast of cool air hit her back and she shivered. "Smoke, stop hogging the covers and give me some," she murmured, half asleep. I was feeling ignorant, so I kicked the covers back until everybody was buck naked and shivering and the covers were on the floor. "Smoke!" She popped up and gave me a nose full of middle of the night breath.

We stared.

"Were you asleep?" I said.

"You know damn well I was asleep. What is your problem?"

"Ulysses Palmer, that's my motherfucking problem. So you might as well wake your ass up and start talking."

"Start talking about what?" She had the nerve to be looking at me like she was confused.

"Don't make me hurt you, Anne. You called him and you better have a damn good reason why."

ISAIAH

Aw shit, five times.

Nobody had to tell me it was going to be a minute before things settled down enough for me to get some sleep. I rolled over and looked at the alarm clock. Two-fifteen A.M. I was surprised it had taken them this long to toss it up.

I picked up the remote, aimed it at the television and froze, listening. Then, I jumped up real quick and went to get Iris. She was standing up in her crib eyeing the doorway when I walked in her room. She stopped devouring her binky long enough to give me a lovesick grin.

"Damn, you stink."

I changed her diaper and then I tiptoed past my parents' room and flipped on the kitchen light. We warmed up a bottle, found some chips and some powdered donuts to snack on and went back to my room. I set her up in the middle of my bed and passed her a donut when she handed me the bottle that she had no intention of drinking.

We chilled like that for a few, watching late night adult cartoons and sitcom reruns, and then things really got live. Something hit the wall, somebody cursed and then somebody else screamed. My mama, I think. Me and Iris caught each other's eyes, then rolled our eyes to the ceiling at the same time.

"Your parents are crazy," I told her and she laughed. "Plan on being up half the night on the regular and hearing some curse words that you never heard before in your life. Things get out of control around here. And ain't no sense in you running to the phone calling me either, because I can't help you. I'ma be too busy driving my own kids crazy."

I had a chip halfway to my mouth and her little fat fingers came at me, pinching that mug and snatching it right out of my hand. She didn't have a lick of home training. I reached for another one and dodged her hand, holding the chip out of her reach and looking at her like she was crazy. "Hold up, little girl. Who do you think you are?"

Why did she slap the shit out of me, bounce up on my chest, and snatch the chip from me anyway? I mean, really though. Probably because she knew who she was, looking like my mama and carrying on. She knew she was my heart. Iris had me kissing her little pink feet half the night before she finally stole my favorite pillow and took her little butt back to sleep.

Me? I stayed up so I could listen to the showdown go down from beginning to end. My parents were crazy, but they were cool with it. Funny as hell.

CHAPTER TWENTY

ALEC

"**Y**ou started this mess!" Anne skipped around the bed and almost tripped over the covers on the floor. "You and Diana, Smoke. Or did you conveniently forget?"

I was right behind her, backing her up against wall and getting all the way up in her face. "Oh, so every time you fuck up and do something wrong, you're going to throw up Diana's name like you got a weapon against me or something?"

"The Bible says thy weapon is thy . . ."

"Woman, shut your ass up, okay? You ain't been to church since heck was a motherfucking baby. Now all of a sudden you're quoting the damn Bible? Get out of here with that shit. You weren't thinking about God when you were dialing that chump's phone number, were you?"

"I was thinking about Isaiah," she said. "Ulysses sits on the board . . ."

"I don't give a shit if he sits on the motherfucking throne, Anne," I cut her off with a finger pointed in the middle of her forehead. "I don't give a shit if he brought Martin Luther King down from up on the motherfucking mountaintop. You call his ass again and I'ma take you on a tour down through the valley of the shadow of death. You feeling me?" I caught her around her neck when she tried to slide past me. "Where are you going? I'm still talking to you."

Anne wasn't a punk, I had to give her that. Even if I didn't quite appreciate the way she slapped my hand down and pointed a reciprocating finger between my eyes. "Keep your damn hands off of me, Negro. I can't believe you have the unmitigated nerve to be stomping around here beating on your chest when not too long ago you thought you had another woman pregnant with your child. What was I supposed to do with that, Smoke? Was I supposed to welcome your extra child into my home and keep my mouth shut about the way that made me feel?"

"You know damn well Diana was never pregnant, Anne. She . . ." She slapped the shit out of a brotha and shut me right up.

"That is not the point, motherfucker." She was talking through clenched teeth now, mad as a pit bull and growling like one, too. I took a step back and she took a step forward, ready to kick my ass to hell and back. "That . . . is . . . not . . . he . . . point. If you think I'm about to sit around here and let you run me into the ground and have me growing gray hair, worrying about where you are, who you're with and what you're doing, you better get your mind right, boy. I might not be the finest woman in the world, but I'm nowhere near the ugliest one either. Hell, if you can get yours, I can get mine too, can't I? We can be one of those swinging couples, living the lifestyle."

"Fuck that." It took me a few seconds to fully consider what she said. "Matter of fact, *mother*fuck that. You need to make a decision. If you want to be here, then be here. If you don't, then run along to your little nerdy wannabe white boy."

She stared at me for long seconds and then she cracked a sneaky smile. "Are you jealous, Smoke?"

"Don't play with me, Anne, okay?"

"Well, I'll be damned. Big, badass Smoke is jealous. You can't handle the same shit you dish out, can you?"

"Chill out, Anne. Seriously."

"I think I like this." She smiled and nodded her head. "I might have to . . ."

I had her by her neck, up against wall before I could think about what I was doing. I parked my lips so close to hers that we might as well have been tonguing. "I said not to play with me, didn't I? None of this shit is funny. I fucked up and I told you that."

"You couldn't have thought I forgot."

"I thought you knew how to forgive though."

"Would I still be here if I hadn't forgiven you?"

"I don't know. Would you? You could be here just so you can pay me back or something. Is that what you think you're doing?"

"I didn't let myself think about what I was doing."

"But you paid me back?" She knew what I wanted to know.

"I went to see him."

"At his hotel," I supplied readily. "On the thirteenth floor. And?"

"And . . . nothing. We talked."

"For four or five hours, you talked? What did you talk about?"

"Nothing." My eyes called her ten kinds of liars. "Isaiah. We talked about him for a little while."

"What about the two of you? Did you talk about your situation?"

"A little bit." She swallowed my breath and gave me some of hers. "We talked about how things used to be." My hand involuntarily tightened and she squeezed her eyes shut. She opened them back up and brought tears between us. One of them fell on my top lip and I licked it off. I sucked half of one of her cheeks inside my mouth, catching the next one. "We joked around about me moving back to Mississippi."

"What's so funny about that?"

"Nothing, Smoke . . . please, okay? Nothing's funny about that. Do I look like I'm laughing?"

"Are you planning on leaving me, Anne?"

"I thought about it after you did what you did," she admitted softly. "*Because* you did what you did."

"What did I do, Anne?"

"You know what you did."

"Tell me. Break it down for me."

"You hurt me, okay? It felt like you were trying to kill me."

"I'm sorry. You believe me?"

"Smoke . . ."

"I need you to believe that." Silence. I eased my grip and tipped her chin up, made her look at me. "What's up? What are you thinking?"

"That I'm too old to be getting arrested and carrying on. Too old to be going through this kind of mess with you."

"So am I." I went in search of her tongue and brought it out to play. "See what you got me doing? Sucking on your tongue and shit. Got me all fucked up in the head. Thinking about rolling down to Mississippi and putting some heads to bed."

"You don't need to do that."

"Don't I?" I licked her lips until they were shining. "Did you fuck him, Anne?" Seeing her suck her lips inside her mouth and swallow what I had left behind turned me on. I dipped my head and gave her some more to swallow.

"What if I did? Stop licking me, Smoke."

"So what if you did? Did you?" I kept licking.

"I thought about it," she said around my tongue. She took it inside her mouth, played with it for a minute and then served it an eviction notice. "But I didn't fuck him."

I think I lost ten whole pounds with the sigh I released. "You still love him? You want to be with him?"

"No, Smoke. Don't ask me why, but I love your ignorant ass. Now, stop licking me."

Of course, there were other things that I wanted to know, other questions I wanted to ask, but I decided to leave well enough alone. Some things I didn't even want to conjure up images of. Some things just had to be kicked to the left, to the slush pile, and forgotten about. If I didn't know about Mr. Mississippi before, I knew about him now, didn't I? The thing was though, that chump was completely replaceable and he had been completely replaced. That chump might not have known about Anne and Smoke before, but he knew now, didn't he? She said she hadn't fucked him, but if he had sucked my woman's pussy, then let him survive for the next hundred years on the taste of it, because getting his hands on her again was not an option. And if my woman had tasted him . . . I didn't even take it there. Couldn't. Somewhere in the back of my mind, I knew that Anne was being less than honest with me about just how far things had gone between her and Mr. Mississippi. But I couldn't bring myself to press her and force her to tell me something that I really didn't want to know. I had to drop the subject, before it dropped me.

Then I kissed Anne's lips like I was starving. I dropped to my knees and put in some more lip service that she wasn't going to forget anytime soon. By the time I got through with her, she was delirious from having multiple orgasms.

I chose to look at the situation like this: I'd had my one visit to fuck-up-ville and Anne had had hers. As far as I was concerned, we were neck and neck and the ref had called time. All that other crazy shit was done and over with. It was a wrap.

ISAIAH

I was chilling on the back deck, kicked back in a patio chair listening to Erica tell me about vacation Bible Camp, when my mama came outside where I was. Bold as baby shit, she took my cell phone from me, told Erica that I was going to have to call her back and snapped that mug shut. She pulled a chair up next to me and crossed her bare legs like she just knew she was the bomb. She pulled the hem of a Frederick's of Hollywood silk robe down around her knees and swung her foot in time to a tune that only she could hear.

I stared at her matching high heel house slippers and thought about Demi Moore in *Striptease*. Her toenails were fire engine red. "What's up?"

"You," she said and reached for my hand. I sat back in my chair and laced my fingers through my mama's. I swallowed her dainty hand inside of mine and brought it to my mouth for a kiss. "You know Ulysses saved your butt, don't you?"

"Almost cost you yours, though."

"Mind your own business and stay out of mine, please," she said and then had to laugh. "What's important to remember is that he came through for you and your friends in a really big way, Isaiah. Make sure you never forget it, because I know I won't."

"He talked to Grandberry?"

"He talked to somebody and that's all I know. Your housing allowance is being revoked for one semester, for the fighting episode, but other than that, you and your friends should be fine. The school is dropping all of the other allegations and putting you on academic probation for the next semester, so you had better walk the line. I can't keep flying in like Superwoman and saving your butt. I'm getting too old to be whipping asses every other minute. Plus, I need to keep something in reserve for when Iris gets older."

I had a thought and cracked up. "You remember the time you hopped on my Home Economics teacher's head for sending me home with a brown egg?"

She blew out a strong breath and rolled her eyes. "That bitch. How was she going to send all of the other little white kids home with white eggs to take care of and then send you home with a brown egg? Now don't get me wrong, I need to see some brown grandchildren and everything, but she was just out of order with that mess."

"You had to be escorted out of the building," I reminded her.

"Making me perpetuate stereotypes and carrying on. Why do white folks make us do that mess?" We couldn't stop cracking up. "I mean, I'm just saying. Half of the stereotypes about black people that white people run off at the mouth about are the direct result of some black person having to step off in one of their asses. It's the law of supply and demand." I was laughing so hard that she slapped me on my arm. "You know I'm telling the truth, Isaiah. Call me a black bitch and what am I supposed to do if not ram my black foot down your throat? Then, suddenly and out of the clear blue sky, I'm a violent black woman. Nobody forced my hand, did they? And I'm sorry, but I have *never* liked watermelon."

"I love you, mama," I told her when I could talk. "You know I loves me some my mama, don't you?"

"I know you do, boy." She took my hand with hers and settled it in her lap. "That's how come I am who I am, because you love me."

"Aw, here we go." My mama wiped tears from her eyes and sniffled. Damn, I hated when she cried. Couldn't handle that for nothing. "Look, please don't start balling and falling out, okay? Do I need to call Smoke to come out here and get you?"

"Shut up, I can cry if I want to." Next thing I knew she was really getting down. Covering her face with her hands, shoulders shaking and the whole nine.

"Mama . . ."

"You have a girlfriend and everything. . . ." Sob, sob and sniffle. "Next thing I know, you'll be talking about getting married and having babies." The thought of me having babies had her gasping and trying to choke herself. She really was putting on a show. "Who told you, you were old enough to be grown, boy?" More sobs and another sniffle. "Damn, where did the time go?"

"It stood still for you," I said and pushed her locks back from her face. I lifted her chin. "You still the prettiest woman I ever seen."

"Erica's pretty." She shot me a sideways look and sniffed, looking off across the backyard like she didn't know what she was doing.

I burst out laughing. "You need to quit. You know you my boo, forever and always. The love of my life."

"Well, that's all right then. Lock up when you come in?"

"Yep." She stood and leaned down to give me some sugar. "Are you and Smoke going to be all right?"

"You let me worry about me and Smoke. You better call Erica back before it gets too late."

"Mama." She had one foot inside the house and one out. I looked at her over my shoulder and winked. "Thank you."

"You're a man now, Isaiah." She pointed at me and raised her eyebrows, and we passed some love back and forth with our eyes. "Show me what you got, you hear me?"

"I hear you."

I pretended to catch the kiss she blew me and put it in my pocket to keep with me forever.

Daddy, granddaddy, uncle, aunt, sister, brother or cousin, I didn't care. There was nothing like a mama and that was for real. I knew I wouldn't take nothing for mine.

ANNE

The phone rang and I glanced at the caller ID on my way out of the laundry room and into the bedroom. I dumped a load of whites on the bed and started folding with trembling hands. Smoke and Isaiah were around the house somewhere, so I was letting either of them answer the phone. Letting the men of the house handle all the little pesky details while I stayed in the background and kept things running smoothly. I figured clean clothes and squeaky-clean toilets were necessary for everybody's general well-being. People tended to think better when their environment was tidy and they could smell Downy in the clothes on their backs.

I had been doing a lot of thinking since Smoke accused me of not needing him and I had come to the conclusion that that was simply not true. I needed him all right. I just had to learn how to let him see my need and be comfortable with him seeing it. Being vulnerable to a man was scary. I didn't know one woman in the whole wide world who wouldn't agree with me on that. If your mind wasn't right, you'd drive yourself crazy worrying about whether or not that man knew what he had and if he truly appreciated it.

That was why I was getting my mind right. I was busy reading a chapter or two from a book that I had stolen from Laverne's bookshelf. It was called *The Proper Care and Feeding of a Husband,* and the more I read, the more I scratched my head and said, wh*aaaat?* The woman who had written the book was on point, I had to admit that. Smoke caught me reading and teased me about it. He had wanted to make love right in the middle of a particularly interesting passage a time or two and had been politely put off in favor of higher learning. So now there was a book of bedtime stories for the grown and sexy on the nightstand too, and nobody had ever accused me of being a slow learner.

Poor Smoke hadn't figured out what hit him yet. I was all over the place, all over him, opening up a little more each day and spilling everything in me into him. I was feeling loose and liquid, and free to be myself. Sensing him and sensing him sensing me, with nothing and no one between us. This thing Smoke and me were doing was about more than having multiple orgasms and grocery shopping together. It was about me knowing him and him knowing me. It was about me letting him see that underneath all of my mess was a woman with real needs and fears. So that was what I was doing. I was letting him see me.

I thought I knew all about men, since I had potty trained and raised one myself. Thought I knew how they thought and what they needed in order to keep feeling like men. But I had overlooked one very important lesson during my journey to here. Raising a son and loving a fully grown man were two very different events. One was instinctively trial and error while the other was largely voluntary, but still trial and error. Something like nature versus nurture. It was in my nature to love my son, but grown folks' love needed to be nurtured to keep it going long and strong. My Aunt Bobbi used to say: "If you see a good black man, call a spade a spade and then let yourself be some digging dirt for a minute or two. See what can grow."

"Anne, where are you?"

"In the bedroom."

"That was Doolittle on the phone." Smoke walked up behind me and hung his head over my shoulder. "The hearing was cancelled."

"You better go and tell Isaiah the good news, so he can stop worrying." I handed him a stack of Isaiah's drawers. "Drop these off too, since you're going that way."

"That chump needs to find his own woman to wash his drawers."

"I think he's working on it." I went up on my tiptoes and kissed his lips on my way to the bathroom. He walked out of the room. "Oh, and Smoke?"

He stuck his head back in the room, eyebrows raised. "What's up?"

"I need you." I took a bottle of Soft Scrub from the cabinet under the sink and pushed all the other jars and crap around, looking for the cleaning sponge. I did a double take when I looked up and he was still staring at me. "What?"

"You need me . . . what? To help you with something?"

"No." I squirted Soft Scrub all over the vanity top and aimed a stream of it toward the toilet. One thing I couldn't stand was a nasty bathroom. "Just . . . I need you, okay? Never think that I don't again, because I do."

I pretended not to see him leaning in the bedroom doorway, tearing up and looking like he wanted to start something that I was way too sweaty to finish right now, so I closed the bathroom door in his face.

Half an hour later, I brought a feather duster into the living room and started in on the sofa table. Smoke and

Isaiah were all tangled up in one of their famous bear hugs, both of them sniffling and Smoke kissing the side of Isaiah's face every few seconds. I kept on dusting and straightening, and let them have their moment. Sometimes, you just had to let men be men, right?

Speaking of which. "Isaiah, the trash," I said on my way out of the room.

CHAPTER TWENTY-ONE

ALEC

"*Ssssss . . . aahhh*." A brotha woke up from a deep sleep with my toes curling and goosebumps popping up all over my skin. "Ooohh . . . shit, Anne. What are you *doing*?"

Stupid question. I could see what she was doing and I could feel it, too. When her mouth finished priming me for explosion, she straddled me and had my back coming away from the mattress. She braced her hands on my chest, threw her head back and rode me the way she wanted to ride. I gripped her hips and tried to bring some order to the situation, but she wasn't having it.

She filled my mouth with ten inches of tongue and sent orgasmic sounds down my throat, still riding long, strong and hard, even though she had gotten hers something like twice. Then, I gripped her hips and took mine, sucking on one of her titties until I got through flopping around like a fish out of water.

"Damn." I ran a hand down her damp back and dropped a kiss on her ass cheek. "What was that all about?"

Her response was a soft snore. Anne was asleep before her head hit the pillow good.

I waited until Anne had gone into the bathroom to put her face on to drop my robe and get dressed. Frankie Beverly and Maze were in town and I had snagged two front row seats. I figured she'd be in the bathroom for a hot little minute, primping. For some reason, she thought Frankie's old ass was sexy and she was hoping that maybe he would notice her fine ass in the front row, slobbering all over herself, and bring her up on stage with him or something. She had gone in there mumbling about making sure she was looking extra tight. Even though I couldn't see where she needed to tighten up, I had agreed and let out a relieved breath when she was out of sight. I hadn't counted on her forgetting the hair clip she was going to pin her locks up with and coming back out.

Damn.

Her eyes got big and shocked looking. "Smoke . . . what happened to your back?"

No sense in me running around like a chicken with my head cut off, trying to cover myself up, so I slowed my roll and straightened the hem of my wife beater inside my slacks. I reached for my Hugo Boss dress shirt and caught her eyes. "Probably the same thing that happened to your wrist, baby. Hand your man his cuff links, would you?"

"Um . . . okay." She opened my jewelry valet with unsteady hands. She dropped my gold money clip twice before setting it down carefully and scooping up a pair of cuff links. "You want the . . . um . . . the gold ones or the platinum ones?"

"I want you to calm your nerves and go finish your face," I said as I walked over to her and dropped a hand on top of hers. "You love me?"

"Yes." Here we go with the waterworks. "Smoke . . ."

"Then, do what I asked you to do and go finish your face, Anne."

"You knew?"

"Your man had your back."

"Baby . . ." she tried to sink to the floor, but I caught her and brought her back to her feet.

She started wringing her hands like she wanted her nails to hurry up and dry. "What did we do?"

"We did what we had to do."

I said that shit like I believed every word of it, but really, I was thinking the same thing. What the hell *did* we do? It was mainly a rhetorical question, but, still . . . .

ANNE

I could barely stand to think about the incident, but the whole scene kept swimming around in my head anyway . . .

We heard the key sliding into the lock and looked at each other. This was it. My last chance to back out. The expression on Dino's face told me that I still had time to run into the other room and hide.

He squeezed my shoulder and whispered in my ear. "You sure you down for what's about to go down, ma?"

"I'm sure," I said.

After that, everything was one huge blur.

Hood walked into his studio apartment and came up short. His eyes went from Dino's face to mine and his eyebrows shot up. "What the fuck is this?"

"Come on in and close the door, nigga," Dino growled at him. "Told you about all that showboating and shit before. Lock that motherfucker, too." He tipped his head in my direction. "You can stop staring at the lady, 'cause you know you know who the fuck this is. Sit your ass down right quick, so we can holler at you for a minute."

Hood was just beginning to notice that all of the blinds had been closed and that both Dino and I were wearing gloves. His eyes danced around nervously, tongue darted out to lick his lips. "What's up, Dino? Tell your boy, what's up? Why you coming at a nigga like this?"

I took a good look at the boy, because at the end of the day he was somebody's wayward son. I could appreciate that, but his mother wasn't the issue right now. He had fucked with my son and that was the issue I kept my mind focused on. If his mother had done her job, I wouldn't be here. I would be at home with my own son, continuing the job that I had been given—the job I took so seriously that I had been reduced to this.

I pushed thoughts of the Bible, of prison, of everything from my mind and swallowed.

Then, I stepped up to Hood and slapped the shit out of him. I slapped him with everything I had. I slapped him so hard that I sprained my wrist.

"Bitch!" Hood's voice filled the apartment and the expression on his face went from apprehensive to furious. He drew back to knock me into the middle of next week when Dino cut off his wind from behind.

"Wrong move, youngblood."

"You see what you've got me doing?" I asked Hood, staring him in his eyes. "Why couldn't you leave my son alone? Why couldn't you just keep on doing what you do and take heed when my man warned you the first time? You didn't really think I wasn't going to come after you, did you? You . . ."

Dino cut me off. "Fuck that. This little nigga is past the point of motherly guidance, ma.

Do what you came here to do." We looked at each other one last time. "Get yours," he said. "Then I'ma get mine."

And I did. I picked up the head-banger Dino had supplied me with and proceeded to go upside Hood's hard head with it. Before it was all over, Dino had to pull me off of that boy. He was half-unconscious and I was all the way catatonic.

ALEC

"All right now, ma. I want you to listen to big daddy, a'ight?"

I cracked the bathroom door and listened to Dino talk to my woman. I had to pee badly, but until Anne was gone, I wasn't going to breathe too loudly. She didn't know I was in town, let alone inside the same apartment that she was in. I had taken off driving to Chicago fifteen minutes after she looked me in my face and told me that she needed to visit the *Olive Branch* to tie up some loose ends and sign some legal documents, and hopped on a plane.

Dino kept her busy until I had rolled into town and given him the signal that everything was in order. After that, Smoke came out of hibernation.

"Oh my God," I heard Anne say. "Oh my God."

"God ain't here right now, ma. It's just you and me, you feel me? Now walk your sexy ass right out that door and keep the hell on walking. There's a car waiting at the curb to take you straight to the airport. The rest of this is me." Silence. Then, "Go."

"What were you in here doing, nigga? Feeling my woman up?" I said as I walked out into the main room and over to Hood. He was tied to a chair with a rag stuffed in his mouth and another one tied around his face to keep the first one in his mouth. Anne had seriously fucked up his face and it looked like one of his arms was broken.

"Whatever, nigga," Dino laughed. "Whatever I was doing, she was letting me, you can believe that. Smoke!"

Hood caught a brotha tripping and set his foot right up

in the middle of my back. Probably gave me a nice little
Timberland boot print that I'd have to hide from Anne for
who knew how long. Shit.

I flew across the room and landed upside the wall. I
shook it off and charged it to the game. The chump knew
what time it was, so I couldn't blame him for trying to get
one last shot in. Hell, I would've too. "You didn't tie his
motherfucking feet up, genius?"

"Little nigga got heart, don't he?"

"He's got more than that," I said.

I walked back across the room, ready for him this time.
He rose up like the *Matrix* and tried to show me the bottom of his Timberland again, and I tipped my head to the
side like I was really interested in seeing it. Then I caught
his foot and sent him spinning onto his back. Since his
legs were flying all over the place and his feet were kicking at the air, I circled around him and stood over his
head.

"He's got a problem, too." I dropped down to my
haunches and yanked the rags away from Hood's mouth.
"I told you not to sleep, didn't I, youngblood?"

"Fuck you, nigga," Hood told me. "Fuck you and your
motherfucking mama, too."

"That's what I thought."

I think I cracked his fucking skull open. And that was
just the beginning of the end for stupid ass Hood.

In the here and now, in the midst of getting ready to go
see Frankie Beverly, Anne stared at me for a minute or
two longer, looking for a soul that was missing in action.
Then, she skidded back into the bathroom to throw up
every last bite of dinner. I had a beer sweating on a
coaster over on the armoire and I went to get it, watching
her body quiver and shake over the toilet. She had exhausted her animal instinct by breaking me off something
proper the night the deal went down with Hood. Now, the

reality of the situation was settling in. The animal in her was gone and now, she was remembering she was human.

The rest of the story?

I washed it down with a swallow of lukewarm beer. As far as I was concerned, it was over and done with. Time to put Smoke back into hibernation. For a while, anyway, because I just knew that Iris was going be a number one stunner. And you know her daddy had to be up on his game. Keeping my house in order was my number one priority, trust.

I took a deep breath and looped the tie Anne had laid out for me around my neck. It was one of her favorites, but I wasn't really feeling it tonight. I snatched it off and picked out another one that was more suited to my mood, a smoke gray silk one that matched my eyes. I stood in front of the mirror and hooked up my tie as I stared myself in the eyes. I watched the smoke clear and grinned. Hood was a distant memory.

Ten minutes passed and Anne was still in the bathroom auditioning for an Emmy. I stuck my head in there to see what the hold up was and knocked on the doorjamb. She was standing at the vanity pressing a damp towel to her face. I glanced at my watch. "Anne, step it up a little, okay?"

Unlike Anne, I wasn't tripping off of shit. It was like I had said, sometimes you had to stand over a motherfucker and watch him take his last breath, to make sure that he was really out of your hair. This had simply been one of those times.

CHAPTER TWENTY-TWO

ISAIAH

"Change it to channel twenty-two, Isaiah," Erica said in my ear. "Hurry up."

I took the phone away from my ear and looked at it like it was crazy. What part of *right now I'm looking at Serena Williams's ass in some tight tennis shorts* was she not understanding?

Damn. I knew I shouldn't have answered my cell.

But she was my boo, so I set TiVo to save Serena's ass for me and aimed the remote at the flat screen, even though I was irritated as hell. I was nowhere near interested in seeing her daddy's big old pie face all up in the television screen, talking about the vacation Bible Camp he was running for bad kids. She was excited about it though, so I pretended that I gave a damn and turned up the volume. Hell, I didn't need volume to watch Serena, just eyes.

"Did you turn it yet?"

"Yes, Erica," I droned. I tossed the remote to the side and lay back on the bed. Channel twenty-two was one of those all news cable channels. No commercial breaks, no nothing, just straight news. I could hear myself snoring already. "What are they showing down there in Mississippi, because this dude doesn't look anything like your daddy up here in Indiana?"

"I think he's coming up next," she said. "Stop being so impatient."

"I'm impatient for you to get to Indiana, that's what I'm impatient for," I told her and felt my dick tighten at the mere thought. "Your man is suffering here. Been touching myself under the covers late at night."

"Oh, for real? I thought it was just me down here running to the bathroom every five minutes. Only three more days left and then it's on, I'm telling you that now, so you better be ready. I told Donna I was arriving five days from now." Her voice lowered. "But I reserved us a room at the Ambassador for two nights and I'll really be there in three days. I thought we could use some . . . alone time."

"I told you that I like the way you think, didn't I?"

"You like the way I do a lot of things."

"You're right." I chuckled under my breath, imaging one thing in particular. "The first thing I want you to do when I walk in the room is take booga-bear out of his cage and . . ."

Something caught my attention on the television screen and I stopped talking so I could hear what the reporter was saying. A blast from the past hit me as I stared at a picture of Hood surrounded by a group of his homies on the screen. They were all throwing up gang signs and cheesing for the camera like they didn't have a care in the world. I recognized the picture, because somebody had taken it with Hood's camera at one of the crazy parties that I had sneaked out of the house to go to back in the day. If I hadn't been hugged up in a corner with a girl I barely knew at the time, I would've been cheesing for the camera, too.

"Isaiah? Are you still there?" Erica. I had forgotten I was on the phone just that quick.

"Hold on, baby." I put the phone down and then I picked it right back up. "Are you watching this?"

"I am now."

"Hold on," I said again and dropped the phone in my lap.

"We went to school together," a tired looking young woman was saying. She looked into the camera and experienced a moment of stage fright. Then she smiled and I groaned. Why did they always find the craziest, worst looking black folks to interview on national television? Just like most of the others they found, this one was missing her two front teeth and her hair was sticking out from her head like she had stuck her finger in a light socket. Behind her, a crowd of similarly silly looking black folks crowded around, some waving to the camera and mouthing hellos. The phone was down in my lap, but I could still hear Erica loud and clear, cracking up. She was a straight fool.

"He didn't never finish or nothing," snaglepuss kept talking, " 'cause I guess he thought selling drugs was better than learning or something. Anyway, I hate to hear about what happened to him, but if you live by the sword . . ." She turned to the dude standing next to her. "That's what they say, right? I mean, I got it right, didn't I? 'Live by the sword, die by the sword.' Like on that Tupac song." He looked just as clueless as she did and she shrugged, turning back to the camera. "Anyway . . . I heard that somebody had took him out from one of my girls. Keisha girl, where you at?"

The camera swiveled back around to the reporter, but the woman didn't yet realize that she was back on camera. She was staring at the girl who had just finished talking with her mouth hanging open and a horrified look on her face.

"Ho, what the hell you looking at?" the girl asked the reporter.

I closed my eyes and shook my head, listening to Erica sounding like she was about ready to piss on herself she was laughing so hard.

"What? Oh, oh . . . um." The reporter snapped to attention and ran a hand over her head, checking to make sure that her hair was still pinned in place. Then, she ran her tongue around her teeth, checking to make sure that they were all there. After all that, she smiled into the camera. "All right now, back to the story. To recap, the victim has been identified as twenty-two year old Justin Patterson, better known as "Hood" to those who knew him. At this point, police are relatively certain that the young man's death was drug related, possibly a drug deal gone bad. They have no leads or suspects at this time."

"Mary, have police been able learn anything helpful from interviewing potential witnesses?" an off-camera reporter asked.

"No, Stanley, they haven't. In fact, I spoke to the chief of police a little while ago and he told me that, at this point, there seem to be no witnesses and no one has come forward with any information. Sadly, this appears to be another example of the random violence that is so prevalent today. Back to you, Stanley."

"Damn," I said into the phone. "Just . . . damn."

"Is something wrong, baby? Did you know that guy?"

"Used to know him. I used to think he was my friend. You know what, baby? I, um, I need to call you back, okay?"

"Wait a minute, Isaiah . . ."

"I'll call you right back," I said and hung up.

Damn. Hood was dead? What the hell? I didn't know why, but I was suddenly remembering all the times that I had hung out with him, smoking blunts and getting blown out of my mind. It took me a while to figure out that he wasn't really my friend, but before all that, I had spent enough time with him to be stunned by the fact that he was dead. I wasn't the type of person to wish ill will on another person. Even though Hood had tried to put a hurting on a brotha, probably was trying to kill me, I still hated to hear that he had been snuffed out.

I already appreciated the hell out of my parents, but now even more so than ever. It seemed like every other night the news reports were filled with stories about young brothas dropping like flies. I was thankful that my mama wasn't the type to stand around and let me drift down the same path as a lot of those brothas. She had kept her foot on my neck the whole way through and when that wasn't enough, she went and found Smoke. And if my mama was no joke, Smoke was damn sure nothing to laugh at.

Here I was, a hot little minute away from graduating from college with a degree in Architectural Engineering and Hood was dead. All the same opportunities that were available to me had been available to him, but while I was probably going to enter the NBA draft, they were going to be digging a hole in the ground for him. When playing ball was no longer an option for me, I was planning on chilling with my wife and kids, planning on designing some bomb ass houses and business parks, resorts and institutions of higher learning. I was planning on living like a king and Hood's mama was picking out a casket for him.

Damn.

Some things just weren't worth it. Doing dirt to folks and thinking you were invincible was a fool's fairy tale and it looked like somebody had read that fairy tale to Hood, just before they put him to sleep.

I thought about going to his funeral and then I decided against it. I hated that the brotha was dead, but I hadn't forgotten what he had tried to do to me back in the day. I still remembered laying up in a hospital bed, hearing my people talking to me and not being able to open my eyes or my mouth, so they'd know I was going to pull through. My mama had cried and cried, until she couldn't cry no more, and you know I couldn't forgive a nigga for making my mama cry like that.

Plus, I wouldn't be able to sit through a funeral and keep the thoughts running through my head from showing on my face. One thought, anyway. Check it. Was I a bad person for feeling like I had just lost ten pounds of dead weight? No pun intended. A brotha was feeling like any and everything in the world was suddenly possible. Like the past was finally dead and gone and there was nothing but the future to look forward to. I came up short and crossed myself. Again, no pun intended and may Hood rest in peace.

ALEC

Now see, this was what I was talking about. Family wall-to-wall, everybody relaxed and having a good time, good food and much laughter. I looked to my left and then to my right, and sat back in my patio chair, nodding my head to some Ice Cube that Zay had just put on. He pulled Erica out of her chair and tangled her up in some low-key bumping and grinding that had Big Mama and Don's wife, Liz, raising their eyebrows and sending out catcalls.

I lifted my beer and saluted my son. He was a chip off

of the old block, for real. "There you go, Zay. Do what you do."

Anne came up behind me and popped me on the back of my head. "Don't encourage him, Smoke. I'm trying not to be embarrassed as it is." She situated her booty right where it belonged, which was in my lap, and snuggled in. She sighed when I wrapped my arms around her and squeezed.

"Tired?"

"Little bit. This feels good."

"What?"

"You holding me," she said and turned her head for a kiss. "Can't seem to get enough of your hands on me." I slid my hands up her arms and massaged her shoulders. Then, I made my way down her back. I hit one of her spots and she giggled. "Smoke, this is not the time."

Across the backyard, I locked eyes with Anne's mother and we smiled at each other. She was reared all the way back in a lounge chair with Iris spread out on her chest, sleeping. Every now and again, she brought a plastic cup of something a little stronger than fruit punch to her lips and sipped delicately. Since she and Anne had started spending more time together, she was spoiling my baby girl to death. Now, she was sitting over there getting her buzz on, too. She thought she was slick.

Laverne was a different story though. She didn't care who knew that she was feeling good. I hadn't met her husband but a few times counting tonight, but he seemed like a cool enough brotha. Cool enough to stop at three beers and switch to Pepsi, because his woman was having a good time and somebody had to drive home. Cool enough to let her sip her ass off, because anybody with two eyes could see that he wasn't going to get too much sleep tonight. Laverne was all over him, damn near about to give him a lap dance. Alice caught my eyes and rolled hers to the sky. She shook her head and laughed behind her cup.

I was feeling a little sorry for her and wishing that old Silas was still alive to light her fire when Jeff came stumbling through the patio doors and into the backyard. "All right now, the party can start now that I'm here," he called out and threw his hands up in the air, waving them to the beat.

Wherever he had been before busting up in my spot, he'd already had a drink or two. I looked over Anne's head at Don and raised my eyebrows. Did a double take and put one of my eyes on Liz's face when his date came stumbling out behind him, wearing a tight mini-skirt and a halter top that wasn't hiding much. Anne and Liz looked at each other and sucked their teeth, and I cracked up. At least, she wasn't Sister Hempstead. Now, that would've really been funny.

The music changed up and went old school on me. Sheila E started beating her drums and singing about some chick wanting to lead a glamorous life, and what did she do that for? Laverne lost her mind. She made her way to the makeshift dance floor, which was really a flagstone patio, and dragged her daughter along with her. I did some more looking and shook my head in time with her husband's wagging head. Shit was getting out of control and funnier by the minute.

Laverne and Tracey got halfway through the dance routine that they were jacking up and then Laverne was screaming for Anne to come and join them.

"Bree, come on out here and do it with me. Tracey keeps messing up the one-two-step and kick."

"Oh, hell no," Anne mumbled under her breath. "I don't *hardly* think so. Is she out of her mind?"

"Go on, baby," I whispered in her ear. "Dance for your man. Show me how you get down."

"Smoke, please."

"Bree, get your ass out here! Wait a minute, wait a minute, start that song over!"

All eyes turned to Anne. She put a hand over her face and shook her head. "Oh my God. She cannot be serious." Laverne screamed her name again and she cringed. "Vern, shut up! I don't even remember that dance, so leave me alone." She sat back against my chest and parked her lips next to my ear. "With her drunk ass."

Laverne rolled her eyes at Anne and hopped to it when the song started over. She was talking loud and snapping her fingers even louder. "Come on, Tracey. Do it like I showed you now. And a one and a two, ready, set and go."

Anne snatched my beer from my hand and took a sip. "Vern never could dance worth shit," she said. "I was the one putting together all the dance routines." She took another sip and passed it back to me. "That ain't even the way the step goes. She's just . . ." She hopped up and took off like a rocket. "Vern, sit your ass down, okay? You're teaching her the wrong dance routine, anyway. That one goes to Lisa Lisa and Cult Jam."

I tried to swallow and laugh at the same time and choked myself. I had to cough it off.

"Start the song over!" Anne snapped her fingers as she shook her booty.

"Aw, sookie sookie, now. Hold up, let me get the camera!" Zay flew inside the house so fast that I heard the wind he made.

I sat back and watched Anne clown with her sister, knowing she was having fun, but trying to act like she wasn't. She and Laverne practiced their dance routine from yesteryear for an hour nonstop, and then they broke out with a routine to an ancient Kid 'N Play cut. Every time one of them missed a step, they fell out laughing, falling against each other and holding their sides.

"What's this move, Bree?"

"That's the Cabbage Patch!" Anne shouted like a kid and hopped around barefoot. "Do the Wop, Vern! Do the Wop!" Laverne did the dance and Anne laughed so hard that her knees buckled and she had to sit down in the grass to catch her breath. I liked seeing her like that. I liked seeing her face light up with laughter, her eyes sparkling and every last one of her teeth on display. The longer I stared at her, the more I wanted to kick everybody out of my backyard and throw her sexy ass up on a patio table. If she was happy, I was happy and when I was happy, I eventually wanted to make love. That would have to wait though because Big Mama was taking over and, as usual, blowing all highs.

"All right now, if I hear that song one more time somebody might have to die," Big Mama shouted out into the backyard from the kitchen. She and Alice had gone inside a while ago to get the food ready for serving. "Me and Alice are in here working our butts off, so somebody better come and eat! And whose little girl is this in here sticking her fingers in my banana pudding?"

"Brittani," Isaiah said on his way past me. Erica followed behind him, looking like somebody had set her down in the middle of the Land of Oz and clicking her heels wasn't working.

Two hours later, most of us were back outside and lying around like a bunch of slobs; full as ticks and half ass miserable with it. Since it was getting dark, Anne had switched on the patio lights and ordered Isaiah to slow the music down. Everyone under eighteen was inside the house doing who knew what, while all the old heads had gathered around the table where Zay, Jeff, Don and Jake had a lively game of Dominos going. Somebody was arguing with somebody else over points when my cut came on. Teena Marie singing "Ooh Wee." I found my woman and coaxed her into the circle of my arms, slipped my tongue in her mouth and started a slow drag the way grown folks did it.

"Uh-oh," Jeff said. "Do your do, Uncle Al."

"You don't know nothing about this, youngblood," I said as me and Anne fell into a smooth groove together and got closer than close. I filled my hands with her ass and pressed my face into the curve of her neck. Then, I really went old school and tapped her ass to the beat.

". . . *I knew that fairy tales do really come true,*" I sang in Anne's ear and heard her giggle. "I ain't lying I was sweating . . ." I raised my head and licked her lips.

"Smoke, this is not cute."

"This is me and you, baby. Loving into the next millennium and beyond. You feeling me?"

"*Talk to me . . .*" she sang to me. "Baby what's cracking?"

"Aw, now see that's what I'm talking about. Sing to me, baby." I kissed a soft spot on her neck and closed my eyes against the groove. I had to say it and I didn't care who heard me. "I love you, baby."

"Love you, too," my woman said on a soft sigh. Then, she threw her head back and really started singing to me. She hit a high note like Lady Tee herself. "Don't let him corrupt you now," she crooned.

CHAPTER TWENTY-THREE

IRIS

My mommy couldn't seem to figure out what was wrong with me. I didn't know how to tell her that I was so upset with her—screaming at the top of my lungs in her ear was the least I could do. I was too through with her. Far as I was concerned, she had sold me out. All that talk about me being her number one boo-boo, her favorite girl in the whole wide world. Yeah, right.

She was walking me round and round my room, patting me on my back and singing my favorite song, but I wasn't having it. I didn't want to hear nothing she had to say. I pretended like I was patting her chest and grabbed her nipple through her tank top, squeezed it as hard as I could and stuck my bottle in my mouth to keep from laughing out loud when she gasped. She tapped me on the back of my hand and it was on. I went back to screaming, even though she had barely touched me.

"Is she running a fever or something?"

My daddy walked into my room and I really started cutting up, swinging my arms and kicking my legs. I grabbed his finger when he touched my forehead to see if I had a fever. I was hot all right, but my heat had nothing to do with being sick.

"I don't know what's wrong with her," my mama told him. I was working her last nerve, which meant that my plan was working. "I wish she would go to sleep, I know that much. It's two o'clock in the morning and every other baby in the world is asleep . . . but your child," she looked at my daddy like it was all his fault, when she was really the one, "*your child* refuses to cooperate. Why is that not surprising?"

"Let me see her," my daddy said as he reached for me. I fell into his arms and sighed from the relief of it. Finally. Then, he started deviating from the plan.

Don't kiss her, I screamed! Stop kissing my mommy! We're not being friends with her right now, so stop it! He wouldn't listen. He kept right on kissing her, so I kept right on screaming.

"Hey, hey, little girl. What is all this noise about?"

He lifted me high in the air and chewed on my belly, and I cracked all the way up. I wrapped myself around his head and giggled, so he'd know that I wanted him to keep on chewing. He went from chewing on my belly to chewing on my neck and I went from screaming with anger to screaming with laughter. My daddy was crazy like that, always making me laugh. I tried to get his attention by biting him on his cheek. Wait, daddy, listen, I have to tell you something. Stop kissing on me and listen!

"I bet you better stop biting me."

I went limp with indignation. This was not going like I had planned. My daddy was thicker in the head than I thought he was.

"She's quiet with you, Smoke, so I'm going to bed." My mama patted me on my bottom and went staggering out of my room. 'Cause she needed her rest, no doubt. Whatever.

I caught a movement out of the corner of my eye and

whipped my head around to see if my eyes were playing tricks on me. I had my suspicions but . . .

Isaiah! Oh, thank God. Someone who understood me.

"Hey, boo-boo. Let me see her, Da."

I was so happy to see my big brother that I broke down crying like a baby. Not screaming, mind you, but really crying. Sobs were coming from deep down inside, because I was absolutely devastated. Everything was falling apart right before my eyes and all of a sudden, everybody was acting like they couldn't understand nothing I was saying. Even Isaiah was playing stupid, bouncing me up and down as he walked back and forth singing 'Go to sleepy little ba-ay-by.' Where did these people come from, anyway?

You know what? That was all right though. At least I had succeeded in running my mommy away. I just couldn't look at her right now. I didn't have the slightest problem hanging out with my daddy or with my big brother, but my mama? Hah! Me and her was probably gonna be on the outs for the next nine months or so.

ANNE

"What is this?"

Here we go, I thought as I set the book I wasn't reading aside and looked at the home pregnancy test that Smoke must have dug around in the bathroom trash can to find. Couldn't hide anything from him, that was for damn sure. Wait . . . who was I kidding? I left it lying on the vanity so he'd see it as soon as he walked into the bathroom. I couldn't bring my lips to say what my mind was still having trouble comprehending and I had been relying on his excellent observational skills to relieve me of the task. Now here he was, holding what was obviously a positive pregnancy test out to me and wanting to know what it was. Scratching the back of his neck and peering at me through the one eye that wasn't squeezed shut. It looked like he wasn't as sharp as I had given him credit for.

"It's a pregnancy test," I said and craned my neck to get a better look at it. "With a pink line for positive."

"And did the pregnancy test fairy leave it in our bathroom?" He stared at the pink line for several seconds and then he locked eyes with me. "With your smart alecky ass. If I catch you sipping out of my beer again, it's going to be me and you."

"I didn't know then."

He took the test to the bathroom trash can and came back. "When did you know?"

"Just now," I said. "Tonight. I took the test before I got in bed. Look . . . I know you're probably pissed off and everything, but I am not in the mood to fight with you tonight, okay? I need to get some sleep."

"Fight about what, Anne? You thought I would be mad about you being pregnant?"

I took a deep breath and released it slowly, looking around the room. "We didn't talk about this, Smoke. We didn't plan for this."

"Did we plan for Isaiah?" I opened my mouth and he put up a hand. "And don't even get me started on Iris, because you know we didn't talk about her little butt. We were too busy making love from one end of Costa Rica to the other to worry about planning." He read the expression on my face and nudged my legs aside so he could sit down on the side of the bed and get up in my face. "If anything, I'm the one who should be looking all long in the face, not you."

That got my attention. "What do you have to be long in the face about? I'm the one who's going to be all stretched out of place and sweating like a pig all day, every day. Dammit, I just now got my six pack back."

"You think I planned on being a forty year old man with a baby's mama?"

"You think I planned on being somebody's baby's mama?"

"You ain't gotta be nobody's baby's mama and you know it. But you're too chicken to step up and do what you know you need to do."

"Oh, so now I'm chicken?" Eyes wide, I pointed at my chest and looked at Smoke like he had lost his last little piece of mind. It was too late at night or morning or whatever it was for him to be talking crazy. "Is that what you just called me? A chicken?"

"I didn't stutter, Anne. And ain't nobody scared of you, so you can lower your squeaky voice, too. Acting like you don't know what I'm talking about. A chicken?" he mimicked me with a silly expression on his face. He stood up and flapped a hand at me on his way out of the room. "You talk more shit than the law allows, but when it comes down to it, you're scared of your own shadow."

I hopped off of the bed and followed him to the kitchen. "How do you figure?"

"Well, let me see." Smoke rooted around in the refrigerator and came out with a pitcher of lemonade. He poured himself a glass and drank half of it, staring at me over the rim of the glass. "Last year, when we had that mouse, you locked yourself in the bathroom until I caught it."

"So?"

"Every time we take Iris to the zoo you refuse to go inside the snake house, because you're a punk."

"So what? Two headed snakes are unnatural. I don't need to see that mess."

"If birds are on the interstate exit ramp you slam on brakes and damn near cause a ten car pileup to keep from hitting them."

"Why would I want to run over innocent birds?" I wasn't seeing the problem.

"They always fly away, Anne. You can't hit them, because they instinctively know to fly away."

"Some of them don't, Smoke. That's how people run over squirrels and stuff, too. They don't move out of the way fast enough and . . ."

"I have asked you to marry me thirty-eight times and you punk out every time," he said and shut me right up. I watched him watch me. "If you don't want to be a baby's mama all your life, then take the ring and let's do it." He tossed back the rest of his lemonade and set the empty glass in the sink.

"Me not taking your ring doesn't make me a punk, Smoke." I spun on my heels and led the way out of the kitchen. "And asking me to marry you at the same time that you cum is not my idea of a romantic proposal," I said over my shoulder.

"You laughed and told me to get the hell up so you could vacuum underneath the bed when I got down on one knee. You thought I was doing that shit again?"

I turned the lamp off, snatched the covers back and climbed in bed. Smoke walked around to his side and did the same thing. We settled pillows underneath our heads and straightened the covers around us. He took a deep breath and yawned and then I yawned and took a deep breath.

He had some damn nerve, calling me a punk. Like he didn't always call for me to come running with one of my shoes when he spotted a house spider hiding in a corner. The man could make me cum six different times in one night, but he was arachnophobic. Iris went to throwing up and he wanted to immediately race her to the emergency room, but he thought catching a mouse was a big deal? Hell, pushing an eight-pound baby out of his ass would send him into cardiac arrest.

Real strength was in knowing one's own weaknesses,

not in keeping track of somebody else's. I was just glad he hadn't been home when I walked out into the garage and saw that slug. I screamed so loud that Kenny from across the street had to come over and shut me up. Now that was a decent young man for you. He had taken the slug away and never mentioned that little episode again. But Smoke? Oh, hell no, Smoke would've teased me about that mess for days.

"You could've at least tried getting down on one knee again," I said and rolled over on my side.

"Nah, I figured you liked just being my baby's mama, so everybody would think that I didn't think enough of you to marry you. So they would think I was just going to keep pumping babies in your belly and shit. I put the ring over there in the armoire and forgot about it." He stretched like a lion and beat his pillow into submission. "The only reason I keep asking you is so I can watch you punk out. Like you always do."

"I don't punk out." I rolled my eyes even though he couldn't see me. "You know, you're really starting to piss me off saying that. I have a right to take as much time as I need to think about marrying some damn body."

"You're right, baby. You're right." Smoke had the nerve to reach out and pat me on my hip and soothingly, at that. "Take all the time you need. And please lower your voice before you wake up Weeping Wanda."

"She's with Isaiah and you know it. And stop patting me like I'm eighty years old, too. I don't care if you have an attitude with me, Smoke, and what I especially don't care for is the condescending tone you have. You can cut that shit out right now."

"Anne, take your punk ass to sleep, would you?"

"What?"

"This is another one of your punking out episodes. I know it, you know it and Zay is probably in his room

eavesdropping like he always does, so he knows it too."
There was the patting again. "It's okay, boo. Lay down and
relax your nerves."

I thought I saw lightning crash through the window and
strike me in the crack of my ass, I was so angry. I sat up
and slammed the covers back. Then I switched on the
lamp and glared at Smoke. "Get me the damn ring, so I
can shove it down your throat!"

Smoke rolled out of bed like he had never been in it in
the first place. "I'm getting you the damn ring so you can
put it on, that's what I'm getting ready to do." He threw
the armoire doors open and started tossing out clothes
left and right, searching for the ring. I caught it on the fly.
"Put it on."

"I didn't say I was putting it on, I said I was shoving it
down your throat, didn't I? See . . . yeah . . . that's what
I'm saying. I'm not falling for your little bully routine."

"Punk."

"Your mama's a punk."

"Oh, she is? Well, call her and tell her that so I can start
planning your funeral. And at least my mama still has all
of her real teeth."

I slapped a hand over my mouth and gave him a wild-
eyed look. "No, you didn't go there. Please tell me you didn't
just go there, Smoke."

"I went there, I came back and now I'm going again. Because if you think you're going to lay up on your ass
around here, having babies and not man up, then you are
officially insane. Your mama's got your ass scared to do
what you need to do, so both of you are punks, as far as
I'm concerned. And yes, I will call her and tell her that myself, because she can't whip no ass over here and you
can't either."

"Kiss my ass."

"Kiss my ass right back and put the damn ring on, punk."

"Oh, I'm putting it on all right," I said as I tore the little black velvet box up snapping it open. "I'm putting it on right now and then I'm using it to scratch your face up so badly that your own mama won't even recognize you." I shoved the ring on my finger and held my hand out to look at it. "Satisfied?"

"Not quite," he said on his way across the room.

"What are you doing?"

He dropped the suitcase he had pulled from a shelf in the closet and ignored me as he stomped over to the doorway. He threw the door open and stepped out into the hallway. "Isaiah!"

I hopped up and blocked his way. "Do you hear me talking to you? What do you think you're doing?"

He slid past me and stepped inside the closet. "Pack your shit, Anne."

"Excuse me?"

"Enough for a weekend, at least. I might want to run through a couple of casinos while we're in Vegas." He carried pants and shirts on hangers over to the bed and went back for another load. My eyes popped out when he emerged with my clothes. Acting like he didn't see me standing there staring at him.

Isaiah knocked on the door and stuck his head in the room. "What's up?" Iris pushed the door open wider and put her face next to Isaiah's.

"Isaiah, it's almost four in the morning. Why is she still awake?" Smoke passed me a pair of navy pinstripe slacks and a white silk shirt and I took them reflexively. "Now she'll sleep all day and stay up half the night tonight."

"You won't be here staying up with her."

"The hell I won't," I said and handed the slacks back to

him. "The gray ones, baby. They look better with the shirt you picked out and, plus, I can wear those new gray sling-backs I just bought." He went in search of the slacks that I requested and I turned my attention back to Isaiah. "I have her on a schedule and every time you bring your butt home you jack it up."

"My bad," Isaiah said, grinning from ear to ear. "What are ya'll doing in here?"

"Well, Smoke is obviously drunk and I'm . . ."

"Don't mind your mother, Zay. She's talking much shit," Smoke cut me off. He was digging around in my under-wear drawer, looking for what, I didn't know. "She's preg-nant again, which, don't get wrong, is cool, but I'm making her marry me or else we're going to have to do something different. I can't be having all these babies without a ring on my finger, you feel me?" He pushed a bra and matching panties in my hands and gave Isaiah a shitty grin on his way into the bathroom. Isaiah looked thunder-struck for a second and then a slow grin spread across his face.

"Aw, sookie sookie now," he singsonged.

I rolled my eyes at him. "Shut up."

I grabbed a lace trimmed ivory skirt suit from the closet and laid it across the bed. I needed to be sharp, as usual, even if Smoke was making me marry him in an all-night wedding chapel. That was just like his behind, too. Vegas, of all places.

"And don't think Vegas is going to be my honeymoon, either," I called out. "Cheap Negro."

"Uh-uh, boo. You're taking me to the Virgin Islands or someplace like that and we're staying gone until after Christmas," Smoke called back. "As soon as you take my last name, we'll talk about where I want to go. You just keep packing and don't forget to pack that sexy red night-gown that I like to eat off of you every now and again."

"TMI, Da," Isaiah drawled sarcastically. "TMI."

Smoke flushed the toilet, opened the door and stepped up to the vanity to wash his hands. "Whatever. Call your grandmother and tell her that we'll be dropping Iris off in a few."

"Which one?"

"Big Mama," Smoke said.

"Alice," I said at the same time.

We stared at each other.

"Ok*aaay*, so which one am I calling?"

Smoke held my eyes for a long time. "Alice," he finally said. "Call your Grandma Alice. Then, you need to go and pack a bag, too. I need you to be my best man, Zay."

"Bet," Isaiah said and left us alone.

Until right this second, I hadn't thought about the fact that I needed a maid of honor. I pushed a hand through my locks and blew out a strong breath. "You think I should call Vern and see if she'll be my maid of honor?"

"That's cool, but tell her she's buying her own plane ticket."

I rolled my eyes at Smoke and reached for the phone. With his cheap behind. A few seconds later: "Vern? It's Bree . . ."

Smoke was butt naked and waiting for me in the bathroom doorway when I hung up the phone. "Come and scrub my back for me, baby. With your punk ass."

"I got your punk, punk." I closed the bedroom door, locked it and jumped out of my gown.

"Let's do this, then."

"Let's do it, then. I'm not scared of you, Smoke." I followed my soon-to-be husband into the shower.

"You need to be. What do you think? You like the sound of Anne Avery?"

"I like the sound of Anne Phillips hyphen Avery even better."

"Look, don't start that women's lib shit, okay?"

"Whatever." I took the shower gel and sponge Smoke passed me and worked up a thick lather, then started in on his back. "Maybe we could set a precedent and go with Anne and Alec Phillips? What do you think, boo?"

He laid his head back and laughed long and hard. "Woman, you must be out of your damn mind."

IRIS

Wait a minute, wh*aaaaat?* This was not how things were supposed to be going down. My daddy was not supposed to be bragging about my mama having another baby. He was supposed to be telling her that there was only room for one baby and that was me. Nobody needed another somebody stealing the spotlight, especially not me. I definitely didn't need another somebody trying to be cute and taking all of my sugar. Everybody knew that new babies stole everything from the ones who had come before them.

I had my game all planned out, had my car all picked out and I already knew what color I wanted my room to be when it came time for me to pick out my waterbed and everything. Dang! But that was all right though. That was quite all right. I was getting ready to make somebody's life as miserable as I possibly could. I was probably going to move in with my big brother and his wife when I got older, just because I could.

That would show my mommy and daddy who was running the show. And it was going to be either me or that other person, or else I wasn't ever moving back home. Erica was already wrapped around my finger, so I wasn't seeing a problem with her and my brother adopting me. Just like Martin Luther King, Jr., I had been to the mountaintop and I already knew that her and my big brother were going to have three little bad, funny looking, gray-eyed boys, so I was going to be her favorite, anyway. She was thinking that she was going to have a girl somewhere along the way, but I knew better, now didn't I?

And my mommy was carrying another boy, too? Ugh. Time to get my fighting skills in order, because I was getting ready to be whipping his little tail all over the house and grinning like an angel when my daddy caught me doing it.

Oh, yeah, it was about to be on. Wait a minute. What's that you said? *Two* boys? Twins? *Aw naw. Say its not so.* I couldn't do nothing but fall out and start crying all over again.

ISAIAH

I stole some of Iris' sugar while I listened to Erica's cell phone ring and waited for her to pick up. She finally did and I said: "Baby, change of plans. We have to cancel the weekend trip we planned, because we're going to Vegas."

Iris went to clowning and I plopped her little butt down in the middle of my bed. I couldn't hear what Erica was saying for all the whining and gibberish talk my baby sis was doing. I took the phone with me over to the closet and stood there looking at my clothes, trying to decide what I needed to pack. Here I was a grown man and my parents were getting married? That shit was too cute and just about damn time, too. But what I couldn't help wondering was, just who did they think was going to be worried with all these babies?

Speaking of which, Iris was so out of control that I had to take the phone from my ear and stare at her little demonic butt for a second. "Girl, would you be quiet? You ain't got nothing in the world to be crying about like that. What? Yeah, boo, she's clowning like it's the end of the world or something . . . and I don't think so. You might get lucky and get one kid out of a brotha before I put the family jewels on lock down, but that's about it. I can't deal with all the noise . . ." She said something crazy to me, something about trying and trying until she got a little girl out of me and I threw my head back and cracked up. "Girl, you must be out of your damn mind . . ."

ABOUT THE AUTHOR

Terra Little is a native of Missouri, where she is a teacher and the mother of a wonderful daughter named Sierra. She is a graduate of the University of Missouri; Lindenwood University; and the University of Phoenix. Her first title, *Running from Mercy*, was released in January 2008 and her second title, *Where There's Smoke*, was released in January 2009. *Where There's Smoke 2: When the Smoke Clears* is her third title. She is also a contributor to the *Gumbo for the Soul* anthology, *Here's Our Child, Where's the Village?* She welcomes feedback from readers at writeterralittle@yahoo.com. Visit her online at www.terralittle.com and www.terralittle.blogspot.com.